"When one of the most creative minds I know gets the best idea he's ever had and turns it into a novel, it's fasten-your-seat-belt time. This one will be talked about for a long time."

—Jerry B. Jenkins, co-author of Left Behind

"A most fascinating story! Full of heart, suspense, and intelligence, Saving Alpha engagingly illustrates the futility of man- made beliefs as well as the world's desperate need for a God who offers hope, guidance, and help."

—Tim LaHaye, co-author of Left Behind

"Bill has written another heart-wrenching, mind gripping novel that delivers on so many levels. Like the Gospel, Saving Alpha is more than just a great read. I highly recommend it!"

—Doug Fields, teaching pastor, Saddleback Community Church, and bestselling author of Fresh Start

"An original masterpiece. Saving Alpha reopens our eyes to God's absolute justice and His unfathomable love."

—Dr. Kevin Leman, bestselling author of Have a New Kid by Friday

"If you enjoy white-knuckle, page-turning suspense, with a brilliant blend of cutting-edge apologetics, The God Hater will grab you for a long, long time."

—Beverly Lewis, New York Times bestselling author

"I've never seen a more powerful and timely illustration of the Incarnation. Bill Myers has a way of making the Gospel accessible and relevant to readers of all ages. I highly recommend this book."

—Terri Blackstock, New York Times bestselling author

"Once again, Myers takes us into imaginative and intriguing depths, making us feel, think, and ponder all at the same time. Relevant and entertaining, Saving Alpha is not to be missed."

—James Scott Bell, bestselling author of Deceived and Try Fear

"A brilliant novel that feeds the mind and heart, Saving Alpha belongs at the top of your reading list."

—Angela Hunt, New York Times bestselling author

"Saving Alpha is a rare combination of Christian fiction that is both entertaining and spiritually provocative. It has the ability to challenge your mind as well as move your heart. It has a message of deep spiritual significance that is highly relevant for these times."

—Paul Cedar, chairman, Mission America Coalition

SAVING ALPHA

BILL MYERS

AMARIS MEDIA

Published by Amaris Media International

Los Angeles, CA

Saving Alpha formerly titled The God Hater © **2010 Bill Myers**

Library of Congress Cataloging-in-Publication Data

Myers, Bill

Originally published as The God Hater: a novel / Bill Myers, p. cm.

1. College teachers—Fiction. 2. Atheists—Fiction. 3. Artificial intelligence —Fiction. I. Title.

PS3563.Y36G63 2010 813' 54—dc22

2009054115

ISBN - 978-0-9991077-2-0 (paperback)

ISBN - 978-0-9991077-3-7 (ebook)

Manufactured in the United States of America

Edited by Dave Lambert

Scripture quotation are taken from New American Standard Bible.

❀ Created with Vellum

For: Roger and Paula,
Jim and Pat,
Eric and Lynda,
Penny, Sandy, and Terri,
Mike and Laura,
Cam,
And the Lafoou and Laulile families.
No one could ask for better neighbors.

Then the Lord answered Job out of the storm and said, "Now gird up your loins like a man; I will ask you, and you instruct Me. Will you really annul My judgment? Will you condemn Me that you may be justified?"

JOB 40:6-8 NASB

AUTHOR'S NOTE

The following is fiction.

I've tried to make the science and theology reasonably accurate. But, just as I'm sure I've made scientific blunders in the writing, I'm equally positive I've stepped on theological land mines. Then there's that whole pesky issue of allegories. They only capture pieces of truth and are way too slippery to do much more. So, just as I would encourage you not to base your science upon this science, the same should go for your theology. As I said in my novel Eli, which in many ways is the flip side of this project, if something doesn't sound right or sticks in your throat, don't waste your time reading this. Go to the original Source and see what it says.

I'd like to thank Ray Kurzweil for his insights into mapping the human brain, as well as James Kennedy and Jerry Newcombe for their research; Angela Hunt, James Scott Bell, Peggy Patrick Medberry, Simon Chow, Nicci Jordan Hubert, and David Lambert for their input; Lee Hough, Paul Arroyo, David Wimbish, and Greg Johnson for their help; and Lee Strobel, whose information was also invaluable and whose quote of Robin Collins I used on page 20.

And finally, most importantly, my thanks to you, the reader. As always, I appreciate your investment of time and money as we take another journey together. And, as always, I hope you find this as provocative in the reading as I did in the writing.

Thanks again,
Bill Myers
www.Billmyers.com

PART I

CHAPTER 1

SAMUEL PRESTON, a local reporter with bronzed skin and glow-in-the-dark teeth, turned to one of the guests of his TV show God Talk. "So what's your take on all of this, Dr. Mackenzie?"

The sixty-something professor stared silently at his wristwatch. He had unruly white hair and wore an outdated sports coat.

"Dr. Mackenzie?"

He glanced up, disoriented, then turned to the host, who repeated the question. "What are your feelings about the book?"

Clearing his throat, Mackenzie raised the watch to his ear and gave it a shake. "I was wondering…" He trailed off, his bushy eyebrows gathered into a scowl as he listened for a sound.

The second guest, a middle-aged pastor with a shirt collar two sizes too small, smiled. "Yes?"

Mackenzie gave up on the watch and turned to him. "Do you make up this drivel as you go along? Or do you simply parrot others who have equally stunted intellects?"

The pastor, Dr. William Hathaway, blinked. Still smiling, he turned to the host. "I was under the impression we were going to discuss my new book?"

"Oh, we are," Preston assured him. "But it's always good to have a skeptic or two in our midst, wouldn't you agree?"

"Ah." Hathaway nodded. "Of course." He turned back to Mackenzie, his smile never wavering. "I am afraid what you term as 'drivel' is based upon a faith stretching back thousands of years."

Mackenzie removed one or two dog hairs from his slacks. "We have fossilized dinosaur feces older than that."

"I'm sorry?"

"Just because something's old doesn't stop it from being crap."

Dr. Hathaway's smile twitched. He turned in his chair to more fully address the man. "We're talking about a time-honored religion that millions of—"

"And that's supposed to be a plus," Mackenzie said, "that it's religious? I thought you wanted to support your nonsense."

"I see. Well, it may interest you to know that—"

"Actually, it doesn't interest me at all." The old man turned to Preston. "How much longer will we be?"

The host chuckled. "Just a few more minutes, Professor."

Working harder to maintain his smile, Hathaway replied, "So, if I understand correctly, you're not a big fan of the benefits of Christianity?"

"Benefits?" Mackenzie pulled a used handkerchief from his pocket and began looking for an unsoiled portion. "Is that what the thirty thousand Jews who were tortured and killed during the Inquisition called it? Benefits?"

"That's not entirely fair."

"And why is that?"

"For starters, most of them weren't Jews."

4

"I'm sure they're already feeling better."

"What I am saying is—"

"What you are saying, Mr... Mr.—"

"Actually, it's Doctor."

"Actually, you're a liar."

"I beg your pardon?"

Finding an unused area of his handkerchief, Mackenzie took off his glasses and cleaned them.

The pastor continued, "It may interest you to know that—"

"We've already established my lack of interest."

"It may interest you to know that I hold several honorary doctorates."

"Honorary doctorates."

"That's correct."

"Honorary, as in unearned, as in good for nothing ... unless it's to line the bottom of birdcages." He held his glasses to the light, checking for any remaining smudges.

Hathaway took a breath and regrouped. "You can malign my character all you wish, but there is no refuting the benefits outlined in my new book."

"Ah, yes, the benefits." Mackenzie lowered his glasses and worked on the other lens. "Like the million-plus lives slaughtered during the Crusades?"

"That figure can be disputed."

"Correct. It may be higher."

Hathaway shifted in his seat. "The Crusades were a long time ago and in an entirely different culture."

"So you'd prefer something closer to home? Perhaps the witch hunts of New England?"

"I'm not here to—"

"Fifteen thousand human beings murdered in Europe and America. Fifteen thousand."

"Again, that's history and not a part of today's—"

"Then let us discuss more recent atrocities—towards the blacks, the gays, the Muslim population. Perhaps a dialogue on the bombing of abortion clinics?"

"Please, if you would allow me—"

Mackenzie turned to Preston. "Are we finished here?"

Fighting to be heard, Hathaway continued, "If people will read my book, they will clearly see—"

"Are we finished?"

"Yes, Professor." Preston chuckled. "I believe we are."

"But we've not discussed my Seven Steps to Successful—"

"Perhaps another time, Doctor."

Mackenzie rose, shielding his eyes from the bright studio lights as Hathaway continued. "But there are many issues we need to—"

"I'm sure there are," Preston agreed while keeping an eye on Mackenzie, who stepped from the platform and headed off camera. "And I'm sure it's all there in your book. Seven Steps to—"

* * *

ANNIE BROOKS CLICKED off the remote to her television.

"Mom," Rusty mumbled, "I was watching..." He drifted back to sleep without finishing the protest.

She looked down at the five-year-old and smiled. He lay in bed beside her, his hands still clutching Horton Hears a Who! Each night he'd been reading it to her, though she suspected it was more reciting from memory than reading. She tenderly kissed the top of his head before absentmindedly looking back to the TV.

He'd done it again. Her colleague and friend—if Dr. Nicholas Mackenzie could be said to have any friends—had shredded another person of faith. This time a Christian, some megachurch pastor hawking his latest book. Next time it could just as easily be a Jew or Muslim or Buddhist. The point was that Nicholas hated religion. And heaven help anybody who tried to defend it.

She sighed and looked back down to her son. He was breathing heavily, mouth slightly ajar. She brushed the bangs from his face and gave him another kiss. She'd carry him back to bed soon enough. But for now she would simply savor his presence.

Nothing gave her more joy. And for that, with or without Nicholas's approval, Annie Brooks was grateful to her God.

* * *

"Excuse me?" Nicholas called from the back seat of the Lincoln Town Car.

The driver didn't hear.

He leaned forward and spoke louder. "You just passed the freeway entrance."

The driver, some black kid with a shaved head, turned on the stereo. It was an urban chant, its beat so powerful Nicholas could feel it pounding in his gut. He unbuckled his seat belt and scooted to the open partition separating them. "Excuse me! You—"

The tinted window slid up, nearly hitting him in the face.

He pulled back in surprise, then banged on the glass. "Excuse me!" The music was fainter but still vibrated the car. "Excuse me!"

No response.

He slumped back into the seat. Stupid kid. And rude. He'd realize his mistake soon enough. And after Nicholas's call to the TV station tomorrow, he'd be back on the streets looking for another job. Trying to ignore the music, Nicholas stared out the window, watching the Santa Barbara lights soften as fog rolled in. Over the years the station's drivers had always been polite and courteous. Years, as in Nicholas was a frequent guest on God Talk. Despite his reclusive lifestyle, not to mention his general disdain for people, he always accepted the producer's invitation. Few things gave him more pleasure than exposing the toxic nature of religion. Besides, these outings provided a nice change of pace. Instead of the usual stripping away of naive college students' faith in his classroom, the TV guests occasionally provided a challenge. Occasionally. Other than his duties at the University of California, Santa Barbara, these trips were his only exposure to the outside world.

He had abandoned society long ago. Or rather, it had abandoned him. Not that there was any love lost. Today's culture was an intellectual wasteland—a world of pre-chewed ideas, politically correct causes, sound-bite news coverage, and novels that were nothing more than comic books. (He'd given up on movies and television long ago.) Why waste his time on such pabulum when he could surround himself with Sartre, Hegel, Kierkegaard, Nietzsche — men whose work would provide more meaningful companionship in one evening than most people could in a lifetime?

Nevertheless, he did tolerate Ari, even fought to keep her during the divorce. She was his faithful companion for over fifteen years, though he should have put her down months ago. The golden retriever was deaf and blind, and her hips had begun to fail. But she wasn't in pain. Not yet. And until that time, he didn't mind cleaning up after her occasional accidents or calling in the vet for those expensive house calls. He owed her that. Partially because of her years of patient listening, and partially because of the memories.

The car turned right and entered a residential area. He glanced down to the glowing red buttons on the console beside him. One of them was an intercom to the driver. But, like Herbert Marcuse, the great neo-Marxist of the twentieth century (and, less popularly, Theodore Kaczynski, the Unabomber of the 1980s), Nicholas mistrusted modern technology as much as he scorned the society that created it. How many times had Annie, a fellow professor, pleaded with him to buy a telephone?

"What if there's an emergency?" she'd insisted. "What if someone needs to call you?"

"Like solicitors?"

"They have do-not-call lists," she said. "You can go online and be added to their—"

"Online?"

"Okay, you can write them a letter."

"And give them what, more personal information?"

"They'd only ask for your phone number."

"Not if I don't have one."

And so the argument continued off and on for years ... as gift occasions came and went, as his closet gradually filled with an impressive collection of telephones. One thing you could say about Annie Brooks, she was persistent—which might be why he put up with her company, despite the fact she doted over him like he was some old man who couldn't take care of himself. Besides, she had a good head on her shoulders, when she chose to use it, which meant she occasionally contributed something of worth to their conversations.

Then, of course, there was her boy.

The car slowed. Having no doubt learned the error of his ways, the driver was turning around. Not that it would help him keep his job. That die had already been cast. But the car wasn't turning. Instead, it pulled to the curb and came to a stop. The locks shot up and the right rear door immediately opened. A man in his early forties appeared—strong jaw, short hair, with a dark suit, white shirt, and black tie.

"Good evening, Doctor." He slid onto the leather seat beside him.

"Who are you?" Nicholas demanded.

The man closed the door and the car started forward. "I apologize for the cloak-and-dagger routine, but—"

"Who are you?"

He flipped open an ID badge. "Brad Thompson, HLS."

"Who?"

"Homeland Security Agent Brad Thompson." He returned the badge to his coat pocket.

"You're with the government?"

"Yes, sir, Homeland Security."

"And you've chosen to interrupt my ride home because ..."

"Again, I apologize, but it's about your brother."

Nicholas stared at him, giving him no satisfaction of recognition.

"Your brother," the agent repeated, "Travis Mackenzie?"

Nicholas held his gaze another moment before looking out the window. "Is he in trouble again?"

"Has he contacted you?"

"My brother and I seldom communicate."

"Yes, sir, about every eighteen months, if our information is correct."

The agent's knowledge unsettled Nicholas. He turned back to the man. "May I see your identification again?"

"Pardon me?"

"Your identification. You barely allowed me to look at it."

The agent reached back into his suit coat. "Please understand this is far more serious than his drug conviction, or his computer hacking, or the DUIs."

Nicholas adjusted his glasses, waiting for the identification.

The agent flipped open his ID holder. "We at HLS are very concerned about his involvement with—"

Suddenly headlights appeared through the back window, their beams on high. The agent looked over his shoulder, then swore under his breath. He reached for the intercom, apparently to give orders to the driver, but the Town Car was already beginning to accelerate.

"What's the problem?" Nicholas asked.

The car turned sharply to the left and continued picking up speed.

"I asked you what is happening," Nicholas repeated.

"Your brother, Professor. Where is he?"

The headlights reappeared behind them, closing in.

"You did not allow me to examine your identification."
"Please, Doctor—"

"If you do not allow me to examine your identification, I see little-"

"We've no time for that!"

The outburst stopped Nicholas as the car took another left, so sharply both men braced themselves.

The agent turned back to him. "Where is your brother?"

Once again the lights appeared behind them.

Refusing to be bullied, Nicholas repeated, "Unless I'm convinced of your identity, I have little—"

The agent sprang at him. Grabbing Nicholas's shirt, he yanked him to his face and shouted, "Where is he?"

Surprised, but with more pride than common sense, Nicholas answered, "As I said—"

The agent's fist was a blur as it struck Nicholas's nose. Nicholas felt the cartilage snap, knew the pain would follow. As would the blood.

"Where is he?"

The car turned right, tires squealing, tossing the men to the other side. As Nicholas sat up, the agent pulled something from his jacket. There was the black glint of metal and suddenly a cold gun barrel was pressed against his neck. He felt fear rising and instinctively pushed back the emotion. It wasn't the gun that concerned him, but the fear. That was his enemy. If he could focus, rely on his intellect, he'd have the upper hand. Logic trumped emotion every time. It was a truth that sustained him through childhood, kept him alive in Vietnam, and gave him the strength to survive in today's world.

The barrel pressed harder.

When he knew he could trust his voice, he answered, "The last time I saw my brother was Thanksgiving."

The car hit the brakes, skidding to a stop, sliding Nicholas off the seat and onto his knees. The agent caught himself, managing to stay seated. Up ahead, through the glass partition, Nicholas saw a second vehicle coming toward them—a van or truck, its beams also on high.

The agent pounded the partition. "Get us out of here," he shouted at the driver. "Now!"

The Town Car lurched backward. It bounced up a curb and onto a front lawn. Tires spun, spitting grass and mud, until they dug in and the vehicle took off. It plowed through a hedge of junipers, branches scraping underneath, then across another lawn. Nicholas looked out his side window as they passed the vehicle that had been behind them, a late-model SUV. They veered back onto the road, snapping off a mailbox. Once again the driver slammed on the brakes, turning hard to the left, throwing the vehicle into a one-eighty until they were suddenly behind the SUV, facing the opposite direction. Tires screeched as they sped off.

The agent hit the intercom and yelled, "Dump the Professor and get us out of here!"

The car continued to accelerate and made another turn. Pulling Nicholas onto the seat and shoving the gun into his face, the agent shouted, "This is the last time I'm asking!"

Nicholas's heart pounded, but he kept his voice even. "I have already told you."

The man chambered a round. But it barely mattered. Nicholas had found his center and would not be moved. "I have not seen him in months."

"Thanksgiving?"

"Yes."

The car made another turn.

"And?"

Nicholas turned to face him. "We ate a frozen dinner and I sent him away." The agent searched his eyes. Nicholas held his gaze, unblinking. The car took one last turn, bouncing up onto an unlit driveway, then jerked to a stop. There was no sound, except the pounding music.

"Get out," the agent ordered.

Nicholas looked through the window. "I have no idea where we—"

"Now."

Nicholas reached for the handle, opened his door, and stepped outside. The air was cold and damp.

"Shut the door."

He obeyed.

The Town Car lunged backward, lights off. Once it reached the road it slid to a stop, changed gears, and sped off. Nicholas watched as it disappeared into the fog, music still throbbing even after it was out of sight. Only then did he appreciate the pain in his nose and the warm copper taste of blood in his mouth. Still, with grim satisfaction, he realized he had won. As always, logic and intellect had prevailed.

CHAPTER 2

ALPHA 11 INCHED around the cottage wall of dried mud and straw. He squinted across the plaza through the smoke, careful to stay out of sight. With the infant in his arms, he could not defend himself. He took a breath for courage, then bolted into the open, racing to the other side. Once he arrived, he pulled back into the shadows of another cottage. To his immediate left, flames spit and crackled through the windows of a larger two-story home. Its raiders cursed and laughed as they stepped over the home owners charred corpse. The dead man's women fought and screamed as the men carried them off on their shoulders to kill or rape or sell. Lurking to the side, a handful of gaunt scavengers waited, the breathglow from their mouths and nostrils so faint it was barely visible. They were the old, the sick, the infirm. Those who could no longer pillage on their own, who could only feed upon leftovers.

Although Alpha was young and strong, just entering his eighteenth season, he seldom participated in such raids. And certainly not today. Today he had a much different mission. Silently, he moved along the front of the cottage, then darted to the next dwelling, and the next, doing his best to remain in the lengthening shadows. Eventually he arrived at the far end of the plaza. He looked over his shoulder to make sure he hadn't been seen. So far, no one had noticed. Ahead of him, he heard the sound of crying babies.

Good. He was close.

Of course, his woman had made the usual protests. "No, Alpha!" she had begged him. "Please!" She had tried rising from her wooden pallet, clutching his arm, but the birthing had taken too much from her, reducing her strength and her glow.

The breathglow was no problem. He would swing by the Grid on his way home and auction off more of his life for additional units. Her strength would return. She would heal. But there was another healing he worried about. For reasons that made no sense, he had become concerned for what she felt. Even though she had deceived him, even though she had given birth to a female, he somehow felt concern.

More and more frequently this was happening—thinking about her. Not as he had his other women, as the providers of pleasure, or the potential bearers of male children—but as someone who had feelings. He knew this type of thinking was dangerous, a sign of weakness. But no matter how often he pushed it from his head, it returned. As unlikely as it seemed, he found himself wondering what she thought of situations, even what she thought of him. And even more troubling, he began to discover that he was the happiest when she was happy.

The baby in his arms began to fuss. Trying to muffle the sound, to avoid drawing attention, he pressed it closer to his chest. He felt its warmth. His woman's warmth. Just hours earlier, it had been part of her.

"Alpha! I beg you!" The memory made his heart heavy. But this was necessary for survival. He rounded the final cottage, and there, across the dirt street, rose the Killing Wall. The cryings and screamings were much louder now. Throughout the day, female babies had been abandoned on the ledge built into the other side. Their fathers gave no regard to the suffering they would endure under the hot, blistering sun. But Alpha 11 could not do that. In deference to his woman he had waited until the end of the day, until the sun was nearly down. It was a more dangerous time to travel, but he hoped it would lessen her pain.

He crossed the street, arrived at the Wall, and began scaling it. The stones were cold and slick from an earlier rain. It was twelve lengths high, tall enough to keep out even the most determined animal. It circled the entire village. But only this section had the lower, outside ledge.

Once he reached the top, he looked out over the meadow. White bones and skulls peeked through lush green grass. Beyond the field lay the forest, with its beasts and unimaginable terrors. He glanced down to the ledge eight lengths below. It was covered with babies, strewn up and down on either side, all in various degrees of living and suffering and dying. But only until the darkness settled. Only until the animals emerged.

He unfastened his coarse wool cloak and pulled the infant out from under it. This was nothing new. He'd been here two times before, when his other women, now stolen, had given birth to females. Two times he had placed their failures upon the Wall to be disposed of. If they had been born male, their fate would be different. But, like all the poor in the village, who lived from life unit to life unit, an extra mouth to feed could not be tolerated. Unless, of course, it was a boy, who could be taught to steal and plunder and provide.

The baby looked up at him, flushed cherub cheeks, pale blue eyes, bright breathglow radiating from its nose and mouth. Feelings stirred inside him and he cursed his woman for it. She was the one responsible. Not him. He climbed down to the ledge and placed the thing at his feet. In spite of himself, he stooped down and adjusted the thin quilt to better cover it, as if the covering would offer protection. Another sentimental act of foolishness.

He rose and scanned the meadow. Already he could see darker shadows rippling through the grass, beginning to approach.

The baby started to cry.

Refusing to look at it, he turned and climbed to the top of the Wall and started down the other side.

The crying grew louder.

He arrived at the dirt street. It was darker now. And colder. It was too late to auction life units. Besides, he had no heart for it. He'd do it tomorrow. Tonight, he would return to his woman. He would try to comfort her and forget what he'd done. But even as he headed down the road, he could hear the desperate screams of the baby. Her baby. Their baby. And he would continue hearing them, long after he was gone.

* * *

NICHOLAS HESITATED, then pulled the key from his front door. It had been unlocked. There were no marks on the frame, no sign of forced entry, but it had been unlocked. His pulse quickened as he looked over his shoulder to check the street. The dull predawn light revealed nothing unusual. No unmarked cars on stakeout. No mysterious vans with hooded men preparing to leap out and kidnap him. Just his taxi disappearing around the corner a block away. He eased the door open a crack and listened. Nothing. If someone had been there, chances were they were long gone.

Once again he thought of contacting the police, and once

again he chose not to. If what had happened to him really had been the work of a government agency (which he seriously doubted), they'd simply deny their actions. And if they were money collectors or other unsavory characters interested in his brother, Nicholas had made it abundantly clear he had no information. It was unlikely they would risk contacting him again. Besides, bringing in authorities would mean filling out reports, answering questions, and dealing with more invasions of privacy.

He pushed the door open farther. Everything in his tiny living room was as he had left it—the sofa he never used, coffee and end tables with their thin coating of dust. In the far corner sat his recliner and his reading table stacked with books. Nothing had been touched.

He stepped inside and paused again to listen. Quietly, he moved through the room. He poked his head into the kitchen. His plate, cup, and bowl, along with his fork, knife, and spoon, all sat in the dish drainer exactly where he'd left them.

With confidence building, he turned and entered the hallway. He stole a quick glance into the bathroom. It was also undisturbed. That left the bedroom. He crossed to it, flipped on the light, and entered.

As usual, Aristotle lay on her bed, sound asleep.

"Hey, girl."

Of course, she didn't respond. She'd been deaf over a year. Still, it never prevented them from carrying on deep philosophical discussions. As a puppy she had been a Christmas gift to Mikey— seven months before the accident. During that time the boy and dog were inseparable. Ari loved Mikey and Mikey loved Ari. And because of that love, Nicholas did not have the heart to put her down. In many ways, she was his lifeline, the last remaining connection to his dead child.

Nicholas moved to his desk. Once again, everything was in order—his in-box full of students' papers, his writing blotter, his stationery, the pen-and-pencil set Annie had given him for his birthday. Relief set in. And exhaustion. He eased himself into his black leather chair. Almost as an afterthought, he reached for the top drawer of his desk and opened it. Again, everything was in order. Except the book of stamps, which he always placed in the left front corner. It now lay in the middle of the drawer. And his address book, which was always in the center, was... He frowned and pulled the drawer farther open. He looked back to the desktop in the unlikely possibility he had left it out.

No. The address book was gone.

He sighed heavily. Well, at least they were professional, cleanly retrieving only what they needed. He gave another sigh and glanced over to Aristotle.

"Some watchdog you are. So what did you do, lick them to death?"

Of course she didn't respond. But there was something about the way she lay on her bed, the way her head was cocked.

"Ari?"

He pushed himself from the chair and moved to the end of the desk. He knelt down, gave her side a pat and a little rub. But she did not move.

"You okay, girl?"

He glanced down to her belly. No movement, no breathing. A heaviness spread through him. He held his fingers to her nostrils and felt nothing. Sadly, he stroked the top of her head, running his hand down her neck. But then he stopped. Something felt wrong. He cupped both hands under her head. He raised it, gently moving it from side to side. The stiffness of rigor mortis was already setting in, but was it possible? Had her neck been broken? He couldn't tell for certain.

Feeling very tired and drained, he laid the animal's head back down and sat beside her on the floor. He rested his hand on her side as his throat began to tighten. And there he remained. For how long, he didn't know, nor did he care. And if he had a wish, it was simply that he could cry.

* * *

ANNIE TOOK another sip of her mocha grande (nonfat of course) and looked out over the students in Amberson Lecture Hall. Whoever assigned eight A.M. for Molecular Biology 201 gave new meaning to the term cruel and unusual punishment. Poor babies. Blurry-eyed, barely coherent, many still wore their sleeping sweats. Some even wore their slippers—when they weren't sporting the standard-issue flip-flops. Still, with midterms coming next week, the hall was the fullest she had seen it since the first day of class.

She continued her lecture. "Now, remember there are over thirty areas that have to be in precise balance to create and sustain life in the universe. If even one of those areas had been off by the slightest margin, life never would have come into existence."

She pressed on, piling fact upon fact, hoping the sheer weight of information would somehow keep her students awake. "Take the cosmological constant, for example—the density of energy in outer space. If it were off by just one part in a hundred million billion billion billion billion billion, you and I would not be sitting here today."

A loud snorting filled the auditorium. It was followed by a smattering of giggles.

Unable to resist, Annie glanced back over to big Gus Zimmerman, UCSB's starting tackle. He sat in the second row, head back, out cold. She didn't mind him sleeping. And if she played it right, the snoring could actually add some comedy to a boring lecture. But she was concerned at the way he kept listing farther and farther to his left.

She continued, "Dr. Robin Collins is quoted as saying the odds of the universe being this finely tuned are the same as throwing a dart from outer space and"—she found her place in the notes she had copied and read—"'successfully hitting a bull's eye that's one trillionth of a trillionth of an inch in diameter. That's less than the size of one, solitary atom.'"

Another snore. Another round of giggles. Annie glanced from her notes to see Zimmerman teetering on the edge of his seat.

"Then there are the mind-boggling odds of all the factors lining up to begin and sustain life here on our own planet—water and the narrow temperature range to keep it liquid, the right amount of gravity, our location within the galaxy let alone the solar system, the right-size sun, the arrangement of other planets to protect us from asteroids, electromagnetic fields to protect us from UV rays, not to mention—"

Another snore. Annie looked up to see the young man waver once...twice...

"Mr. Zimmerman!"

Her shout startled him awake—and sent him crashing to the floor.

The hall broke into laughter, even applause, as Annie rushed to his side. "Are you okay? Are you all right?"

He nodded sheepishly and climbed back into his seat.

"You're sure?"

"Yes, ma'am," he muttered, his face growing bright red.

Unsure what to do, she tried to make light of the moment. "Here." She set her coffee on his desk. "You need this more than me."

Chuckles filled the room as she turned and headed back to the podium. There were only a few minutes left in class and there was plenty more to cover.

"Now, for nearly fifty years, origin-of-life experts have pretty much rejected the concept of life forming on our planet by random chance."

She turned back to the class. Those who were awake frowned as if they'd misheard. Good, she'd finally gotten their attention. In fact, a young Asian near the center of the auditorium actually raised her hand. "Yes?" Annie nodded.

"Is that true?"

"Absolutely. And it's been true since the 1960s. Every origin- of-life expert worth his or her salt has rejected the concept that life formed by random chance."

The girl's frown deepened and Annie answered the unasked question.

"You didn't learn this in your high school biology class because it's an inconvenient truth." With a smile she added, "One of our dirty little secrets. But if you plan to pursue biology and want to play with the big kids, it's a paradox you'll have to accept."

Another student, blond, disheveled hair and meticulously dressed to look like he didn't care what he wore, raised his hand. "How can they be so sure?" he asked.

Annie crossed to the overhead video projector. Picking up a pen, she wrote the number 1 in the top left-hand corner of the screen. After it she scribbled a long list of zeros, filling an entire line:

100,000,000,000,000,000,000,000,000,

000,000,000,000,000

"Remember, to form even a short functional protein we need to have, at the very least, seventy-five separate amino acids." She started a second row of zeros. "These must be the exact amino acids lined up in exactly the right sequence."

She finished the second row with the number now appearing as:

100,000,000,000,000,000,000,000,000,000,

000,000,000,000,000,000,000,000,000,000,

000,000,000,000,000,000,000,000,

But she wasn't done and started a third row. "This puts the odds of a single protein coming together by chance at one in a hundred thousand trillion trillion trillion trillion trillion trillion trillion trillion trillion trillion."She paused until she finished the number:

100,000,000,000,000,000,000,000,000,000,

000,000,000,000,000,000,000,000,000,000,

000,000,000,000,000,000,000,000,000,000,

000,000,000,000,000,000,000,000,000,000,

000,000.

"And keep in mind that's just one molecule. For a complex cell we'd need three hundred to five hundred molecules."

"But..."

She turned back to the girl.

"... it could still happen randomly, I mean."

Annie shook her head. "No."

For the first time that morning she had the entire room's attention. Even Zimmerman's.

"With these odds it's inconceivable for life to begin within the hundred thousand million years the earth has been hospitable to life."

"So what are you insinuating, Doctor?"

It was an older voice from the back. One she recognized instantly. She hadn't seen Nicholas Mackenzie slip into the hall and take a seat, but there he was, with his unruly hair and the same sports coat he wore on last night's TV show. By some trick of lighting his face appeared swollen.

"Dr. Mackenzie." She smiled. "So nice of you to join us."

Most of the students turned to him. More than a few exchanged looks and arched eyebrows.

"You didn't answer my question," he said.

"Which was?"

"By stating the odds are inconceivable for life to occur by chance, what are you insinuating?" It was an old ruse. One he had used over the years when he braved the treacherous bicycle lanes and crossed campus to visit her lectures. But that was okay. She had a few of her own that she used when visiting his.

"I'm insinuating nothing, Doctor," she replied. "I'm merely stating facts."

"In such a manner that these poor impressionable minds will reach your own unsupported conclusions."

"I was unaware I stated a conclusion."

He sighed wearily. "A conclusion based upon your Judeo-Christian bias that life cannot be self-generated and therefore owes its existence to an 'intelligent' creator."

She tilted her head. "Interesting that even you would reach such a conclusion, Doctor, when all I did was state undisputed facts."

A couple of the students snickered. They'd no doubt heard of the rivalry and these occasional mock debates between the dueling professors.

"Facts come and go," Nicholas said.

"Do they, now?"

"Two hundred years ago you scientists were attaching leeches to people to suck out their sickness."

"That was two hundred years ago."

"And given what little you still know of the universe, don't your conclusions calling for an intervening god simply stem from an immense ego—one that feels it has enough information to know all truth?"

She smiled. "I couldn't agree more, Doctor. The same

immense ego that insists it knows enough not to believe in God's existence."

More chuckles. But this was old ground, too easy. Annie knew Nicholas had something else up his sleeve.

"Then we are in agreement," he said. "The only absolutes are not facts, but how we perceive those facts. Making personal belief and philosophy the only real truths."

Annie was impressed at this new approach, but he gave her no time to respond.

"Therefore, philosophy, not science, is the real study of truth, is it not?"

A couple of the kids oohed. Someone whispered, "Gotcha."

And he did have her. It was an attack she'd not seen coming and it was a clear success. Now, of course, he would take his victory lap.

"So," he said, addressing the students, "I expect all of you who are interested in a real education to drop these silly courses where learned facts change with the wind, and join me in the Philosophy Department for the study of real truth."

More chuckles, even a brief scattering of applause as Annie struggled to hold back her own smile. The class buzzer sounded and the students rose, closing notebooks and reaching for backpacks.

"Make sure you review chapters twenty-three through thirty for Wednesday," she shouted. "And bring your questions. We've got one more class before midterms. One more class."

She was politely ignored.

As she turned to gather her notes, Zimmerman approached. "Here you go, Dr. Brooks." He handed her the coffee, sniffing back a nosefull of congestion and swallowing.

She glanced at him, then at the cup, then smiled. "That's okay, you keep it."

"You sure?" He coughed up a wad of phlegm and swallowed again.

"Uh, yes, but thank you."

"No prob." He turned and swaggered off.

She finished gathering her papers and started up the steps to join Nicholas, who rose stiffly to greet her.

"Very nice," she conceded. "I didn't see that one coming."

"I do what I can."

As she approached, she noticed his face. The swelling wasn't a trick of lighting after all. Nor were the dark rings around his eyes. "What happened?" she asked.

He shrugged.

"You look terrible."

He steadied himself against the desk. There was dirt around the cuticles of his nails. "Annie?" He seldom used her first name and it caused her alarm.

"Are you all right? Nicholas, what happened?"

"I believe . . ." He looked up. She saw his face more clearly now—nose swollen and off-center, bruises around his eyes. "I may be in need of your assistance."

CHAPTER 3

R USTY RAN ACROSS the backyard to greet Nicholas, who had just stepped onto the brick patio with Annie. "You look awful!" the boy exclaimed.

Nicholas nodded. "I was beaten up by a very bad man." Then he added, "What's your excuse?"

Without missing a beat, the boy replied, "Genetics. Mom says it's from a dominant gene on my father's side."

Nicholas threw Annie an amused look. "I see."

"Does it hurt?" Rusty pulled up a wicker chair and stood on it, taking a closer look at the broken and newly taped nose. "It looks like it hurts." He reached for it and Nicholas shied away.

"Russell," Annie admonished.

"Of course it hurts," Nicholas groused.

The boy nodded. "That's 'cause the synapses are shooting electrical signals to your brain. Did you know that?"

"Actually, I did."

"'Cause you know everything, right?" He turned to his mother. "That's what you always say, right?" Nicholas replied, "Your mother's very observant."

27

"Actually," Annie corrected, "I say it's because he thinks he knows everything."

"Are you staying for lunch?" Rusty asked.

"If that meets your approval."

"Cool!" The boy hopped off the chair and headed for the house. Then, remembering, he turned back to Annie. "There was a bee in the backyard. Like a giant bumblebee. It was so cool. It landed right over there on the swing."

Annie looked with concern to the swing set. "You didn't go near it?"

"I wanted to, but you know Grandma." He shrugged in resignation.

"You know you're allergic," Annie said.

"I know, I know—ana-anaphal—"

"Anaphylactic," she said. "One sting and you go into anaphylactic shock." She reached out, pushing the hair from his eyes. "And that's very, very dangerous."

He turned to Nicholas. "And you got it too, right?"

Nicholas nodded. "We're the lucky ones."

"Do you have an EpiPen?" Rusty asked.

"Comes with the territory, Squirt."

"Yeah, we got 'em all over the place." Rusty yanked open the screen door. "I'll tell Grandma you're staying for lunch."

"I'm sure she'll be thrilled," Nicholas said. As the screen door slapped shut, he eased himself into the chair. "He's getting bigger."

Annie crossed to the edge of the patio and smelled the star jasmine weaving its way through the lattice. "You feed 'em, give 'em a little water, it happens."

"What is he, six now?"

"Five."

"And still not too irritating."

"Amazing."

"Who would have thought?"

Annie nodded. A single mom with a five-year-old? Who would have thought, indeed? Certainly not her. After all, she was the good girl. The Goody Two-shoes Christian who never slept around. Well, except for that one time after a third glass of Chardonnay. But she and Mr. Right had been dating nearly eight months and the evening was so perfect, the moment so natural, and the love so true. They'd even begun talking about marriage. Well, until the little dot came up blue. And yes, she was sure. And no, she would not get an abortion. And yes, she would raise it with or without him.

Six weeks later, Mr. Right not only checked the box labeled "Without," but disappeared from her life without a trace and no penny of support. Ah, yes, true love.

And who helped her through those next months? Certainly not her friends, not from either side of the moral aisle. After all, she was a college professor, an advocate of the faith, a role model to young women. So, while her nonreligious friends secretly gloated, her religious ones subtly evaporated. It was only Dr. Nicholas Mackenzie, the curmudgeon she publicly debated on campus, who stayed at her side. Never once did he point out her hypocrisy. Never once did he do anything but offer help. A surprising paradox, for the crank that both faculty and students went out of their way to avoid.

The screen door creaked open and Rusty appeared with the game Go. Nicholas had given it to him last Christmas. It was a Chinese game of logic created some four thousand years ago—popular today with the computer geeks and eggheads. Not exactly the exploding action figure Rusty had requested, but not surprising considering the source of the gift.

The boy plopped the game board down on the patio table in front of Nicholas. "I figured out how you beat me last time," he said.

"As if that will make a difference."

"It will. You just watch."

"Big words for a little man."

"Just watch." Rusty produced two cups—one filled with white round stones, the other with black.

Annie started toward the house. "I'll give Mom a hand with lunch."

Nicholas made no reply. Neither did Rusty.

She stepped into the house and turned to steal a look through the screen. They had already hunkered down to play, Nicholas resting his bony arms on his knees, chin in hands ... and Rusty imitating him to the letter.

"Any century you feel like starting, let me know," Nicholas said.

"I'm thinking, I'm thinking."

"I thought I smelled smoke."

It was all routine, part of their start-up banter.

Annie's thoughts were interrupted by her mother's voice.

"If that man insists upon freeloading, the least he could do is buy food once in a while."

It wasn't that her mother disliked Nicholas. She loathed him. Actually, loathe might be too kind of a word ... But it was a beautiful day and Annie wanted to think positively.

She turned to see her mother at the kitchen island, slicing carrots on a chopping block. She was a stout person in a summer dress whose taste in clothes was almost as bad as Nicholas's.

"Rusty likes him," Annie said, walking over to join her. "It's good for him to be around another male."

"It would be good if the male had a shred of manners. Did you see him on TV last night?"

"He was a little blunt."

"Blunt? He was a jerk."

"Mom." Annie motioned for her to keep her voice down.

But, in vintage Mom style, she repeated even louder with a final chop, "Jerk!"

Annie headed to the cupboard for the salad plates. Changing subjects, she asked, "Are you all set for your trip to Aunt Myrtle's?"

"Packed and ready to go. Just as soon as I'm done waiting on you and your friend."

Annie glanced over to the pot of boiling spaghetti and adjacent saucepan. "What can I do to help?"

Blowing the hair from her eyes, the woman nodded to a small desk across the room where Annie had set up the family computer-close enough to keep an eye on her ever-inquisitive son. "You can figure out what's wrong with the Internet."

"It's down again?" Annie asked, crossing toward it.

"Not if you call getting the same message three dozen times 'down.'"

At the desk, she clicked on the screen. Sure enough, there were a good thirty to forty e-mails, all with the same topic:

Urgent: Read immediately.

Unconcerned about viruses (the kiss-up kids in her class always made sure she had the latest protection), she brought up the e-mail and read:

Bro!

2430 Hyperion. DESPERATELY need you.

T.

She stared at the screen. Earlier, when she had taken Nicholas to the campus infirmary and stayed with him (he was as frightened of modern medicine as he was modern technology), he'd told her all about his encounter with the so-called Homeland Security agent and the agent's insistence upon finding Nicholas's brother Travis. Annie reread the message, thinking, T as in ... Travis?

She'd never met the man, but had heard enough stories.

For Nicholas he was a source of both embarrassment and pride. Embarrassment because of his multiple run-ins with the law. And pride because, according to Nicholas, he was one of the best computer minds in North America.

Without a word, she turned from the computer and headed back through the kitchen toward the screen door.

"Did you find the problem?" her mother asked.

She didn't answer, but pushed open the door. "Nicholas?"

The boys were deep in thought over the game.

"Nicholas, I think you might have an e-mail from your brother."

He looked up. "What? Here?"

"See for yourself."

"On ... the computer?"

She nodded.

He hesitated, pushed at his glasses.

"You don't have to touch anything," she said. "Just read the screen."

He took a silent breath and rose, obviously not liking the idea.

"What about our game?" Rusty protested.

Nicholas shoved an index finger at him. "I know where every piece is, so don't you even think of cheating, Squirt."

Rusty folded his arms with the same contempt she'd seen Nicholas exhibit a thousand times. She opened the door, allowing Nicholas to pass. Only then did she spot the reflection at the fence through the bougainvillea. A glint of light that suddenly disappeared on the neighbor's side, then became a moving shadow.

"Hey!" She started across the patio. "What are you doing?" She caught a glimpse of a man racing through the yard, heading toward the street. "Hey!"

"Mom ..." Rusty called.

She didn't reply. Someone was spying on her kid and he

was going to answer for it. She ran to the side gate and threw it open. She could see the man clearly now, young, T-shirt and jeans, with a camera in his hands. He scurried across the neighbor's front yard, heading toward a white Ford Escalade across the street.

"Hey!"

He picked up his pace.

So did Annie. "What are you doing?"

The Escalade fired up as he crossed around the front and hopped into the passenger seat. The rational side of Annie's brain told her to be careful, to remember Nicholas's recent encounter. But that was no match for the other side, the mother bear protecting her cub.

"I'm talking to you!"

The Escalade's tires squealed as it took off.

With adrenaline pumping, Annie started after it, thinking she could somehow chase it down.

"Hey! Hey!"

It wasn't until it reached the end of the block that reality finally set in. She came to a stop, panting. What was she thinking? She could have been hurt. They might have had guns. Suddenly her knees felt a little rubbery. She leaned over, catching her breath, clearing her head.

"Are you all—"

She screamed and spun around. A tall, good-looking man stood behind her.

"Sorry, I didn't mean to startle—"

"Who are you?"

He reached into his sports coat and she took a half step back.

"Matthew Hostetler," he said, pulling out his wallet. He opened it and produced a business card that he handed to her. "FBI."

She took the card and pretended to read it, though she

was shaking too hard to focus. She motioned toward the departed Escalade and demanded, "Are you with them?"

"Uh, yes," he cleared his throat. "Yes, I am, Dr. Brooks."

"You know my name."

"Yes, maam."

She scowled, fear giving way to anger. "What do you want?"

"You're a colleague of Dr. Mackenzie?"

"Yes, we both teach at UCSB. What's—"

"Have you seen him in the past twenty-four hours?"

She glanced up the block to her house.

"Dr. Brooks?"

"No," she lied. "Why do you ask?" She turned to him, trying to hold his gaze. He had sad, sensitive eyes.

"We believe he was kidnapped last night."

"Kidnapped?"

"He appeared on a television show."

"And?"

"And the TV station's limo was reported stolen. We found the body of the driver in a dumpster early this morning."

"Dead?"

He nodded.

For a moment Annie was speechless. "Who would—"

"I'm afraid that's proprietary information."

Once again she felt her anger starting to rise. "And that's why you're sneaking around taking photos of my family? What, are we suspects? Are we—"

"You're one of the few people close to Dr. Mackenzie."

She stared at him, making it clear she expected more.

He hesitated, then explained, "We have reason to believe his brother, Travis Mackenzie, is involved in an operation that could prove very dangerous if it fell into the wrong hands."

"What's that got to do with Dr. Mackenzie?"

"In order to get to his brother, they may try to get to him."

"That still gives you no right to go around spying on my family!"

"Actually, Doctor, we have every right."

Her look hardened to a glare.

He attempted to sound more reasonable. "Listen, Dr. Brooks... when it comes to national security, we have more than a right, we have an obligation—to you and everyone else in the country."

She felt herself cooling, but just slightly. He seemed honest enough. And those eyes, so sad and sincere. Still, it would have to be Nicholas's decision to trust him, not hers.

She swallowed and demanded, "Is there anything else?"

"No, Doctor."

"I'm free to go back to my own home?"

"Yes, maam."

She pulled herself from his eyes and started back to her house.

"Oh, and Doctor ..."

She slowed and turned.

"If you should see Dr. Mackenzie, please give him my card. My cell number is on the back."

She glanced down at the card, still not able to read it.

"Have him contact me immediately. For his own safety. And his brother's."

Without a word, she turned and continued toward the house, feeling him watching her all the way. She knew when they got back to the lab or office or wherever they worked and checked the photos, they'd discover she'd lied. But at least it would give Nicholas time to decide what he wanted to do.

Only after she entered the door and shut it did she call out, "Nicholas?" She passed through the living room and into the kitchen, where Mom was draining the spaghetti. "Nicholas?"

Rusty stood at the screen door.

"Where's Nicholas?" she asked.

The boy scowled hard at the ground, obviously not happy.

"Sweetheart? Where's Nicholas?"

"He's ... gone."

CHAPTER 4

"HELLO?" NICHOLAS BANGED on the old oak and glass door. "Hello?"

A faded cardboard clock with the words WILL BE BACK AT: hung inside. Its hands were set at 1:00. It was now 1:52. No wonder the world was falling apart.

Earlier, at Annie's, when she was yelling at the photographer and chasing his SUV down the street, Nicholas had slipped out the back and headed up the alley. A more gallant friend might have come to her rescue, but from what he had seen, she was definitely holding her own.

He banged harder on the door, causing it to rattle. "Hello!"

Still no response.

He cupped his hands against the glass and peered into the unlit shop. To the left was a wall of used paperbacks. Ahead of him stood four rows of old, overstuffed bookcases that stretched into darkness. And to his immediate right was a glass case filled with comic books, used board games, and hookah pipes of various shapes and sizes. From what he could see, everything was covered in a thin patina of dust.

"Don't waste your time, brother." He turned to a bearded wino shuffling toward him. He was stooped, dreadlocked, and wore a wool overcoat and smudged pants that might have been beige at one time.

"They never 'round here no more."

Nicholas turned back to the shop, hoping to avoid further contact with the man. No such luck.

"You gots any change? Help a brother out?"

Nicholas pulled an address from his pocket and without looking at him said, "Do I appear to be your brother?"

"What choo say?"

Nicholas unfolded the paper and double-checked the information he'd written from Annie's computer: 2430 Hyperion.

The man sidled up closer. "I could leave a message if you want."

Nicholas stepped back and checked the address above the door. The blistered numbers read 2430. Still not looking, he replied, "What I want is for you to go haunt somebody else."

"Sorry, man, ain't gonna be that easy."

Finally Nicholas turned his full contempt upon the vagrant. He generally tended toward the cranky side when he didn't get his eight hours' sleep. Last night he'd gotten zero. To make matters worse, the wino had shoved his hand into his overcoat pocket and pretended he was holding a gun.

"Oh, please," Nicholas scorned.

The man pulled out his hand just enough to reveal the walnut grip of a pistol.

Nicholas stiffened, but with no less contempt replied, "Unless you take Visa or American Express, I'm afraid you're out of luck."

"Let me see your wallet."

"I have used all my cash on a taxi."

"Your wallet."

"You're obviously not paying attention. I've just explained —" The man pushed the barrel into Nicholas's ribs.

Having no intention of repeating last night's unpleasantries, Nicholas pulled his wallet from his pocket and opened it. "See?" He spoke as if to a child. "No money. I have no—"

The wino snatched the wallet from him and flipped through the plastic folders. He stopped at the driver's license. Squinting at the name, he raised it to eye level, comparing the photo to Nicholas's face.

Nicholas looked around, hoping to catch the attention of a passerby, some dutiful citizen. The place was deserted except for a middle-aged woman across the street at the bus stop reading a paperback.

The derelict pulled a small walkie-talkie from his pocket. All trace of ghettoese was gone as he spoke into it. "We have him."

A tiny chirp followed, and then the reply. "Copy that."

Nicholas took a half step back, preparing for the worst.

The man closed his wallet and handed it to him. "Here you, go, Dr. Mackenzie."

Nicholas stared at him.

"I apologize for the scare, but we had to be certain."

Nicholas yanked the wallet from him. "Who are you?"

"That will all be explained in a moment."

The vagrant glanced to the woman at the bus stop. She was on her feet now, checking the street to the right, then the intersection to the left. Nicholas followed her gaze to a skinny bald man at the intersection who was doing the same with the opposing street. Satisfied, the man turned toward the vagrant and gave a discreet nod.

"What's going on?" Nicholas demanded. "Who exactly are—"

"Hey, bro, what's happening?"

Nicholas turned to see a silver Lexus approach, its back window rolled down. As it slowed, the door opened, and there, all smiles, wearing an obnoxious Hawaiian shirt, white cargo shorts, and flip-flops, sat his brother, Travis Mackenzie.

"'Sup, dude!" Travis called as the car rolled to a stop. "How you doin'?"

Nicholas was both relieved and angry. "What is this about?"

Travis waved for him to join him. "Come on, man."

Nicholas dug in and folded his arms . . . until the derelict placed his hand in the middle of his back and eased him forward.

"Please, Doctor, we haven't much time."

"Come on, bro." Travis motioned. "Hop in."

Reluctantly, Nicholas started forward. As he arrived, Travis scooted across the seat to make room. The derelict remained at his side and, with more than a little annoyance, Nicholas climbed in.

"What nonsense are you involved with this time?" he asked.

"Good seeing you too. What's it been, a year?"

"I am asking you a simple question. What's going on?"

The derelict shut the door, patted the roof, and the car pulled onto the street.

"Not much. Just something you've been waiting for like your entire life."

Noting the leather seats, the walnut interior, Nicholas concluded, "You're involved with narcotics again."

"Nah." Travis flashed one of his famous lopsided grins. "Something better, man. A whole lot better."

"What is going on?"

"I told you—"

"Travis!"

"After all these years, you finally get to be the big kahuna."

"What are you talking about?"

"You heard me. You, Dr. Nicholas Mackenzie... you're finally gonna get your chance to play God."

* * *

THE MUFFLER of Annie's rusting Honda Civic rattled away as she approached Hyperion Street. Not that her beater drew much attention in this section of town. Not with the thrift shops and liquor stores. Still, like most of Santa Barbara, with its Mediterranean charm and Beverly Hills property value, even this stretch was relatively safe. In fact, when she first moved here as an associate professor (i.e., bottom of UCSB's food chain) these were her old stomping grounds.

It had been thirty minutes since Nicholas left. She knew he wouldn't hitch a ride, which probably meant a taxi. If not, he'd walk. Anything to distance himself from the house. Her mother insisted it was because he was a coward. Maybe. Though Annie preferred to think he was trying to protect her family by removing himself from their presence.

Then there was the matter of his brother. Nicholas never went into much detail about the man. That would involve discussing feelings and personal history; both he detested. Still, she had pieced together enough to know that they had shared a widower father who anesthetized his pain with booze, while wholeheartedly embracing the concept of not sparing the rod. As the older brother by nearly ten years, it was Nicholas's job to intercede and protect Travis—until one late-night brawl led to Nicholas breaking his father's arm, which was followed by an agreement to join the military so the old man wouldn't press charges.

Annie reached for the business card she'd tossed on her dashboard. The one from the FBI agent. What arrogance ...

"That gives you no right to go around spying on my family!"

"Actually, Doctor, we have every right."

The card certainly appeared official enough, with its gold embossed FBI seal in the top corner, and the name Matthew Hostetler—Supervising Special Agent centered below. She tossed it on the seat and began turning left onto Hyperion when a Lexus pulled in front of her out of the blue. She slammed on her brakes, seat harness digging into her chest. She barely missed hitting the Lexus's rear passenger door when, for a millisecond, she stared directly at the passing profile of Dr. Nicholas Mackenzie.

Shocked, flustered, and angry, she fumbled to find her horn. By the time she blasted them with its anemic beep, the Lexus was halfway down the block. She turned the Honda hard to the right, barely missing a skinny bald man, and began pursuit. Now that she found the horn, she gave it no rest. . . though she doubted they could even hear it.

The Lexus continued accelerating and pulling away. Wherever they were going, they were in a hurry. And if it was for any distance whatsoever, that would mean the freeway. But Hyperion was peppered with stop signs. Knowing they couldn't barrel through every one, Annie took a chance. She turned right on Ventu and dropped down two blocks to Milpas for a clearer, faster shot to the freeway entrance.

"If this is a joke, I am not amused."

"No, no, no." Travis crammed a piece of Juicy Fruit into his mouth. "You know how paranoid them big corporate boys can be."

Nicholas stared with contempt at the red and white cowboy bandanna his brother held out to him.

"It's outrageous, man. When you see what we got, you'll be blown away."

"You said you were in trouble."

"No way. I distinctly said, 'I desperately need you.' Big difference, bro."

Nicholas glanced back at the sweat-stained bandanna. "You expect me to wear that?"

Travis nodded.

"And if I refuse?"

Travis shrugged. "Then I'll ask Syd to let you off right here. No harm, no foul. There's plenty of philosopher types around. I just figured you'd want to be in on the ground floor."

"The ground floor of..."

Once again Travis held out the bandanna. Nicholas turned and looked out his window.

"It's totally legit, man," Travis said.

"Which explains this ridiculous game—not to mention your driver, who thinks he's racing NASCAR." Nicholas leaned forward, calling to the big man behind the wheel. "Is it possible to slow to a speed that avoids vehicular manslaughter?"

The driver ignored him and Travis resumed his sales pitch. "When it comes to new technology and IPs, corporations get totally nuts."

"And that's what all this is about? A corporation protecting some intellectual property?"

"Not some intellectual property, bro. The queen mother of all intellectual properties. The big boys will pay billions for it." He gave his gum a couple snaps. "Buco billions."

Nicholas pondered the thought. If that was true, it would account for his treatment last night. And the break-in at his house. He glanced down at the trace of dirt still under his nails from burying Aristotle. Travis was a con man and a habitual liar. But never once, in all of their years, did he purposely endanger Nicholas. Instead, he looked upon Nicholas as a surrogate father, a true north on his erratic and ever-changing compass. Like it or not, they were family, a fact that didn't change even when Nicholas had started his own. On more weekends than not, Travis would swing by for free meals. Often he would lavish expensive gifts on Stephanie or, even more frequently, some new electronic gizmo on Mikey. Thanks to Travis, their little boy was operating joy sticks before he could walk. And, as the child grew older, Travis would sneak top-secret beta-version computer games he was creating over to the house. The two of them would test and play them well into the night—laughing, gorging on junk food, sharing conspiratorial secrets. Often Nicholas felt like he was raising two children, and in some ways they were closer to each other than he could ever be.

But those times had come and gone. A lifetime ago.

"So, which will it be, Neo?" Travis grinned, holding the bandanna and paraphrasing his favorite movie. "The blue pill or the red one?"

Nicholas stared at him.

"Blue or red?"

Finally, Nicholas reached up and removed his glasses.

"All right!" Travis scooted closer and wrapped the bandanna around Nicholas's eyes. "You're gonna like this, bro. You're gonna like it a lot."

* * *

ANNIE HAD BARELY PULLED over at the intersection next to the freeway when the Lexus shot past. Without hesitation, she turned back onto the street and cut off a VW bug, its horn sounding even more pathetic than hers.

"Sorry!" She waved as she fell behind the Lexus, following

it onto the 101 southbound ramp. She stayed close on its tail, flashing her lights and honking. If they had any doubt she was serious, they knew it now.

Which might explain why they picked up speed.

But Annie would not be put off. She also accelerated.

As soon as the Lexus entered the freeway, it swerved around a utility van to enter the fast lane. Annie followed suit. But the car continued pulling away. She glanced at the speedometer. They'd just cleared seventy, with no signs of slowing. Where was a cop when you needed one?

It was an older section of freeway, with only two lanes. The Lexus quickly approached a pickup and veered back into the slow lane, cutting off an elderly couple on a Harley. The man and woman both swore and gave accompanying hand gestures. Annie pushed the accelerator to the floor, also cutting off the couple and drawing the same tokens of ill will.

The Lexus came up to a Jeep Cherokee. Once again it swerved into the fast lane, nearly hitting a slower, lumbering SUV, before it squeezed back in, cutting off the Jeep. By the time Annie arrived, the Jeep and SUV were side by side, boxing her in. She had to wait for the Cherokee to clear before hitting the gas and following. She gripped the wheel tighter, wishing she'd played more of Rusty's video games.

To her left the sprawling lawn of the Montecito Country Club appeared. Beyond that lay the exclusive city of Montecito, where Oprah and the like lived. She noticed the front wheels of her Honda beginning to vibrate. And for good reason. She was approaching ninety. Some part of her knew this was crazy, that she should be calling the police on her cell. The other part doubted it would do any good.

The Lexus swerved around a U-Haul, then an RV. Annie followed. The road bent sharply to the right and under a canopy of eucalyptus. It straightened, and suddenly a cement truck loomed in front of her. The adjacent lane was blocked by another pickup and she hit the brakes, tires squealing, the Honda sliding. She would have lost control if it weren't for those icy Chicago streets she'd learned on. She pulled out of the skid and slowed, heart pounding, the tingle of adrenaline spreading through her arms and into her fingers. But once again she was blocked by two vehicles. Wiping the sweat from her hands, she pulled behind the pickup, flashing her lights, making it clear she wanted to pass ... just as another set of lights began flashing in her rearview mirror. The far brighter and more colorful ones of the California Highway Patrol.

Annie could only stare. Unbelievable. Once again the bad guys got away while the good ones got stuck with, what—a $150, $200 ticket? Her gut clenched in anger as she blew the hair out of her eyes, then signaled and pulled to the side.

Unfortunately, she was about to discover Santa Barbara's traffic fines were as inflated as their real estate.

CHAPTER 5

WITH THE BANDANA over his eyes, Nicholas turned toward his brothers voice. "You created what?"

"That's right, man . . . artificial intelligence, AI. Emotions, pattern recognition, free will, the ability to hold contradictory views—"

"You mean the mimicking of those attributes."

"Nope." Travis gave his gum an extra snap. "I mean human consciousness. The whole enchilada."

"That's not possible."

"Come out of your cave, dude. Computer circuits already operate a million times faster than human neurons."

"That may be the case, but—"

"And most of our brain drain is used just to survive. The trick was to find a computer big enough to duplicate all the redundancy. Then, of course, there was that whole digital/analog thing."

Nicholas frowned, not entirely sure what Travis was talking about. The car slowed and took another hairpin curve, one of dozens since they had left the freeway.

"But we've done it, man. Signed, sealed, and delivered."

"You've constructed some giant computer?"

"Yes and no. But that's only for starters."

Nicholas sighed in obvious irritation.

"Patience, big brother. You'll see the whole picture when we get there."

"And that will be in ..."

"Just a little longer."

Nicholas sighed louder. They'd turned off the freeway thirty minutes ago. Now, with the ocean at their backs, they were winding through the Santa Ynez mountains—the same range that once served as home for Ronald Reagan's ranch as well as Michael Jackson's Neverland. The wilderness was expansive and secluded enough for any person or organization to buy up property and go about their business unnoticed.

Fifteen minutes later the car slowed, turned onto a dirt road, and started a steep climb.

"Hey, Syd?" Travis called to the driver. "Can we lose the blindfold now?"

"Don't see why not," the big man said.

Nicholas pulled off the bandanna and squinted in the bright afternoon light. He reached into his pocket for his glasses. He barely had them on before the car crested a ridge and an old ranch house came into view—one story, weathered wood, and blistered paint. Behind it rose a steep, grassy hill, so close that the house could have been built into its side. And beyond that, more hills, higher and steeper.

Travis opened the car door before the vehicle even stopped. He stepped outside and stretched. "Here we are. Home, sweet home." He crossed around the front of the car to join Nicholas.

"It doesn't look like much," Nicholas said.

"Not suppose to." To the north, the sun shimmered off a

row of towering eucalyptus trees. Their smell always reminded Nicholas of medicated cough drops ... or a cat box that needed emptying. Beyond them rose more hills with golden grass, gray-green chaparral, and randomly scattered oak. The driveway was coated in tiny red berries from two pepper trees that hovered over either end of the house, their twisted branches offering shade from the relentless sun.

They walked toward the back porch, gravel crunching under their shoes, as the car pulled away to join two SUVs and another sedan under a grove of oaks. Nicholas noted the camouflage netting stretched across the trees above the vehicles. They climbed the steps and Travis pulled open a dilapidated screen door, which groaned in protest. He knocked and waited, then gave Nicholas one of his lopsided grins.

The door opened. A well-cut Latino, mid-thirties, with dark blue pants and a white polo shirt, stood before them.

Travis greeted him, all smiles. "Hey, Norm, what's up?"

The man said nothing as he produced a handheld metal detector. Travis raised his arms, allowing the wand to pass over him. Once again he threw a grin to Nicholas. "They do have their paranoia."

The guard motioned Travis inside and Nicholas stepped forward, raising his arms for a similar search. Satisfied, the guard motioned him inside to join his brother. It was a large state-of- the-art kitchen, Viking stainless steel oven and grill, matching refrigerator, stainless steel sink, and black marble counters.

"Come on." Travis motioned him to follow. "My lair's in the basement."

"Since when do California houses have basements?" Nicholas asked.

"Since when did you think this a house?" They entered a hallway leading toward the back. At the left was the living room. To the right were four doors.

"I suppose these are offices?" Nicholas asked.

"And sleeping quarters, yeah."

They reached the end of the hallway and Travis opened a door to reveal yet another passageway. Unlike the first, it had fluorescent lighting, stark white walls, and two steel doors, each with an electronic number pad beside it. As they approached the closest door, Travis pulled out a plastic ID. He slid the card through the box.

"What's down there?" Nicholas motioned to the other door.

"R.E.," Travis said as he entered a six-number code.

"R.E.?"

"Reverse Engineering. Long story. I'll show you later." The door gave a dull click. "But down here ..." He turned the handle and pushed it open. "Down here is where the magic happens."

* * *

ANNIE PULLED into her driveway and shut off the engine. Even though she'd received a traffic ticket the size of the national debt, it was Nicholas who remained on her mind. She retrieved the FBI agent's card, checked the number, and dialed it on her cell. The call was answered after the third ring.

"This is the Federal Bureau of Investigation ..."

"Yes, I'd like to speak to—"

". . . the Santa Barbara Resident Agency. If you know your party's extension, please dial it now."

Annie blew at the hair in her eyes and waited.

"For Agent Harold Gibson, please press four."

She double-checked the name on the card.

"For Supervising Agent Matthew Hostetler, press five. If you are unsure of—"

She pressed five and waited.

"Hello, this is Agent Matthew Hostetler."

"Hi, this is Dr. Brook—"

"I'm sorry, I'm not in the office right now, but please leave a message."

She closed her eyes, summoning patience.

"If this is an emergency, my cell number is 555-9051. Thanks." She flipped over his card to confirm the cell number, then disconnected. She dialed the number and waited. And waited.

A loud rap on the drivers window caused her to jump. She turned to see her mother standing outside, small suitcase in hand, anything but happy.

"Oh, Mom." She pressed the button to the window, remembered it didn't work, and opened her door. The door chime began to sound loudly. "I'm so sorry. Time just got away from me."

"Your spaghetti's in the fridge." Her mother turned and headed down the driveway toward her car. "Rusty's on a computer game, and I'm forty minutes late. I'll see you Monday."

"Hello?" the voice from her phone was barely discernible over the chiming. "Hello, Matthew Hostetler, here."

She raised the phone to her face. "Oh, yes, hello, uh, hang on a minute." She opened the door wider and took a half step out. "Mom, is there any way you could wait another hour? I've got some important business regarding Nicholas and—"

"I'm going to hit rush hour as it is."

"Right, but if you waited, you'd—"

"Hello?" the agent asked.

Annie returned to the phone. "Yes, just a minute."

"I'm not giving that man another minute of my time." Her mother opened the back door to her car and threw in the suitcase. "And if you were smart, you wouldn't either."

"Hello..." The door chime continued.

"... Dr. Brooks?"

Annie spoke back to the phone, "Will you just—" Then, to her mother, "Mom?"

Her mother got in the car. "You and Rusty have a wonderful weekend."

"Mom—"

She closed the door and started the ignition.

"Hello.."

Annie turned to the phone and demanded, "What is it?"

"Uh, actually, you called me, Dr. Brooks."

She watched as her mother pulled away. "Right. How do you know my—" Guessing the answer before she finished, she changed gears. "We need to talk."

"Do you have more information?" he asked.

"Yes."

"Great. I'll be over at your house in twenty minutes."

"No, no more house calls." She stared at the card's address. "Your office. I want to meet you at your office."

"All right. When would you like to do that?"

The chiming continued. She rubbed her head. "Now. I want to meet you now."

* * *

COOL DRY AIR hit Nicholas's face as he stepped through the door. "Did we just enter the hillside?" he asked.

"Very good," Travis said. "Now, hang on to the railing, these steps can be tricky for an old man like you."

Nicholas ignored him and eased down the steep girder steps into the darkness. It was a small room, ten by twenty, and lit only by the blue-green glow of a dozen monitors. They were mounted on steel scaffolding directly in front of a control console, where a young man and woman sat taking notes and occasionally typing information on their keyboards. The side walls were lined with ribs of black foam, the type found in sound studios. At the back stood a row of cupboards and a small counter.

"Hugh?" Travis called. "Rebecca?" The two turned toward him. "Here he is ... Dr. Nicholas Mackenzie."

The young man was on his feet so quickly his chair rolled backward across the concrete floor. He was a pudgy kid, grad school age. "It's an honor, Doctor. We've heard so much about you." They shook hands. His grip was as soft and doughy as his body.

"Yes." Nicholas scowled. "I wish I could say the same."

"Hugh's my main man," Travis explained, "our lead programmer, right out of Stanford." He motioned to the young woman. "And this is Rebecca Staffer, who you may or may not remember."

Nicholas turned to her. She was bony, with stringy blond hair.

"I'm sure you don't," was all she said before turning back to the monitors.

"She was one of your undergrads," Travis explained. "All set to be a seminary student, till you talked some sense into that pretty head of hers."

Nicholas stared at her back.

Travis continued, "She teaches philosophy at the University of Washington now. We thought she could give us a hand. And she did, beautifully. But—"

Still not facing them, she finished his phrase. "No one can compete with the great Nicholas Mackenzie." She punched a button on the console for emphasis.

Nicholas turned to his brother. "I want to know what all of this is about. And I want to know now."

Travis snapped his gum and grinned. "You've been patient, I'll give you that." He moved to the counter at the back wall. On it sat a coffeemaker, mugs, a small refrigerator, various snacks, and a basket of fruit. "Hugh, you want to do the honors?"

"With pleasure." The kid motioned to the only other empty chair. "Please, Doctor, have a seat."

Nicholas remained standing. Hugh cleared his throat. "Travis has no doubt explained that we've finally managed to create artificial intelligence. But not just a single individual, as you would suppose. Instead, we've created an entire community."

"I've seen those sort of things," Nicholas said. "My students waste their time playing with them on the Internet."

"No, Doctor. This is a million times more complex. We are talking very specific and very distinct consciousnesses. Nearly a thousand of them."

"One wasn't enough?"

"Not if we want to study evolving human social interaction."

For the first time Nicholas could find no words.

Obviously pleased at the impact, Travis poured himself a mug of coffee and took over. "Actually, the first AI was the hardest. But once we got him nailed, the others were a piece of cake."

"How so?" Nicholas asked.

"We humans aren't all that different, bro. Using the first as the prototype, we simply made tweaks and adjustments to create the others—older, younger, male, female."

"And for this, corporations would pay billions?"

"Or more."

Nicholas showed his skepticism.

"It's a way of seeing into the future. Want to know how people are going to act in a situation? Just enter the variables and see what happens. Want to win an election? Run the program, look into my crystal ball, see what works."

Nicholas frowned, intrigued but still doubtful.

"And this is the coolest part." Travis leaned forward. "Where the real bucks are. You want to know what laundry soap will sell? Run my program. Seriously, man, imagine what would have happened if some corporation knew in advance how popular the hula hoop would be. Or Barney the Dinosaur. Or whether to go eight-track or cassette. HD-DVD or Blu-ray. We're talking billions, bro. Hundreds of billions."

Nicholas paused, thinking it through. Then, turning to his brother, he asked, "And the computer power we discussed?" He looked about the room. "Where does that come from?"

Travis took a moment to sip his coffee. Nicholas waited.

At last, he answered. "You know about the SETI project, right? All those radio telescopes pointed into outer space hoping to eavesdrop on aliens talking to each other?"

The name stirred a vague memory.

"Anyway, our project has way too much data for just one computer to handle, no matter how big it is. And since supercomputers are just thousands of home computers wired in parallel, SETI had this bright idea of actually connecting the computers in people's homes."

Nicholas frowned.

Hugh explained, "Volunteers download a simple program and whenever they're not using their computers, SETI takes over and employs those computers to process the data."

Nicholas gave a half nod. "How many home computers is SETI using?"

"About eight million," Travis said. "Around the world."

"And that's just the SETI program," Hugh said. "Similar projects have been implemented to predict the three-dimensional tangle of proteins, the weather, models for possible universes. Actually there are currently fifty-one different projects using this type of cluster computing."

"And yours makes fifty-two," Nicholas said.

"Actually, no." Travis sipped his coffee.

"Why not?"

"Because we don't exist."

"Then how do you..." Nicholas saw the grin flicker across his brother's face. He turned to Hugh, who found an excuse to look away. Slowly, the realization sank in. "You've hacked into one of them?" Travis's grin grew bigger.

"You've hacked into all of them?"

Travis gave a shrug. "If you're going to create a world, you need all the help you can get."

Nicholas shook his head. Apparently the prison time Travis had served for breaking into computers had done little toward his rehabilitation. Nicholas turned toward the wall of monitors and for the first time he began to study them. The largest screen filled the center area. It was surrounded by a dozen smaller ones. As best he could tell, they were all different angles of some medieval village at nighttime. "And that's your world?" he asked.

"That's what we've created until now," Hugh explained.

Finally, Rebecca spoke. "At least this time."

"You've done this before?" Nicholas asked.

Hugh sighed. "More times than you want to know."

"And that's why you're here," Travis said.

Nicholas glanced to his brother, then back to the screens. "Where is everybody? Where is this community'?"

"Right now they're in sleep mode," Hugh said.

"Just like humans," Travis added. "They're busy processing the data they got while they were awake."

"And what exactly does all of this have to do with me?"

"I'm glad you asked." Travis leaned back against the

counter and took another sip of coffee. "Okay, boys and girls, let's bring up the morning and show the man what we got."

The assistants went to work, typing and punching information into their keyboards. But Travis wasn't quite finished. "And, bro?"

Nicholas turned to him.

For the first time that day, Travis appeared uneasy. "You're going to see some things that may upset you at first—but just be cool."

"What do you mean?"

"What I mean is I acted out of love, okay? You know me, man. Nothing but the best intentions."

"What are you saying?"

Hugh called over his shoulder, "We're ready."

"Just... be cool. Remember that famous logic of yours, all right?" Nicholas scowled as Travis took a final swallow of coffee and turned to the monitors. "Okay. Let the games begin."

CHAPTER 6

A LPHA 11 WOKE to the red light filtering through his window. The day's fires had already begun. He lay for a moment listening to his woman's deep, rhythmic breathing. She'd finally drifted off to sleep. Good. He could have beaten her, demanded she stop the sobbing, but he hadn't the heart —another sign of his weakness. And, even worse, though it was entirely her fault for birthing a female, her ache over the loss of the baby had become his ache.

He rose silently from their pallet and slipped into his wool tunic and parchment-thin sandals. She would protest his going out this early, but her breathglow had become dangerously dim. The sooner he was able to purchase life units from the Keepers, the more likely she would survive. Already he could hear the shouting of men as they killed and plundered, the screams of women being stolen and ravaged. The attacks would only grow worse as the day progressed.

* * *

"WHAT HAVE YOU DONE?" Nicholas stared at the screen, barely able to speak.

"Just let me explain," Travis said. Nicholas reached out to the back of a nearby chair to steady himself. There, on the monitor in front of him, was an exact replica of his dead son ... the black hair with the goofy cowlick, the dark, penetrating eyes of his mother, even the pale scar above his left brow from a skateboard accident.

"It was supposed to be a gift." Travis's voice was far away, barely discernible through the pounding in Nicholas's ears.

The young man on the screen was no more than three or four years older than Mikey—eighteen at most. His narrow chest and gangly arms were thickening into a man's—becoming what Mikey should have been if he had lived.

"For his birthday. It was going to be a surprise for his birthday."

Nicholas stared at the screen, barely able to breathe, watching the man-boy move about the dirt floor, preparing to start a fire in the small, stone fireplace. Emotions flooded in from every direction—guilt, pride, sorrow ... and rage. The trembling started in his hands. By the time he turned to Travis, it had filled his body.

"Before the accident. I was gonna give him this program, you know, before you—"

Nicholas lunged at him, a roar escaping from somewhere deep in his gut. He grabbed Travis, yanking him toward him.

"What was I supposed to do?" Travis shouted.

Nicholas hit his brother hard in the mouth. He felt the jar of pain all the way into his elbow.

"What could I do?" Blood spurted from Travis's split lip. "What would you do?"

Nicholas swung again, but Travis blocked him. "The program was complete!" He grabbed Nicholas's arm. "What could I do?"

Adrenaline pumped, fueling Nicholas's fury, enabling him to break free and hit Travis again, but only a glancing blow off the head. Travis returned with a powerful punch into Nicholas's stomach, knocking out his air. Before Nicholas could recover, Travis threw his arms around him, pinning his hands to his side. "I loved him too!"

Twisting, squirming, Nicholas threw them both backward, slamming into the counter and toppling to the floor. Travis hung on as they rolled across the cement. The assistants shouted, but Nicholas barely heard. A moment later, he was on his back, Travis straddling his chest, pressing his arms to the concrete with his knees.

"What was I supposed to do?"

Nicholas wiggled and bucked, but in vain.

"Destroy him?" Travis shouted. "Is that what you want?"

More squirming.

"Stop it." Travis was crying now. "Stop it."

At last, Nicholas slowed—chest heaving, sweating.

"I couldn't destroy him." Travis continued to cry. "That's all we got left. You understand me?" He motioned to the screen. "That's all we got."

Nicholas tried breaking free one last time, but it was hopeless. Exhausted, he lowered his head to the floor, fighting for breath under Travis's weight. He turned to the side and looked back up at the screen. The image was blurred from his tears, but he kept watching, he had to watch.

"Freeze it," Travis said. "Freeze the program."

Hugh hit a set of keys and the image on the screen came to a stop.

* * *

ANNIE SAT LOOKING around the small reception room. Directly in front of her was a steel-gray desk occupied by a plump black woman in her forties. Behind the woman stood two wooden doors, circa 1930, complete with frosted glass panes and painted lettering. Above one, the acoustic tiles sported what looked like a tea-colored Rorschach ink-blot test, courtesy of a leaky roof.

"Not very many agents," Annie observed.

The office manager looked up from her computer. "How's that?"

"For an FBI office, it's pretty small."

"This is just a residency office, honey. Our main office is in Los Angeles, the 9200 Wilshire building."

"Ah."

"And believe me, this is the Ritz compared to the cages they got down there. Sure I can't get you some coffee?"

"No, I'm good." Annie stared down at the business card in her hand. She recrossed her legs, barely conscious of her bouncing foot.

The office manager turned to Rusty, who was engrossed in his latest Nintendo game. "What about you, son? We've got a soda machine just down the hall."

He answered without looking up. "Yes, please."

"No, thank you," Annie corrected. "He's fine." Spotting her foot, she brought it to a stop. "What time do you think he'll be here?"

"Friday afternoon? This is his weekend with the kid, so he should be here any—"

The door opened and a seven-year-old redhead, in white shorts and a flowered peasant blouse, appeared. Agent Matthew Hostetler followed—his dark hair falling into those sad, puppy-dog eyes.

"Sorry I'm late," he said, pushing back the hair. "We had a little impromptu parent-teacher conference."

The office manager arched an eyebrow at the girl. "What'd you do this time?"

"It wasn't my fault," the girl protested, "honest."

Hostetler explained, "Seems little Jimmy Riordan didn't know when to stop teasing."

"And?" the office manager asked.

The girl shrugged. "I dropped him with a spin kick."

"And?"

The girl glanced down.

The office manager cleared her throat.

"And I sorta broke his nose."

The woman could only shake her head.

Looking to change topics, Hostetler turned to Rusty. "And you must be .."

Rusty was too mesmerized by the girl to answer. "Did you really break someone's nose?"

"Not on purpose," she protested. "Well, not really."

"Was there lots of blood?"

Hostetler crossed to his office door. "Should we get started? Can I get you anything?"

Annie rose. "No, we're good."

Spotting the Nintendo in Rusty's hand, the girl stepped closer. "Which one is that?"

"Lord of Conquest."

"Cool." She moved in closer.

Annie looked at her son, hesitating.

"He'll be fine," the agent assured her. "Sabrina will take good care of him."

Annie gave the girl a dubious look.

"Don't worry." The office manager chuckled. "I'll be here."

With a tentative smile, Annie pulled her hair behind her ear and followed the agent into his office. The place redefined the term cramped. The multiple stacks of files and paperwork on his desk and filing cabinet didn't help. Hostetler moved behind the desk and motioned to a chair in front of it. "Please," he said, then noticed the McDonald's wrappers scattered on the seat. "Oh, sorry."

"That's okay," she said, "I just stopped by to—"

He crossed to the chair and gathered the debris. "Sorry."

"Really, there's no need."

"There you go." He headed back to his desk and dumped the trash into an unseen basket. There was a nervous energy about him that she couldn't define.

She sat down and he followed suit, until the stack of folders on his desk blocked their view and he was back up. "Sorry." He scooped the folders into his arms and looked for a place to set them. "So, did you give any more consideration to our little chat?"

She watched him juggling the papers and suddenly realized what she was witnessing—self-consciousness. Was it possible? She had sensed the attraction in front of her house. Hers and his. Felt his eyes follow her all the way to her front door. But this? She almost smiled. It had been a long time since she'd had this type of effect upon a man, especially one so, well, so easy on the eyes. She cleared her throat. "I came to tell you I saw Dr. Mackenzie."

"Right," he said, stopping and juggling with the stack in his arms as he flipped through it. "We know."

"You know?"

He found a file and handed it to her. She took it and opened it to see a series of eight-by-ten color photos of Nicholas on her patio playing the board game with Rusty.

She made little effort to hide her displeasure. "Since then. Probably with his brother."

Hostetler turned to her so quickly he nearly spilled the files. "He was with his brother?"

"I'm not sure. Somebody picked him up from an address they left on my computer. I followed them onto the 101 heading south. I tried to chase them down, but they were going too fast."

Hostetler frowned. "That should really should be our job, shouldn't it?"

She gave no reply.

"Did you happen to get the make of the car?"

"A Lexus. Silver."

"License number?"

"No."

"No part of it? A number, a letter?"

"That should really be your job, shouldn't it?"

He nodded, taking the barb. "Right." She watched as he continued to search for a spot to set the files. "Travis Mackenzie may be in a very dangerous situation."

"So you said."

"And you have no idea where they were going?"

"None."

"Is there a way to contact Dr. Mackenzie?"

"He doesn't own a cell, but you probably know that."

Hostetler nodded and finally dumped the files back on his desk, exactly where they'd been in the first place. Annie barely hid her smile.

"Do you think he'll contact you again?"

"I don't know. If he does, what should I say?"

"Have him call me." He reached for his billfold. "Let me give you my card."

"Actually, I've got it." She showed him the business card she'd been holding.

"Oh, right." He replaced his billfold. "Make sure he calls me."

"Will do."

He nodded and started to take his seat. "Is there anything else?"

"No." She rose. "That's about it."

Again he was up and out of his chair. "Well, okay, then."

She turned for the door and he hustled around the desk to join her. "Now be sure to call me if you hear anything. You have my cell number, right?"

"It's on your card."

"Right. Well, day or night, just call."

"I will."

He opened the door and she stepped back into the reception area, where Rusty was watching in awe as the girl played his Nintendo game.

"Anytime," Hostetler repeated.

Annie nodded.

"Day or night."

Once again she nodded, then stole a look at the office manager, who glanced away, obviously trying to hide her own amused smile.

* * *

AN EXHAUSTED NICHOLAS stared at the cup of tea in his hands. The ripples across its surface betrayed the emotions he was still feeling. Hovering on the screen above him was the frozen image of his son.

"I couldn't just destroy him," Travis repeated. "He's all I had. He's all we had."

"So ..." Nicholas kept his voice flat and even. "You exploited him. To sell your soap, you exploited the memory of my son."

"No, it's not like that. Not at all."

Nicholas looked up to his brother, who was leaning against the back counter. "Then how is it?"

"I thought it would be an honor. You know, to have him at the center of the most important advancement of the decade. It was supposed to be an honor, man."

Nicholas looked back at his tea. "How much—" He swallowed and tried again. "How much of him is there? Besides his appearance, I mean."

"I had to give him a personality. We couldn't just make cardboard cutouts. I had to give each of them—"

"How much?"

Travis hesitated.

Nicholas looked up and waited.

"Emotions, attitudes, likes, dislikes, little character quirks —as much as I could remember."

Nicholas quietly nodded. "And the others. You said they were all based on him?"

"Yeah... he was the prototype." Nicholas glanced back at his tea, letting the truth sink in.

"It wasn't for the money. I swear to God. It wasn't the money."

Nicholas stared at the tea a long moment before finally asking, "Is there more?"

"What?"

"Of the program. Is there more?"

"Well... yeah. Plenty."

He took a deep, silent breath. "Then let's see it."

"You sure?"

Nicholas's nod was barely perceptible.

"Okay. Well, I mean if you're sure."

Finally he lifted his eyes back to the screen. And waited.

"Okay." Travis turned to Hugh. "You heard the man."

The pudgy programmer looked over his shoulder, obviously questioning the judgment.

"Come on," Travis said impatiently. "Let's do it."

Hugh turned back to the console. He punched a single key and the screen came to life.

* * *

ALPHA CROSSED BACK to the pallet to check on his woman one last time. She continued to sleep soundly. He hoped that was a good sign. Moving across the room, he fetched his battle-ax and hoisted the weapon onto his shoulder. He moved to the door and released the bolts. The heavy wooden planks creaked as he pushed them open to check outside.

Other than a thick fog and the acrid smell of smoke, the street was deserted. He slipped through the opening and into the morning chill. Turning, he began to bolt his woman indoors where she would be safe. He had barely finished the task before he heard them approaching: father and son. He spun around just in time to see the father, a giant, barrel-chested man, swing his broadsword. Alpha leaped back, but the blade still caught him, slicing through his tunic and deep into his chest.

Immediately, light blazed from the wound as the man-child, no more than ten seasons old, clubbed Alpha behind the knees and dropped him to the ground.

But Alpha still had his ax. And as the father raised his sword to finish the kill, Alpha rammed the pointed top deep into the man's gut. Light gushed out, spilling from him like a fountain.

"Father!" The boy ran toward him.

Rising, Alpha pulled the ax from the man and spun it around, catching the boy's neck, nearly severing his head. Brighter light exploded from the boy's wound as Alpha turned back to the horrified father and delivered his death blow, higher up and deep into the chest. The man staggered backward, dragging the ax with him, and fell not two lengths from his son, dead before he hit the ground.

Alpha stepped closer and raised his hands. He opened his mouth and palms toward the father and child, greedily feasting upon their glow. But their wounds were too severe and the light escaped too quickly. He barely had enough to heal the gash in his chest and seal it before their bodies grew dark, their energy gone.

Placing his foot on the father, he pried his ax from the man's chest. Then, checking on the door one last time, he turned and started down the street.

* * *

"Wait a minute," Nicholas said. "Hold it."

"Freeze," Travis ordered.

Hugh hit a few keystrokes and the image of Nicholas's son came to a stop.

Nicholas rose to his feet and stepped closer to the screen to examine the carnage. No one spoke. Finally, he turned to his brother. "Why is there so much violence? Why did you make him so barbaric?"

"I didn't make him anything," Travis said. "This is how they naturally evolved."

"They?"

"The community."

Nicholas frowned, not understanding.

"Survival of the fittest," Hugh said.

Rebecca, the female assistant, added, "Charlie Darwin would be proud."

"This is how we're wired, man," Travis explained. "You know that."

Nicholas turned back to the screen, quietly marveling. "Remarkable. Absolutely remarkable."

"And absolutely our problem."

He turned to his brother, waiting for further explanation.

"Every time we run this model, or any other, for that matter—"

Rebecca stepped in, "Epicureanism, Machiavellianism, Marxism, existentialism—"

"You've tried all those systems?" Nicholas asked.

She shook her head. "They thought up those systems—in one form or another; it's always been their doing."

"And?"

Travis shrugged. "And it's like a broken record, dude. They always wind up killing each other off."

"Until they evolve," Nicholas corrected. "Until they become civilized."

"Yeah, right," Rebecca scorned.

"What do you mean?"

Travis explained, "We can push these systems, fast-forward them. We don't get an exact future that way, but a rough idea."

"And?" Nicholas asked.

"And every system we've tried eventually winds up destroying itself."

Nicholas stared in disbelief.

Travis shrugged. "Evolving technology equals fancier weapons. Fancier weapons equals greater destruction."

"And this happens every time?" Nicholas repeated.

"Like clockwork," Rebecca answered.

He looked to the screen, thinking. "So why don't you add a touch of compassion to your models? Some element of morality?"

Travis nodded to Rebecca, who gave the explanation. "Every model we've used must come from the community's own thinking. Each philosophical system must grow naturally and organically from within."

Nicholas continued the thought. "And to impose any outside influence..."

"Would be cheating," Travis said.

"Actually"—Hugh nodded toward the screen—"you're watching the most compassionate member of the group now. At Travis's insistence, Alpha 11 here always has the most heart."

Nicholas looked to Travis, who shrugged.

Rebecca sighed in boredom. "Which usually means he's the first to be destroyed."

Nicholas scowled. "How? You've certainly made him strong enough. He's obviously a warrior."

Travis turned to Hugh. "Fast-forward us to the Grid."

Hugh nodded, turned to the console, and entered a dozen keystrokes.

* * *

THE KEEPER STOOD on the platform before the crowd, his breath luminous, his white silk robes shimmering in the breeze. Below him and to the left was the Grid, which hummed and crackled. To the untrained eye it appeared as nothing more than a finely woven iron-mesh fence.

"The bid is eight seasons?" he shouted.

All morning Alpha 11 had pushed and worked his way through the crowd until he reached the bidding line—the front row of twenty or so citizens allowed to participate.

The Keeper waved his arm to the life units on the altar before him. There were six of them. Blazing, gelatinous bricks, manufactured from the Grid.

"The bid is eight seasons. Do I hear nine?"

"Nine!" the man beside Alpha shouted. "I'll give you nine seasons."

The number was high. Higher than most on the line were willing to commit. But the breathglow of Alpha's woman had been barely visible, her need urgent.

"Eleven!" Alpha shouted. "I will give you eleven seasons."

A quiet murmur rippled through the crowd.

"Twelve!" another yelled from the end of the line. "Twelve seasons!"

Alphas heart sank. He looked up to the platform and saw the Keeper grinning broadly. He was new. Alpha guessed he and his priests had seized control of the Grid only a day or two earlier. As always the battle had no doubt been fierce, the loss of life severe. How long this new Keeper would last, no one knew. But while in charge he would gain as many seasons and as much glow as possible ... until he was challenged and destroyed by the next band of raiders.

Seeing no other alternative, Alpha shouted, "Fourteen! I will give you fourteen seasons!"

The crowds murmur grew louder.

"Fifteen!" the bidder at the end yelled.

Alpha leaned past the line to see who was bidding against him. It was an old man, stooped. His strands of hair were oily and dirty white, the leather skin of his face etched in deep lines. It was obvious he'd given up many seasons in past bids. Alpha doubted he had more than twenty left. Like Alpha's woman, the man's breath was barely visible, which meant he was equally desperate, his time also running out. There was only one way to end this. One way to secure the units and race home before it was too late.

"Twenty-one!" Alpha shouted.

The old man turned to him, his face filling with despair.

Alpha had him and they both knew it. "I will give you twenty- one seasons of my life!"

The Keeper laughed, and rightly so. To Alphas knowledge, few had ever bid so high. But for Alpha, the stakes had never been so great.

"Twenty-one!" the Keeper shouted. "My bid is twenty-one. Is there anybody else? Do I hear twenty-two?"

No one responded.

"Sold!" the Keeper called. "Six life units for twenty-one seasons! Come forward, my son."

Alpha stepped across the bidding line. Although victorious, he already felt the dread. Cold sweat broke out across his face. To his right, a saffron-robed priest appeared and gently took his arm, escorting him to the Grid. It was a small structure, three lengths high, two wide, just big enough to hold a man. He stepped up to it and turned, placing his back against the metal. He spread his feet and hands, allowing a second priest to fasten them with leather restraints to the iron mesh. Sweat dripped down his face, stinging his eyes. He'd been to the Grid twice before. Once as a little boy when his parents had been killed and he was too young to steal life units. And later when he'd been careless and allowed a band of raiders to make off with his first woman and the units the couple had carefully hidden.

"Open," the first priest ordered.

Alpha opened his mouth. A leather pouch filled with sand was placed between his teeth. This would prevent him from biting off his tongue. The second priest turned to the Keeper and shouted, "Secure!"

Alpha braced himself.

He heard the pop and crackle of energy a split second before it struck. Suddenly life was sucked from his body, curling his hands and his feet, throwing him into convulsions. He tried to scream, but the pain was too great. He could not move, he could not breathe. He could only feel his life and consciousness drain away.

When he came to, the priests were already unstrapping his hands and feet. He tried standing, adjusting to his older body. But other bidders were waiting their turn, so the priests half walked, half dragged him toward the altar.

"Here you go," the first said as he lifted the life units.

Alpha stretched out his arms to receive them, startled at his loss of muscle tone, surprised at how weathered his hands appeared. And the units, they were much heavier than he remembered.

"I don't—I don't think I can carry these all the way home."

"Carry them?" The second priest laughed. "You won't make it past the gates."

"I'll be fine," Alpha said.

"Maybe in your youth," the first priest said. "But that was many seasons ago. The younger ones will rob and kill you before you're out of sight."

* * *

"STOP PROGRAM."

At Travis's command, the images froze on the monitors. "Explain this machine to me," Nicholas said, "those glowing blocks."

Travis popped a breath mint into his mouth and nodded for Hugh to answer.

"The machine—they call it the Grid—is the community's source of energy, their nutrition, if you will."

"And those blocks of light are—"

"How the energy is traded and stored."

"It's their food," Travis said. "What they eat to survive."

Nicholas repeated what he understood. "So the blocks replenish their life. And that's the light we see around their mouths and what they bleed when they're injured."

"You got it," Travis said.

"And... Alpha... has purchased them with, what, twenty-one years of his own life?"

Hugh nodded. "It's simply another form of currency. In our world it takes portions of our life to make money—you know, so many dollars per so many hours. In reality, spending money is simply spending portions of life."

"And instead of transforming life into currency—"

"They cut out the middle step and went directly to transferring life."

"This was their invention?" Nicholas asked.

"Well, not entirely." Travis rattled the mint in his mouth. "But you gotta admit it's a pretty cool idea. And for our purpose here, it speeds up the whole life cycle thing, plus it saves tons of teraflops by eliminating stuff like digesting, defecating, and all that."

Impressed, Nicholas turned back to the screen.

"Of course, it's still easier to steal life units," Hugh said. "Or kill for them."

"Or"—Rebecca nodded to the screen—"exploit others with good old-fashioned capitalism."

Travis nodded. "But for a few like Alpha 11 here, that type of behavior is tough on the ol' conscience."

Nicholas stared at the image on the screen—at the once-strong young man who, apparently for the love of his wife, had more than doubled his age. It was impossible not to be moved by his dedication. And, though Nicholas kept telling himself it was only a program, he could not help but feel a certain pride over how his son might have behaved in similar circumstances. Pride ... and sadness.

He waited a moment, making sure he could trust his voice. "What's next?" he asked. "For Alpha, I mean."

"Usually he doesn't make it this far," Rebecca said.

Hugh nodded. "He definitely won't make it home. The younger ones will kill him and steal the life units."

"You're telling me he always fails?" Nicholas asked. "That one of the best hopes for the community's survival never succeeds?"

"How could he?" Travis said.

Silence filled the room as Nicholas stared at the middle-aged man on the screen. "So let me see if I correctly understand what you want. I'm supposed to pull a magic trick from my hat—some philosophical model that comes naturally and organically from who they are, that will enable them to survive."

"We've tried everything we can think of," Hugh said.

More silence, except for the rattling of Travis's mint. "We gotta do somethin?'

"Without imposing upon their free will," Rebecca added. "Otherwise the program is irrelevant for our purposes."

Nicholas removed his glasses and cleaned them on his shirt. "That's a tall order."

No one answered.

He replaced the glasses and stared back at the screen. "I'd say nearly impossible."

More silence.

Finally, Travis answered, "If it wasn't impossible, bro, I would have found somebody else."

CHAPTER 7

"MOM, WHAT'S WRONG?"

"Nothing's wrong, baby." Once again Annie turned the ignition and once again the car ground away but did not start.

"Did you run out of gas?"

"No, we didn't run out of gas." She threw a look to the gauge just to make certain. Blowing the hair out of her eyes, she tried the ignition again, with identical results.

"Are you sure?"

"I'm sure." She took a moment, then tried again. Same response, though the battery was beginning to show wear.

"Do you have the right key?"

"Yes, I have the—" The rap on the window gave her a start. She turned to see Agent Hostetler and his daughter standing outside.

"Problems?" he asked.

Flustered, she reached for the power window, remembered it didn't work, and opened the door. The obnoxious door chime began.

"Is everything all right?" he asked.

"It doesn't want to start."

"You out of gas?"7

"No, I am not out of gas."

He nodded. "Do you have AAA?"

She shook her head, then reached for the ignition and tried again. The results were even less encouraging. She glanced back to Hostetler, who was pulling out his wallet.

"What are you doing?"

"We'll use my card."

"No, that's okay. I'll just call a garage and—"

"Nonsense," he said. "Let me help—I never use the thing anyway." He pulled out his cell phone and began searching his AAA card for a number when someone on the sidewalk caught his attention. He smiled. "Better yet..." Raising his voice, he shouted, "Hey, Brenda."

Annie looked over to see the office manager heading up the street.

"Brenda!"

The woman turned.

"We could use a hand over here."

"No, really," Annie said, "I'll just call a tow truck."

"Don't be silly." He motioned for the office manager to join them. "She's like a mechanical genius. Ran a car pool over in Baghdad."

The woman approached. "There a problem?"

"A little car trouble." Hostetler turned to Annie. "Give it another try."

She obliged, with the same results.

"Are you out of gas?"

"No," Annie patiently replied, "I am not out of gas."

Brenda nodded, already moving to the front of the car. "Pop the hood—let's see what you got."

Annie looked back to Hostetler, who nodded. Finally she

reached down and pulled the lever. Brenda dropped her head under the hood and began rummaging away.

After a moment she shouted, "Give her another try." Annie tucked her hair behind her ear and obeyed. Once again the engine ground away.

"All right, hang on," Brenda said. "Oh, yeah, I see it. Hang on..."

"Daddy..." Hostetler's little girl said.

He looked down. "Just a minute, Sabrina."

Soon Brenda was out from under the hood and rounding the car. "It's your coil wire."

"My what?"

"Not a problem. I'll grab my tools."

"Your what? No, really," Annie protested. "I don't—"

"My truck's just around the corner." She turned and started back up the street. "I'll have it fixed in no time."

Annie stuck her head out the door and called, "I really don't think—"

But Brenda waved her off and continued down the street. Annie looked back to Hostetler, who was already shaking his head. "Once she's on a mission, no use trying to stop her."

NICHOLAS HAD LOST HIS BEARINGS. Not a lot, and not for long. But enough. The earlier outburst against his brother both shocked and embarrassed him. The image on the screen was merely digital, he knew that. No more his son than a photograph or a video. But seeing him, seeing it, had struck something inside him, something he thought he had exorcised years ago. But even now, as he wandered the grounds outside the house, he was shaken— a victim of his emotions. And being a victim was something Dr. Nicholas Mackenzie would not tolerate. He'd taken too many precautions to be fooled by some twenty-first century parlor trick.

"Professor?"

He looked up and saw Rebecca, the stringy-haired blonde, clomping down the hill toward him. Behind her, the last trace of blue was disappearing from the sky. He had no idea how long he'd been walking, head down, hands stuffed in his pockets. He'd been in that faraway place where he went to think and evaluate, deep inside his thoughts where no one could bother him.

"Dr. Mackenzie?"

Almost no one.

"Hey, Professor!"

"What do you want?" he barked.

"From you, nothing. But if you're interested, dinner's ready." Before he could respond, the girl turned and traipsed back up the hill, which was fine with him ... until he realized he had no idea where he was. Looking around, he saw no house, no familiar landmarks, not even a path.

"Wait a minute," he shouted. "Hold on!"

She continued walking.

"I said wait a minute!"

She came to a stop. Even in silhouette there was no missing her attitude. The hill was steep, and by the time he arrived he was breathing hard. She turned and they headed back toward the house in silence. But the moment was too good to last. They barely traveled twenty yards before she spoke.

"Anyone ever call you a bully?" she asked.

"Not in the past few hours," he answered. He said nothing more, doing his part to reclaim the silence. His efforts were futile.

"I saw your little performance on God Talk last night," she said, "with that pastor."

"A poster child for imbeciles."

She ignored him. "It's the same, tired information you've used for years."

"Truth is truth."

"No matter how you distort it?"

"Apparently there are still remnants of that wanna-be seminary student."

"Don't worry, Professor, you destroyed my faith long ago."

"I do what I can."

"'There are only facts. Everything else is fantasy and wishful thinking.' Isn't that what you used to say?"

"Still do."

More silence. And more disappointment when she resumed. "So tell me, Doctor, how many were killed in the Inquisition?"

"A pop quiz. How delightful."

"Thirty thousand. And most of them were Christians."

"Figures vary, but you're close."

"And the Crusades?" she asked.

"Over the course of three hundred years, one and a half million lives were senselessly slaughtered."

They crested the hill and the house came into view.

"And the witch hunts in the United States, how many there?" she asked. Before he could answer, she said. "A grand total of twenty."

"If there's a point, you're failing to make it."

They headed toward the side porch and she continued, "Let's see . . . the atheists brought us forty million murders courtesy of Marxism through Joseph Stalin; fifteen million, thank you Nietzsche, through Adolph Hitler."

"Hitler was a Catholic," Nicholas interrupted.

"Yeah, right. Which is why he planned to overthrow them after the war." Before he could argue, she continued. "Seventy-two million from communism through Mao, and an additional seven million in Cambodia. All that carnage in just seventy years." They started up the porch steps. "Granted, there were further atrocities, on both sides—but basically we're talking two million killings over the entire history of Western civilization due to religion, versus a hundred and thirty-four million in just seventy years based upon atheistic systems." She reached for the door. "You tell me which is more toxic, Professor: faith or atheism."

Nicholas was almost impressed.

But the lecture wasn't over. Opening the door, she continued, "And while we're at it, let's not forget those minor positive contributions from religion like hospitals, orphanages, literacy, women's rights, the abolition of—"

Fortunately, she was interrupted by Travis, who sat with Hugh at the kitchen table. "Hey, bro, there you are." A half dozen white cardboard boxes sat before him. "R.E. ordered more Chinese than they could eat, so we got some primo leftovers." He pushed out a chair with his foot. "Take a load off."

Nicholas stepped over to the sink and washed his hands.

"So"—Travis took one bite of orange chicken and then another—"has our resident genius found any solutions?"

Nicholas finished washing, then dried on a towel. "Actually, the problem is at your end."

Travis smiled, mouth filled with chicken. "Why am I not surprised?"

"You've been deceiving them."

Hugh glanced up from grappling with his chopsticks.

"In allowing the community to follow their natural course, you've been dishonest with them." By now all eyes were on him as he crossed the room and took a seat. "Instead of hiding the truth from them, you should be honest with them."

Travis continued chewing. "What truth? What haven't I told them?"

"That they're not real."

He laughed. "No way, to them they're totally real."

Nicholas shook his head. "They may think they're real. But they're certainly not as real as us."

"Ah . . ." Hugh said, nodding in understanding. "Reality is relative."

Rebecca cut him a look. "What bumper sticker did you read that off of?"

Nicholas continued, "Wherever he read it, it's true. Our reality is more real than theirs."

"No way," Travis argued. "Everything about their life is as real to them as ours is to us."

"No. Their reality is a copy of ours." Nicholas tapped the table with his index finger. "A facsimile of this reality."

Without looking up from her food, Rebecca said, "Plato's cave analogy."

"Plato's what?" Hugh asked.

She continued, "The Greek philosopher, Plato, said the reality we live in is just the shadow of a greater reality that is cast on our cave wall."

"A shadow?" Hugh frowned.

She nodded. "What we see, touch, everything we experience ... they're all shadows of original objects... which are more real because they come from some greater reality."

Hugh and Travis traded confused looks.

Nicholas shook his head at the girl. "Children. We're talking to children." With exaggerated patience, he tried. "Instead of allowing your computer creations to think solely in terms of their world, you must tell them the entire truth. You must tell them there is another world beyond theirs."

"Dualism," the girl said.

Nicholas glanced at her. "I see your education wasn't an entire waste."

"Yeah, well..." Hugh gave up on the chopsticks and reached for a fork. "Apparently mine was. What is Duelingism?"

"Dualism, moron," the girl said. "Descartes' model."

"Oh." Hugh nodded. "Right, what was I thinking?"

She continued. "Rene Descartes was a French philosopher who believed the world was made up of two realities. The material world, like what Alpha 11 and the others are experiencing, and another world, the metaphysical one."

"Which would be like ours," Travis ventured. "We're their greater reality."

"Cool," Hugh said.

Travis shifted his weight in growing excitement. "So that would make me like, what, their god?"

"Now, there's a scary thought," Rebecca said.

"Right, but still—"

"No, Travis," Nicholas said.

"Why not? I created them. That's what we're talking about, right? Some religious thing? We're living here in heaven and they're down there on earth."

"No," Nicholas repeated. "We're not talking about religion."

"Then what?"

"Metaphysics. Spirituality. The understanding that there are higher thoughts with higher standards than a simple materialistic world."

Travis frowned, not willing to concede. "You still need a god. How do you have spirituality' without a god?"

"Trust me," Nicholas replied, "your little community has enough problems—they don't need to add God to the equation."

"So we're talking about Eastern mysticism," Rebecca concluded. "Buddhism, Hinduism, that kind of thing."

Hugh scowled. "So how is that different from—"

Nicholas interrupted, "It's a belief in a greater good without the tyranny of a meddling dictator."

"I wouldn't be a meddling—"

"Give it up, Travis." Nicholas said.

"Cool," Hugh repeated. "Very cool."

Nicholas turned to his brother. "Are you capable of programming such a thing into the community?"

"Hey." Travis gave a belch. "I'm God—I can do anything I want."

"Travis…"

"Just playing with you, man. No sweat." He wiped his mouth and started to rise. "Just give them a sense of a greater reality, I get it."

"And an interconnectedness to that reality," Rebecca added. "They need to feel that what they do affects everything—including themselves."

"Like karma." Hugh beamed, pushing back his chair.

Rebecca rolled her eyes.

"Okay, then." Travis gave a stretch, then cracked his neck. "Let's get a move on, kiddies. We got ourselves a world to remake."

He turned and started toward the hallway. The assistants followed, Hugh grabbing two or three boxes of food for the road.

"And don't forget the fortune cookies," Travis ordered.

"Right." Hugh managed to clamp on to one of the bags with a spare finger.

Only as they entered the hallway did Travis turn and see Nicholas remaining at the table. "What's wrong with you?"

"My work is finished."

"What?"

"I've accomplished what you've asked. I've found your solution."

The group exchanged looks.

"What if there's a problem?" Travis asked.

"There will be no problem. I've thought through every permutation."

Travis hesitated.

"You doubt me?"

"No," Travis said, "I'm sure you've thought of everything. It's just that... I mean, with Alpha and all, I thought you might want to stick around. You know, see how things—"

"No." Nicholas's answer was firm. He'd already considered it, thought through the ramifications. And, as much as he wanted to stay, he would not. He could not. The attachment he was already feeling was unhealthy. It was only a computer representation. Nothing more. To read anything else into it was foolhardy. He cleared his throat and continued, "I should like to go home as soon as possible."

Travis frowned, shifting his weight.

"It's an hour drive. Your driver can take me back by myself. And I promise to wear your silly bandanna."

Travis glanced to Rebecca.

She gave a nod.

He turned to Hugh, who shrugged. "I'm down with that. Sure."

Finally, he turned back to Nicholas. "Okay, bro. I mean, if you're sure there won't be a problem."

"I am sure," Nicholas repeated. "There will be no problem."

* * *

THE OFFICE MANAGER's definition of fixing the car 'in no time' had turned into a forty-five-minute job. Long enough for the children to pressure Annie and Agent Hostetler to visit the McDonald's just up the street. Now, as they waited for their food, the kids were climbing ladders, sliding through tubes, and playing in a pit filled with a thousand colored balls. While Annie was... well, she wasn't exactly sure what she was doing. She'd been out of circulation for so long she didn't know if this had somehow turned into a date, or if it was an extension of Hostetler's work, or if it was just a couple adults grabbing a snack.

But, whatever it was, it felt good.

He was definitely showing interest without being a jerk and she was definitely enjoying it. There was something about his mixture of strength and vulnerability she found moving—whether he was playing with the kids, taking charge in ordering the food, or spilling Diet Coke down his front when the lid popped off. "Shoot!" he said, grabbing a napkin. "Doggone it!"

The language (or lack of it) surprised Annie and she did her best to hide her amusement as she handed him a wad of napkins. Once he'd finally toweled off, the four of them sat down to eat. Luckily, the children provided plenty of chitchat. . . what grade were they in, did they like school, what was their favorite subject. There was the added bonus of Sabrina taking acting lessons, and did they see her Barbie press-on nails commercial last year? Other than the acting, none of this really interested the kids, but it was definitely home base for their self-conscious parents. Eventually, however, the children again abandoned them for the play area and the adults were left on their tightrope, all alone, without a net.

Still, old habits die hard and, focusing their attention on the playing children, they began trading kid stories, then parent-of-kid stories, then parent-of-intelligent-and-precocious-kid stories. The dance continued nearly twenty minutes before he made a misstep.

"Is Rusty's intelligence ... is that why he and Dr. Mackenzie hit it off so well?"

Annie was just biting into her soft ice cream cone when she paused and looked at him.

"Sorry." He shrugged. "I stink at leaving my work at the office." Annie looked over to Rusty, grateful she at least had one answer; the meeting had not been work-related.

Hostetler continued, "It's just, I was wondering ..."

She turned back to him.

He took the plunge. "I mean, his own son was pretty smart too, wasn't he? At least according to our records. Does he ever talk to you about Michael?"

Annie shook her head. "No. And, as I'm sure your records also indicate, he hates it when people pry into his personal matters." Hostetler nodded, getting her point.

Thinking she might have been too harsh, she added, "He rarely mentions his son. I'm guessing he disappeared from his life after the divorce. As far as I know, he's never even bothered to contact him." She returned to her cone.

"I'm sorry, what?"

She glanced at him, her mouth full of ice cream.

"The divorce came after the accident, not before."

She frowned, then swallowed. "Accident?"

"Yes, nearly two years later. Actually, it's not that unusual — couples splitting up after the death of their child."

"Their child ... died?"

"He didn't tell you?"

Annie lowered her cone. "I just naturally figured ... I mean, he..."

"It was a private plane crash. Over the San Gabriel Mountains. Coming up on fifteen years, now."

"And the boy, his son—"

"Didn't make it. Pilot error. Mackenzie and his wife were the only survivors."

"Pilot error?"

"Mackenzie was flying. Apparently he made some bone-headed mistake."

The bottom dropped from Annie's stomach. Hostetler turned back to the children. "Poor guy. Can't imagine what that would be like. You know, killing your only child."

PART II

CHAPTER 8

"A S USUAL, YOU have no idea what you're talking about," Nicholas said.

Annie tightened her grip on the steering wheel. "I'm telling you, they say you could be in serious danger. You and your brother."

"Which is why I returned home safely and spent the entire night without incident."

The morning sun drifted into Annie's eyes and she lowered the visor. "Nicholas, hiding out in your office all night is not the same as spending it at home."

"I had little choice in the matter when I saw your FBI friends parked outside my house."

"They were only trying to protect you."

"Which explains the beating I received the night before."

"I seriously doubt that was them."

"You seriously don't know what to doubt."

Annie blew the hair out of her eyes. There was no reasoning with him when he was like this. Along with his usual bullheaded-ness, he was cranky from lack of sleep.

"Where's the boy?" he asked.

"He's fine."

"You didn't leave him by himself, did you?"

"Despite what you think, I'm not a totally incompetent parent. I dropped him off at the babysitter's."

Nicholas gave no answer and looked out the window at the passing boats in the marina.

Annie could understand Nicholas's annoyance, but the last twelve hours had not gone well for her either. After McDonald's, she and Rusty had swung by Nicholas's cracker-box house to see if he was home.

But of course he wasn't.

So she left a note on the door asking him to call whenever he arrived.

But of course he didn't.

All this as Agent Hostetler's warning continued rattling in the back of her head: "Travis Mackenzie may be in a very dangerous situation."

The words stayed in her mind late last night as she listened to Rusty read Horton Hears a Who! And they remained as she tried to sleep, frequently checking the clock, waiting for morning. Then, when dawn finally did arrive and she was fixing a breakfast of bacon and eggs, Rusty had called to her from the computer. "Hey, Mom, come see."

"What's up?"

"We're getting a ton of those e-mails again."

She crossed the room, spatula still in hand, and read the message over his shoulder:

Need N. Another emergency.

Will pick up at pier parking lot ASAP. T

For better or for worse, she chose to find Nicholas before calling Hostetler. Of course, this meant another visit to his house. But not before ensuring Rusty's safety. If there was any danger, she wanted him out of harm's way. So mother and son had climbed into the car and headed to Fran Carlson's, six blocks down the street. Electronics wiz kid and computer gadget tester, Fran was Rusty's favorite sitter.

Annie had to ring the bell twice and practically beat down the door before a groggy voice on the other side demanded, "What? Who is it?"

"Fran, it's me, Dr. Brooks. And Rusty."

"Hang on." After the click of a lock, the release of a deadbolt, and a sliding chain, the door opened. A frumpy young woman appeared in robe, baggy sweats, and a Cousin It hairdo. She had been a grad student until she ran out of money and the credit card companies caught up with her. The two of them had met at a Bible study just after Rusty was born. She was as reliable as the day was long. Well, except for the credit cards.

"What time is it?" she mumbled, searching her robe for her glasses.

"I'm sorry to do this to you," Annie said, "but can you watch Rusty for a couple hours?"

"Yeah, sure. No prob." She found her glasses on the string around her neck, slipped them on, and squinted down at Rusty. "What's up, little man?" She made a fist and they bumped knuckles.

"Same-o, same-o," he said with a shrug.

"I hear that."

Annie continued, "It's kind of an emergency."

"Sure." Fran opened the door wider. "Come on in."

Even in the dark, Annie could see the tables piled with computers, monitors, and who knew what.

"What are we working on today?" Rusty asked as he brushed past Fran and entered the room.

"It'll only be an hour or two," Annie promised.

"Not a problem. Did he have breakfast?"

"Yes," Annie said.

"No," Rusty called back.

"I'll throw in a pizza."

"All right!" the boy exclaimed.

"For me, little guy. Your mom's a health nut. You get a banana."

"Oh, brother..."

"Or a nice sour grapefruit."

The boy whined, "Fran ..."

Annie gave the woman a quick hug. "Thanks." She turned and started down the steps. "I owe you."

Fran nodded as she closed the door. "I'll put it on your tab."

Next stop, Nicholas's house. But when she arrived, he was gone. Along with the note she had left the night before. He had either been home, taken it, and left ... or someone else had removed it. If he had been there, chances were he'd already gone to his office on campus, since those were the only two places he frequented. It was useless to call his office, as part of his morning ritual was to pull out the phone jack that maintenance dutifully plugged back in every evening. She would have to drive there.

Twenty minutes later, just as she expected, she found Nicholas in his office—jacket wadded up under his head, asleep on the floor, even more of a bear than usual. A disposition that did not improve as they approached the Santa Barbara pier.

"You sure you can't tell me what any of this is about?" she asked.

"Can, but won't."

"And the reason is ..."

"You'll run off to your government buddies again." He abruptly changed subjects. "This babysitter. It's not that Fran woman, is it?"

"Of course it is."

"Her place is a death trap. And she doesn't know the first

thing about personal hygiene. You should have had the foresight to at least—" He motioned to the side of the road. "Here, park here."

They were fifty yards from the pier. The veterans were already out on the beach placing thousands of white crosses and tiny flags in neat little rows to honor the fallen in Iraq and Afghanistan. Arlington West, they called it. Like Annie, Nicholas admitted he found the scene moving—at least the flags part. He had an entirely different opinion about the crosses.

She pulled over to the curb. "You know my number. If you get in a jam, call me."

He snorted as he reached for the door.

"Or, Travis," she said. "Have your brother call me."

Without a word he climbed out, slammed the door, and headed for the pier.

Annie stuck her head out the window and shouted, "Anytime! Always glad to help!"

* * *

ALPHA 11 INHALED DEEPLY, savoring the lilac smell of her body lotion. When he closed his eyes, she was almost there. He'd done this in the past, when he missed her so badly he couldn't sleep. When he padded across the floor and opened her cabinet of cheek colorings, lip stains, and the other wiles of womanhood. When he rubbed a small portion of her lotion into his palms, then held them to his face and breathed.

He wasn't sure how long he stood there, lost in memories. But, eventually, he placed the lotion back on the shelf. He turned, sidestepped a rat that was grooming itself in the center of the floor, and headed back to their bedroom. At the foot of the bed lay the mat where they had practiced their meditation. He paused a moment, then crossed to it. He lowered himself to his knees and closed his eyes, trying to let go, to find that deep, silent place within.

He heard their baby's uneven breathing in the crib behind him. He tried ignoring him and focused upon entering that deeper state of peace.

But, as happened more often than not, he failed. Why was this so difficult? Why couldn't he close his mind to the world and its illusions, to its imaginary pains and pleasures? His wife had done it so naturally. Even as she was dying.

He recalled her final day, lying in bed, her skin as dry as paper...

"No need for sorrow," she had whispered.

He had nodded, turning so she wouldn't see his tears.

"Push it aside," she said.

"Shh, save your strength."

"These are shadows, my love—emotions, desires. All illusion."

"Shh..."

"Until you see that—" She broke into coughing.

"Please.."

She caught her breath and continued. "Until you see that, they will always control you. Let go. Connect with the greater reality."

But he could not let go. Instead, he remembered other realities ...

Their first meeting. The way he stared at the ceiling, unable to sleep, thinking only of her. Their talks long into the night. The joy of holding her hand. That first kiss. And those early months of marriage. How deeply they drank from one another. How passionately they gave and took and shared.

But those times soon passed. Even before her illness. As

her faith matured, she slowly and steadily grew beyond such pleasures.

The priests explained it best. "All desire is bad," they said. "It is merely the flesh attempting to trap us in this temporal world of illusion."

He understood their words. Envied his wife for her ability to obey them. And cursed himself for his inability. Even now, as he knelt alone on the mat trying to empty his mind, his thoughts were filled with her. And with his son dying in the crib behind him. It was these attachments that brought him so much heartache— while the devout, like his wife, were able to overcome the world's illusions and be free... even from life units.

"No," she had said in her final hour.

"Just a little. They will give you strength."

She shook her head. "They merely—" She wheezed, then coughed. "They merely prolong the illusion."

"They'll keep you alive," he insisted.

She smiled sadly at him. "And still you don't understand."

"I understand," he lied. "I understand. But you're dying."

"We're all dying..."

"But the baby, he needs a mother. You would make him suffer without a mother?"

More coughing. "If he suffers ... it's because of his past."

"But-"

A whimper, barely louder than a sigh, brought Alpha back to the present. He turned to the crib. There was no movement, save for a rat scurrying across the wooden railing. It had been two weeks since the baby first became sick, from the same disease of the lungs that had taken his mother, that had swept through the entire community.

"You must promise not to interfere," she had said.

"But—"

"This is his reward." More coughing. "Your word, my love. Give me your word."

It had been a bitter promise, but she was right. It was the child's reward for the evil he had committed in past lives. That was why he suffered. And the sooner he paid his debt in this life, the sooner he could leave and return at a higher level. This was truth. A truth his wife was enjoying even now, wherever she may be.

He sensed a sudden stillness. The baby had stopped breathing. He staggered to his feet and rushed to the crib. A pile of rat droppings lay on the pillow near the infant's face. Angrily, he brushed them away.

The baby did not stir. His eyes remained fixed. There was no glow from his mouth.

"No!" Alpha cried. He scooped up the baby. The child's arms hung limply. Alpha felt his head growing light, his legs losing strength. He lowered to his knees so he would not fall. And there, clutching the dead baby in his arms, he buried his face into the little body and began to sob. He sobbed for his wife. He sobbed for his child. And he sobbed for himself, hoping against hope that his turn would soon follow.

* * *

ANNIE PULLED BACK into traffic and passed the pier's entrance, with its fountain of bronze leaping dolphins. Just on the other side, local artisans were setting up booths displaying digitally enhanced photographs of sunsets, watercolors of sunsets, oils of sunsets, shell necklaces, and shell necklaces of painted sunsets. For a change of pace, every fifth or sixth booth sold wind chimes—everything from finely tuned pipes of silver to clanging empty bottles of beer—a cacophony of tinkling highs, midrange jingles, and mystical lows.

Since Nicholas would have a long walk to the parking lot at the end of the pier and since Annie had contributed enough to the California Highway Patrol fund, she took her sweet time heading to the freeway. She entered and drove south three or four miles to where she had lost Nicholas the day before. Once she arrived, she pulled over to the emergency lane and waited. She scooted down in the seat so she wouldn't be visible and adjusted the side mirror to see as far down the freeway as possible. She figured she had five or ten minutes before the silver Lexus would appear—if it was even the same car.

Her thoughts drifted back to the night before, to Agent Matthew Hostetler. To the warm stirring she felt as they sat in the restaurant talking and watching their kids. Of course, she didn't let her imagination run away, she was a grown woman, for crying out loud. Nevertheless, the attention had felt good. It had been a long time and it felt very good. She shook her head and directed her thoughts back to Nicholas. They'd known each other going on eight years now. They'd been friends for five, ever since Rusty's birth. To say he was a complicated man was an understatement. Even after a second or third look, and giving him more benefits of the doubt than he deserved, it was easy to conclude he was simply a cranky old eccentric. But she saw something different, underneath the thorns and crustiness. There was much more to Nicholas Mackenzie than met the eye. And the news of his son's tragic death was the latest case in point.

Through the side mirror, she spotted a silver-gray vehicle approaching in the fast lane. It was impossible to see inside because of the reflection of morning sun and tree shadows. She scooted higher, knowing that when it passed she would only have a moment to catch a look. Unfortunately, she hadn't seen the semi in the slow lane, until it roared by, shaking her little car and blocking her view. She bolted up and turned to the window, desperate for some glimpse of the car. And then she saw it—the silver Lexus, with Nicholas and his unruly white hair blurring past.

She dropped her car into gear and hit the gas. She picked up speed in the emergency lane—twenty-five, thirty, thirty-five miles per hour—before she pulled out onto the freeway.

* * *

"THIS BETTER BE IMPORTANT," Nicholas growled after they had settled back into the lab.

His brother rolled a breath mint in his mouth and turned to the kid sitting behind the console. "Bring 'em up, Hugh."

Nicholas looked at the monitors. Unlike the previous village, these adobe homes were smooth and low. Their gentle beige shapes blended naturally into the surrounding fields and hills. In fact, everything about the dwellings fit into their surroundings, creating a sense of peace and tranquility—a feeling enhanced by the lack of activity in the streets...and the lack of citizens.

"Where are they?" Nicholas asked. "It's daylight, I don't see anyone."

Hugh began punching buttons, bringing up a different set of angles on the screens. Some showed the outside of the homes, others the inside with their simple furniture and decor. Like the streets, most of the structures were vacant. Except for the rats.

"Where are the people?" Nicholas repeated.

"Dead." Travis answered. "Most of them, anyway."

"What?" Nicholas asked incredulously. "How is that possible?"

"Disease. Something like the Black Plague." Travis motioned to one monitor featuring a dozen rodents. "Spread by those cute little critters there."

Nicholas turned to him. "Why did you let this happen?"

"Me? It's their choice, not mine."

"Why create rats in the first place? Or disease, for that matter?"

"If it's in our world, it's in theirs. That's the purpose of this little exercise. The good, the bad, the everything."

"Except," Nicholas scorned, "a means to stop the disease."

"Oh, they have the means," Travis said, "they just didn't bother to use it."

Nicholas looked at his brother, waiting for more.

It was Rebecca who answered. "This far into their development they should have easily discovered the disease and created the antibiotics to stop it."

Nicholas turned back to the screen. "But... they haven't."

Travis rolled the mint in his mouth. "Instead of Door Number One: Science and Technology, they chose Door Number Two: Herbs and Spices.

"Natural remedies?" Nicholas asked.

"Bingo."

"What about research? Clinical science?"

"There's no science here, bro. At least not the hard-core stuff like we have. Everything's organic."

"Because..."

"Because they've decided that it has to be natural. Whatever they do, they don't want to upset the balance of nature."

"Hence, the rats," Nicholas said.

Travis nodded. "You respect nature, even worship it if that floats your boat, but whatever you do, you don't go messin' with it or try changin it."

"Because..."

"A: It's divine. B: You're no better than it is. C: It's really not real. Remember, everything's just a shadow of reality."

"So they take no authority over it," Nicholas concluded.

"Give the man a lotus leaf."

Hugh quietly quoted, "'So heavenly minded they're no earthly good.'"

Nicholas felt his face growing warm. He should have seen this outcome. Predicted it. "And Alpha?" he asked. "Where's he?" Hugh typed in a series of commands and the images reversed direction. The digital readouts at the bottom of the screens began spinning backward. When they stopped, he hit another set of keys. A large bedroom appeared on the main monitor.

And there, kneeling on the floor silently sobbing, was the duplicate of Nicholas's son.

Although he had braced himself, Nicholas was again caught off guard by the image of the man... and his sorrow. "What's that he's holding?"

"His baby," Rebecca said.

Nicholas stepped toward the screen for a better look. "Boy or girl?"

"Does it matter?"

Nicholas paused, closing his eyes. Of course, what was he thinking? What difference did it make? He reopened them to watch Alpha's quiet weeping.

"Is it... dead?" he asked.

"Yes."

He continued watching in silence.

Rebecca explained. "Unlike the rest of his family, Alpha will survive this particular strain of infection."

"And the next strain?"

Hugh and Rebecca traded looks but did not answer.

Fighting off his irritation, Nicholas repeated, "And the next?"

"It's the same ending, bro," Travis said. "Just like all the others. Only instead of destroying themselves... they let nature do it for them."

Nicholas stared at the screen a moment, before pushing up his glasses and looking away.

Hugh turned in his chair. "Now what, Professor?"

He gave no answer.

"Dr. Mackenzie?"

He still did not reply.

Rebecca turned to him. "You see it, don't you?"

Nicholas glanced to her, then down, searching for another option.

"See what?" Hugh asked.

No one responded.

Hugh looked from one to the other, then repeated, "See what? Professor, what do you see?"

Nicholas scowled. The answer was clear, but surely there had to be another.

"What's up, bro?" Travis asked.

"Should I tell them," Rebecca said, "or do you want the honors?"

He shot her a glare.

Unfazed, she turned and addressed the group. "If the doctor can set aside his prejudice, he'll not only admit his mistake, but supply us with the obvious solution. Otherwise we'll just keep chasing our tails until everyone's dead again."

"Admit what?" Travis demanded.

She turned back to Nicholas. "We still haven't been honest with them."

"Honest?" Hugh asked. "About what?"

At last Nicholas spoke. "About us." He nodded to Alpha. "It's time we tell him the complete truth."

"What are you talking about?" Travis said. "We've been totally honest with them. I've reprogrammed everything."

"Not everything," Rebecca said.

"Yes, everything. The interconnectedness, the knowledge

of our world, this super reality you're talking about. They know everything."

"Except..." Nicholas quietly answered.

"Except what?" Travis insisted.

"They don't know about us."

"What?"

Rebecca explained, "You told them about everything except us."

Travis turned to her, then back to Nicholas. "You said that would cause too many problems. You said believing in a god would make things worse."

Nicholas took a silent, controlled breath.

"And he was wrong." Rebecca tried not to gloat but failed miserably. "In order to be entirely honest, they should have the whole truth. Isn't that right, Professor?"

"You're saying we have to tell them everything?" Travis asked. "Not only about our world, but about you and me, about our existence?"

She looked back to Nicholas, goading him on. "And..."

"And what?" Travis demanded.

Nicholas was about to answer, but the victory was too sweet for Rebecca to keep silent. "And that we have the answers to help."

"Help?" Hugh said. "Them? That's cheating."

"How do you figure?" she asked.

"They're supposed to evolve on their own. They're supposed to survive without our interference."

"Says who?"

"Says us," Hugh exclaimed. "We set up clear guidelines that..." He slowly came to a stop, realization sinking in.

Rebecca smiled. "That's the cheat. The real truth, the whole truth, is that we're here ... and we're watching them . .. and we can tell them how to survive."

Nicholas's jaw tightened. She was right, of course. The

solution couldn't be more obvious. At least now. And he hated it. He hated every aspect of it. An outside intelligence, a god, offering them assistance from outside their model. But it was true. They were watching and they could assist. Like it or not, that was the whole truth. And if Nicholas stood for anything, it was truth. Everything else was just fantasy and make-believe.

Slowly, he began to nod. The silence in the lab was deafening— except for the clicking of Travis's candy. But it was short-lived. The intercom buzzed and a husky man's voice spoke through the speaker.

"Travis?"

Hugh reached over and hit the intercom button.

"'Sup?" Travis called over to the console.

"Sorry for the interruption."

"No prob. What's cookin'?"

"We've got company."

CHAPTER 9

F OR THE RECORD, Annie was not thrilled about her reception at the compound. She didn't expect to be greeted with open arms, but the guards' somewhat indelicate treatment (which included dragging her out of her car at gunpoint) and their concern that she was a corporate spy (which included a strip search and the removal of her cell phone) had definitely set her teeth on edge.

Nor was she particularly thrilled about being held prisoner in a small, sparsely furnished office for nearly an hour as the powers that be debated whether or not she should be given further admittance. Only later did she discover the tipping point was Nicholas's refusal to continue his work unless she was allowed to join them. So, after answering a hundred questions (Agent Hostetler did not come into the conversation, nor did she feel inclined to bring him up) and signing a dozen confidentiality forms, she was escorted along two separate hallways, through a secure steel door, and down girder steps into a reinforced concrete bunker that looked like a TV control room.

The first to greet her was Travis. Although he introduced

himself, there was no need. The sandals, shorts, and a bright Hawaiian shirt were a dead giveaway. He also introduced the two sitting behind him at the control board. Hugh, a chunky programmer with the rambunctious charm of a puppy dog, and Rebecca, a thin wisp of a girl, who made no attempt to hide her displeasure at Annie's presence. Travis finished up by motioning to Nicholas across the room, "And, of course, you already know the old fart."

She gave Nicholas a smile. He returned it with a nod. Even at that she saw something in his eyes. It had barely been two hours since they'd separated, but somehow he looked older.

Despite Rebecca's disapproval, Travis gave Annie a quick explanation of the project. She was impressed, to say the least. In fact, If Nicholas hadn't been involved, she might not have believed it. But there he sat, through the entire spiel, not once disagreeing. Though she doubted he heard all of it. He seemed preoccupied, with much of his attention focused on the image frozen on the screen before them.

In any case, after being offered some juice and settling in at the back, Annie silently watched and listened to what sounded like the end of a long debate.

"So, we're in agreement," Rebecca said, pouring herself a cup of coffee. "We tell them that we're here and that we can intervene."

"I'm still not a hundred percent sure why," Hugh said.

She sighed wearily. "To help them survive."

"To become their dictators," Travis countered.

"No." She tore open one, two, three packs of creamer and dumped them into her coffee. "We only give them basic information, the most elementary rules for survival."

"Oh." Hugh's lights finally came on. "Kinda like the Ten Commandments."

Annie shot a look to Nicholas. He remained predictably

stoic, at least to the untrained eye. But there was no missing the workout he was giving his jaw.

"And if they refuse to follow them?" Travis asked.

"We don't give them a choice," Hugh said. "We work it into the program."

Rebecca gave another sigh. "And we wind up with robots."

"Why's that so wrong?"

"It's called free will, moron. If they can't make their own choices, we won't know what they'll buy."

Travis nodded. "Which is the whole point of this little dog-and-pony show."

Finally Nicholas rose to his feet. "No, she's right. It's settled. We inform them of our existence and give them basic guidelines for survival. That's it, nothing more. The rules must be minimal. No laundry list of do's and don'ts."

"Agreed," Rebecca said. "Just the basics."

He turned to Travis. "When you communicate with them, keep it simple. Merely tell them—"

"Whoa, whoa, whoa." Travis held up his hands. "Communicate with them? Not me, bro."

"They're your program."

"You're the philosopher. That's why we brought you in. You talk to them, man, not me."

Nicholas scowled hard then looked back to the screen, thinking.

"He's right," Rebecca agreed. "For better or worse, you're the obvious choice."

Another moment passed before Nicholas slowly began to nod.

"All righty, then." Travis gave his hands a clap and rose from the chair. He stretched long and loud, then turned to Hugh. "Looks like you and me, we got some more programming to do."

"Yeah," Hugh said with a sigh. "But after some eats."

Travis cracked his neck. "Can't rebuild the world on an empty stomach. Let's go topside and grab some lunch."

"No argument there," Hugh said, rising to his feet.

The others followed and headed for the stairs—everyone but Nicholas.

"You comin'?" Travis asked.

Annie turned to see Nicholas still facing the screen. He raised his hand, indicating he'd be there shortly.

"All right," Travis said, "but don't stay down here forever."

Nicholas gave no response as they started up the stairs. For a brief moment, Annie thought of remaining behind, then decided against it. Whatever he was working out, she knew better than to disturb him. And so, with the others, she left him down in the lab as he stared at the broken father on the screen holding his dead baby.

* * *

DURING LUNCH—FROZEN gourmet pizza that wasn't half bad—Travis and Hugh answered more of Annie's questions. As before, Rebecca was not pleased with the sharing of so much information, but Travis didn't seem to mind, and Travis was the boss. There was, however, one item that all three agreed not to discuss: the corporation bankrolling them.

Other than that, they seemed pretty candid. Hugh did most of the talking—particularly when it came to the areas of science. And, always eager to please, he eventually got around to asking Annie if she wanted to see the other lab.

"You have another one?" she asked.

"Oh, yeah. We got an entirely different one for the R.E. team."

"R.E?"

"Reverse Engineering." He finished his second root beer and fought back a belch. "You're a biochem prof, right?"

"Right."

He broke into a grin. "Then you'll love it. I mean really love it." Catching himself, he turned to Travis. "If that's cool with you?"

Travis shrugged. "She's signed all the nondisclosures." He threw a glance to Rebecca.

The assistant sighed. "You've spilled everything else that's proprietary. Why stop now?"

Travis looked back to Hugh and gave him a nod. "But keep it short. I want to start in twenty minutes."

"Will do."

Hugh rose and Annie followed him out of the kitchen. They passed through the hallways to the second set of steel doors. After sliding his ID card through the lock and entering his six-digit code, he led her down the steps and they entered another, somewhat larger reinforced bunker. In many ways it reminded her of the lab in her medical research days—black lab counters, cheap metal desks, dozens of glass cupboards, and plenty of fluorescent lighting. There were some differences. A large monitor hung on the far wall, below it a console not unlike the one Travis had been using in the other lab. And at the opposite end was an assortment of stainless steel cages holding several cats, a couple dogs, and a sleeping chimpanzee.

At the moment, the room was staffed by only two scientists. Dr. Agapoff was head of the team. She was in her late fifties, a plump Ukrainian woman who had little regard for fashion or makeup. She was assisted by Heather, a young brunette who pretended to be as disinterested in Hugh as he pretended to be in her.

Hugh made the introductions, along with some exaggerated claim that Agapoff s team had single-handedly managed to download the human brain. Of course, the woman immediately protested.

"No, no, no. Travis and your team, you are the ones who have done the heavy lifting." She turned to Annie. "Once they solved the storage and computation problems, for us the rest was a piece of cake."

"So you've managed to mimic some part of the human brain's function?" Annie asked.

"Mimic, no. Duplicate, yes."

The statement startled Annie. "Really? And what portion would that be?"

"This is most recent, but..." She hesitated. "Basically, we have duplicated all areas of consciousness."

Annie was certain she'd misheard. "Pardon me?"

The woman smiled. "We have managed to download and duplicate all the areas involved in human consciousness."

It was Annie's turn to smile. "I'm afraid that's not possible."

"At first, no. But, as I have said, most recently, yes."

Annie searched the woman's face, but by all appearances she was serious. "I see." Still striving to be polite, she continued, "So how exactly did you pull off such a thing? What methods did you use?"

"At first we tried noninvasive techniques—fMRIs, PETs, TMS. And in the beginning they came in very handy. Others ahead of us were able to create such things as an artificial hippocampus, the olivocerebellar regions, and of course there was Lloyd Watts's breakthrough in reproducing auditory discrimination."

Annie nodded. "Research employed in speech recognition."

"Yes. These and similar breakthroughs allowed Travis and his team to begin their program—up to and including some of the higher functions: emotional intelligence, morality, and the appreciation of art. But to download an entire personality with all of its quirks and idiosyncrasies—well, that required something that needed to be, how shall I say it, a bit more refined."

"Unquestionably."

Agapoff motioned for Annie to follow her to a large cupboard. She opened the door to reveal what looked like a wine rack, though smaller. And, instead of bottles, each of the dozens of nooks held a stainless steel cylinder. She pulled one out and handed it to Annie. "No offense, but the clever boys and girls at Berkeley really outdid themselves this time."

"Compared to UCSB?"

"No offense."

"What's in here?" she asked.

"Nanobots."

"Miniature robots," Annie said, looking at the cylinder. "People have been hypothesizing about their use for years."

"Yes. Each is the size of a single human blood cell. When injected into the circulatory system, they perform whatever task we design them for. They can track down and destroy disease, repair tissue—"

"But in the future," Annie corrected. "Sometime in the future."

Agapoff shook her head. "As early as 2003 a researcher from the University of Illinois designed a batch he injected into rats to cure their type one diabetes."

Annie nodded. She vaguely remembered reading something about it in one of her periodicals. "But what's this got to do with—"

"Downloading our minds into computers?"

Annie nodded.

"Allow me to show you." They crossed toward the cages. Hearing their approach, the chimpanzee awoke. She quickly stood on her feet and began to chatter, eager for the company.

"Hello, sweetheart," Agapoff said.

The chimp clapped, chattering louder, then began swaying back and forth. Agapoff unlatched the cage door, opened it, and the animal leaped into her arms. The woman staggered under the impact. "Easy, girl, easy. You are getting much too big for this."

Paying no attention to the protest, the chimp threw her arms around the scientist's neck, pursed her lips, and gave the woman a noisy smack on the side of the face.

"Yes, and I love you too." Turning to Annie, she made introductions. "Claire, I'd like you to meet Annie. Annie, Claire."

Still clinging to Agapoff's neck, the animal craned her head and leaned toward Annie, puckering her lips.

"She wants to say hello," Agapoff explained.

"Oh." Annie leaned forward and awkwardly turned her cheek to the animal. "Hello."

She felt a pair of warm, leathery lips against her face, followed by another noisy kiss.

"I think she likes you," Agapoff said.

Annie smiled, resisting the temptation to wipe it off.

Agapoff turned to her associate, who was over at the computer console. "Heather?"

The girl looked up from her conversation with Hugh.

"Will you bring up Claire II, please?"

"You bet," the girl answered. She dropped into her chair and entered information into the computer. A moment later a cartoon chimpanzee appeared on the large screen.

"Let us give her a picture-puzzle exercise."

"Which one?" Heather asked.

"The red ball."

"Pretty easy," the girl said. "Sure you don't want something a little fancier?"

"Perhaps another time. Our guest and Hugh should soon be returning to their work."

Hugh shrugged. "We're cool."

"The red ball, if you please, Heather?"

"Coming up."

Referring to the character on the screen, Agapoff said, "It is not as elaborate as the characters in Travis's lab, but for our purposes, it serves us well." She opened one of the drawers in the counter and pulled out a children's picture puzzle. It consisted of nine little squares—some red, some black, some a combination of both. "Okay, girl," Agapoff said as she lugged Claire to the nearest counter and set her down. "Are we ready, Heather?"

"One more minute."

As her associate entered the last keystrokes, Agapoff explained, "We are giving them both the same puzzle, with the same pieces identically arranged."

"All set," Heather called.

An exact duplicate of the puzzle appeared on the monitor before Claire II.

"Okay." Agapoff handed Claire the puzzle. "Let us begin."

Both animals took the puzzles into their hands.

"Watch and compare their progress," Agapoff said.

Annie nodded. To her amazement, both the computerized Claire and the real-life Claire attacked their puzzles in identical fashion, making the same choices, moving the same pieces in nearly perfect unison.

Annie stepped closer to the screen. "That's incredible. How are you doing that?"

Agapoff chuckled. "We are not doing it, they are. Five months ago, we injected Claire with very specially designed nanobots. They entered every capillary, every section of her brain. As they passed through, they transmitted the information they gathered."

Annie turned to her in astonishment. "You mapped her entire brain? From the inside out?"

"Every region. Every function of every neuron."

"With no vascular damage?"

"None whatsoever." Agapoff continued, "We recorded everything. Within four and one-half hours and multiple passes, we had all the data we needed. Of course, sorting the data was another problem. But, as I have said, thanks to Travis and his computer group, that information came very quickly."

Annie looked back to Claire, then to Claire II. The puzzles were nearly completed, and in identical fashion. Not only that, but both Claires were displaying the same type of excitement. "What about the blood-brain barrier?" Annie asked.

Agapoff shrugged. "As I said, those students at Berkeley, they are a clever bunch."

Annie turned back to the screen just as Claire II finished the puzzle and stood, raising her arms in triumph, shouting a scream of victory. But the scream did not come from the monitor. It came from Claire, who stood on the counter, her arms raised in identical fashion, her face expressing the same joy.

* * *

AFTER THE TOUR, Annie joined Nicholas outside on the side porch. He sat on the steps, lost in thought, mulling over a cup of lukewarm tea.

"You all right?" she asked.

"Me? Always. And you?"

"I just had quite a tour. Fascinating."

He stared down at his tea.

She sat beside him. "And, as much as I'd love to stay, I've got a little boy who's wondering where his mommy is. Just as soon as I can convince the security fellows to return my cell phone and let me go, I'm on my way."

"They'll allow you to leave?" he asked.

"What do you mean?"

"I had to wear a blindfold." He motioned to the house behind him. "You know where they live."

"Yes, I do," she said with a sigh. "And they've made it abundantly clear that they know my address as well."

"Did they threaten you?"

"No. But they made their point."

Nicholas scowled. "They're certainly paranoid, that's for sure. In my day it was countries that attacked and fought each other. Now, apparently, it's corporations."

"Let's hope that's all it is." "You're still thinking about what your FBI friend said?"

"And about those bruises." She reached toward the purple blotch under his right eye until he shied away. Knowing better than to pursue, she withdrew her hand. She tilted back her head, letting the sun warm her face. "So what are you going to tell them," she asked, "this new world you've created?"

"The bare minimum. We must be as nonintrusive as possible."

"You, nonintrusive?"

He ignored the jab. "And it must be verbal, not written. No holy books or religious artifacts to kill each other over."

"Sounds like you're feeling a little committed to that on-screen guy."

Nicholas tossed his tea to the ground. "What we are attempting has nothing to do with feelings, Doctor. It's simple logic. Nothing more, nothing less." He reached for the porch railing and pulled himself to his feet.

Annie remained silent as he turned and climbed the steps toward the kitchen. "We're about to resume. If you stay out of the way, you're welcome to watch." The screen door creaked as he opened it.

Without turning, she answered, "As soon as the security guys are done I'll be heading home."

He came to a stop. "Suit yourself. But with this new direction we're taking, you might actually have something to contribute."

"You don't need me," she replied. "You'll do just fine without—" The screen door slapped shut behind him as his footsteps faded away.

Annie sat for a moment, quietly musing. Only then did she realize that Nicholas hadn't offered her an invitation ... he'd just asked for her help.

CHAPTER 10

A LPHA...
    The voice was as soft as a breeze. Yet so intense it took his breath away. He turned from the heat of his baby's funeral pyre to see who had spoken. Just six weeks earlier, every burning platform in front of the Grid was in use. Day and night they disposed of the bodies, releasing their spirits in the flames . . . and, for more practical purposes, preventing the rats from eating their remains. But now, with so few left to die, the deaths came less frequently. In fact, he saw only one other person, five or six platforms over. A woman slightly younger than himself, lost in her own grief. She could not possibly be the one who had spoken.

Alpha 11 ...

Once again he gasped. It came from every direction. Above. Below. Inside. Taking a moment to summon his courage, he finally spoke. "Who—" His voice caught in his throat. He took another breath and tried again. "Who's there?" he called.

The woman across the pyres glanced to him, then looked away. She pulled up her shawl and shook off a climbing rat.

Don't be afraid, Alpha.

The voice was kind, like his own when he spoke to his son. And yet terrifying because it was everywhere.

"Who are you?" he asked.

There was no answer.

He looked up to the sky. "Hello?"

Nothing.

He scanned the grounds, the surrounding hills.

I am your... The voice seemed to hesitate, *"programmer."*

Alphas mind reeled. The answer made no sense. Yet the exhilaration he felt when the voice spoke, the sense of absoluteness that rose up inside him—it was as if everything suddenly had focus ... meaning.

Seeming to read his thoughts, the voice replied, *We programmed your world.*

Alpha reached out to steady himself on a branch sticking from the pyre. "What. . ." His mouth was as dry as sand. He was unsure what to say. From someplace far away, he heard himself ask, "What do you want?"

I want you to exercise authority.

Alpha frowned.

Over your world.

"I'm sorry, I don't..."

Look down, Alpha.

He glanced to the ground, to the swarm of gray and brown rats crawling over each other, circling the fire, smelling the flesh of his dead child but unable to approach because of the heat.

Those are what killed your wife. Those are what killed your baby. Exercise your authority over them.

The thought was as astonishing as the voice. "But..." he stammered, "they are life, they are sacred."

No. You are sacred.

"Me?"

You must take charge.

Alpha continued staring at the rodents, his head swimming. Was it possible? Were these creatures the ones responsible for killing his wife? His son? For destroying his community? Yes, they were a nuisance, and yes, they were growing and multiplying by the thousands, but to be responsible for such evil? How could that be? They were a natural part of the world, which was the shadow of a much greater world. Even more shocking, how could he possibly be their superior? He lifted his gaze to the crackling flames. Maybe he was losing his mind to grief. He'd seen it happen to others.

I am speaking truth, Alpha.

Alpha closed his eyes, trying to comprehend. If this was truth, if he wasn't going crazy ... then everything he'd been taught was a lie. Everything the priests had told his wife was wrong. A fabrication that brought about her own death. That killed their own baby. Moisture filled his eyes. He swiped at them and focused on the burning bundle in the center of the flames.

You are a steward of this world.

Could it be? Could he have been so wrong for so long? The moisture continued welling up until it spilled onto his cheeks. They were tears of confusion, tears of grief. And now, as his mind raced through the memories, tears of resentment.

You are sacred because you were programmed to be like us.

He began to tremble. It was slight at first. But it quickly grew. Emotions roiled inside him, swelled into his chest. He looked down at his foot and saw a rat scampering over it. Defying everything he knew to be holy and true, he angrily kicked it. His foot caught its belly, lifting it into the air, sending it twisting into the flames. It landed, writhing, squealing, then stopped, its body catching fire and burning alongside his child's.

He cringed at the sight, at the pain he'd just inflicted. But instead of rebuke, or threats of retribution, the voice spoke with calm encouragement.

That's right. Do what I say and take authority. You are the stewards. You are what is sacred.

The tears came faster now. The trembling more violent. How was it possible? To have been so wrong?

Another rat approached. He kicked it harder.

Again, no rebuke.

He kicked another. And then another. And another, until he was no longer kicking rats. He was kicking his foolishness. His stupidity. His superstitious ignorance. That's what killed his family. That's what destroyed everything he loved.

Across the flames he saw the wavering image of the woman. Her grief no longer allowed her to stand. She had dropped to her knees, sobbing, broken, like so many others he'd seen. And the rats, taking advantage of her position, swarmed around her knees, scampered up her robe, climbing onto her back and shoulders.

Treat one another as though you are sacred. Treat one another as you would treat me.

Now, his entire body shaking, he stepped to his son's pyre and pulled a burning log from it. Sizing it up in his hands, he looked back to the woman. Then, exploding with a rage he could not contain, he raced toward her, raising the log over his head yelling, roaring.

She looked up, startled, eyes widening in terror. Her mouth opened in a scream, but he could not hear it over his own fury. She barely had time to cover her face before he arrived and began clubbing them. Like a madman, he batted them off her body, hitting one after another, kicking them into the flames, smashing them, crushing their skulls—all the months, all the years of suffering, all the anger focused and unleashed.

He grabbed the woman by the arm, yanking her to her feet, away from the squealing creatures. She screamed. She kicked and clawed and scratched. But she would eventually understand. If he had not lost his mind, she would understand.

* * *

NICHOLAS REACHED out and steadied himself against the console. It was one thing to observe the character up on the screen, but to actually communicate with it, to interact with it—that had taken more out of him than he had anticipated.

"That's it?" Travis asked from beside him. "Do what we say and and be stewards? Treat each other like you would treat us? That's all you're telling them?"

"It's enough," Nicholas replied. "If Alpha is anything like his prototype, he's a thinker—he'll expand on the words and adjust them where they're needed."

"And that's all it will take to save their world?" Rebecca asked skeptically.

"If we applied it, it's all that would be necessary to save our own."

A moment passed. No one disagreed. He glanced to Annie, who gave him a little nod. Although he knew it was for encouragement, the act irritated him. He didn't need her approval. He turned back to the screen and watched with the others as the woman collapsed into Alpha, exhausted and sobbing—as Alpha wrapped his protective arms around her, pulling her shawl up over her shoulders.

"It's okay," he whispered, "you'll be all right. You'll be okay."

It was a touching scene that no one in the lab dared interrupt. Finally, Travis cleared his throat and turned to Hugh. "Let's push it. Let's fast-forward and see the impact on their future." Hugh nodded and began to type when a voice suddenly shouted through the intercom, "Lockdown!"

Nicholas heard a series of pops through the speaker.

"Lock down! Lock down!"

Hugh spun around to Travis, who shouted, "Do it!"

Leaping to his feet, Hugh crossed to a touch pad at the end of the console and quickly typed in a set of numbers.

"What's going on?" Nicholas demanded.

A dull thud echoed through the room as the air pressure suddenly changed. The lights dimmed and the faint drone of a generator began.

"Travis?"

"Looks like we've got ourselves more visitors," his brother answered. Throwing a glance to Annie, he added, "Apparently it's our day for company."

"Who is it?" Nicholas said. "What do they want?"

"Us, I imagine. Or at least our work." Travis reached to the console and began hitting switches. Glancing back to Nicholas, he flashed his lopsided grin. "You should see your face, man. It's like you think we're in danger."

"We're safe down here?" Nicholas asked.

"The boys upstairs are pros. And we're built like Fort Knox. No way is anybody getting to us. We're totally safe from the bad guys."

"Unless . . ." Hugh coughed. He nodded across the room to Rebecca, who had just produced a serious-looking handgun.

She finished his phrase, "Unless the bad guys are already here."

A moment of stunned silence followed, then Travis broke out laughing. "Come on, Rebecca. What are you doin'?"

"I'm taking you all upstairs." She turned the gun on Hugh and ordered, "Unlock the door."

"Rebecca." Travis started toward her, shaking his head. "Becka, Becka, Be—"

She spun at him and accidentally fired a round. The noise was deafening in the small room.

"What, are you nuts?" Travis shouted. "There's expensive equipment down here!"

Nicholas looked over to Annie. She was frightened, but unhurt. He moved toward her.

Rebecca was trembling, obviously as surprised by the shot as they were. She turned to Hugh. "Unlock the..." She took a breath, trying to calm herself. "Unlock the door."

Hugh hesitated.

"Now!"

"All right," he said. "Just be careful with that."

She took a wider stance, holding the gun on him with both hands, her face shiny with sweat. He turned back to the console and reentered the code, so nervous his fingers slipped, hitting a wrong key.

"Hugh!" she shouted.

"All right, all right!" He tried again. There was another dull thud as the air pressure returned to normal.

She pointed the gun toward the stairway and ordered, "Let's go!"

"Rebecca—"

"Now."

They hesitated.

"Now!"

Without further argument, they shuffled toward the steps. Travis and Hugh took the lead.

Nicholas and Annie followed. "It's all right," he assured her. "We'll be fine." They began climbing the steps, Rebecca bringing up the rear.

"So who are you working for?" Travis called over his shoulder. "How much are they pay—"

"Shut up!"

Nicholas could hear the popping of guns outside. Suddenly the door flew open and the Latino guard who had first searched him stood glowering. In his hand was an automatic rifle.

"Norm," Travis said, "what's going—"

"Let's go!" The man motioned him toward the hall with the weapon.

Travis continued, "You might want to have a little chat with Rebecca. She seems a bit—"

The guard yanked him into the hallway. "Move!"

Hugh followed, his hands already in the air. "I'm cool, I'm cool."

Nicholas and Annie were next. They headed down the first, brightly lit hallway and entered the second, where they moved past the living room toward the kitchen. The shooting was much louder and closer. But Nicholas had already begun focusing his thoughts, overriding his fear.

"Where are you taking us?" he asked the guard.

"Shut up, old man!"

"It's a simple question. Surely you're capable of—"

The butt of the guard's rifle flew up and caught Nicholas's face. For a moment he saw stars. But at least he'd made personal contact—rule number one in any hostage situation. Checking for blood on his face, Nicholas tried again. "If you would merely—"

A series of shots exploded from the living room to his right. The guard staggered, then fell into Annie. She screamed as he grabbed her. The grip was a reflex action—the man was already dead. Nicholas quickly stepped in, prying him away. "It's okay," he said, "you're all right." The corpse fell off her and crumpled to the floor.

A voice shouted, "This way!"

Nicholas turned to see the big driver who'd brought him to the compound. The man stood at the front door, Uzi in hand, blue-white smoke rising from its barrel. "I've got a car!"

He started toward the man, then turned back to Annie. She was frozen in fear, staring down at the body.

"Hurry!" the driver shouted.

She continued staring, unable to move.

Nicholas reached out his hand to her, but she did not respond.

"Let's go!" the driver yelled. Nicholas's tone was soft but firm. "Annie?" She raised her eyes. He gave her a nod. She continued to look at him. Not breaking his gaze, he reached out his other hand.

Another nod. Finally, she took both of his hands, her fingers cold and wet. He gently eased her forward until her eyes faltered and she glanced down. Once again she stiffened.

"Look at me," he ordered. "Look only at me."

But she could not take her eyes off the ripped holes in the shirt, the glistening pieces of bone and shredded tissue ... or the widening pool of blood that was just now touching her shoes.

"Anytime!" the driver shouted.

"Look at me, Annie." Nicholas's voice grew more commanding. "Annie!"

She looked up. He gently pulled, guiding her over the body, one step, then another. They entered the living room and he shifted to her side, both arms around her. The driver moved out onto the front porch, looking to the left, then the right, before motioning that the coast was clear. Nicholas could see the Lexus through the doorway, its engine idling, the back door open and waiting.

He eased Annie onto the porch as a pounding roar suddenly filled the sky. A small midnight-blue helicopter with a yellow corporate logo appeared over the ridge. It headed directly for them.

The driver crossed to his side of the Lexus, raised his rifle, and began to fire. The chopper turned, revealing a shooter in black overalls. He was leaning out of the cockpit for better aim. Immediately Nicholas pulled Annie in to him and covered her head just before the man opened fire. A line of bullets sprayed across the roof and hood of the Lexus, until it found the fuel line.

Blinding white light threw Nicholas backward, slamming him hard against the wall of the porch. He was out before he hit the ground.

* * *

How LONG HE WAS UNCONSCIOUS, he didn't know, but he awoke to the sound of gunfire and Annie and Travis shouting.

"Are you all right? Nicholas! Can you hear me?"

He opened his eyes, saw them staring down at him. He tried to answer, but words did not come.

"Can you stand?" Travis shouted.

He nodded and they helped him to his feet—Annie on one side, Travis on the other. Only then did he feel the searing pain in his right thigh. He looked down and saw the leg of his trousers, bloody and ripped. A piece of shiny black metal jutted through the material. Angrily, he reached down to pull it out, but Travis grabbed his hand.

"Wouldn't do that, bro! Not till we can plug it with something!"

The shooting was much closer. He turned toward the house. The battle was inside now.

"There!" Annie pointed across the burning chassis of the

Lexus to an SUV and a Beemer parked under the trees fifty yards away.

Travis turned to Hugh and shouted, "Here, take him!"

Hugh joined them and Travis transferred Nicholas's weight to him. Nicholas tried to help, but he quickly learned his efforts were more of a hindrance.

Travis raced down the steps to the Uzi lying on the ground next to the smoldering remains of the driver. He scooped up the gun and motioned over to the parked cars. "There! I'll meet you there!"

Nicholas allowed Annie and Hugh to ease him down the stairs, one painful step after another. He wanted to help, but most of his energy was spent trying to stay conscious.

Once they reached the ground, Hugh turned to him and shouted, "Are you okay?"

Irritated at the attention, he tried to answer, but could only scowl.

Annie got the message. "He's fine! Let's go!"

They hobbled across the yard, Nicholas doing his best to help and failing miserably, until they reached the nearest oak. They leaned against the tree to catch their breath. A steep slope dropped off behind them. In front of them, the closest vehicle was still twenty yards away.

"Hugh!"

They turned to see Rebecca. She was sprawled on the ground near the kitchen porch. Her pants were torn and she was bleeding.

"Help me!"

Hugh hesitated.

She cried again, "Hugh!"

He turned to Annie and shouted, "I'll be right back!"

Before she could argue, he dashed into the open. He'd nearly reached Rebecca when the helicopter appeared over the roof. The gunman spotted him and yelled to the pilot. The chopper crabbed to the right, giving him a clear shot.

"Look out!" Annie shouted.

Puffs of dust raced at Hugh until they found him. The bullets tore up his leg and into his chest—his body jerking mercilessly until it toppled to the ground.

"Auhhh!" Another voice screamed from their left, firing a burst from an automatic rifle.

They spun around to see Travis shouting, running at the chopper, shooting the Uzi crazily into the air. What he lacked in aim he made up for in anger. Before the helicopter could rotate, allowing the shooter to take a bead, Travis was underneath the craft, firing away. A series of holes plink-plink-plinked across its underbelly until they reached the tail rotor, creating a series of sparks and some serious damage. The helicopter began turning on its own axis. The engine whined as the pilot struggled to regain control. But the stabilizer was gone and there was little to be done as the chopper tipped to the left, then to the right, until the blades clipped one of the overhanging trees and snapped off.

The entire craft plunged into the house, exploding into a yellow-orange fireball.

Nicholas and Annie turned their heads away from the heat. A moment later, the oak behind them chipped and splintered. Someone had spotted them from the burning house. They ducked behind the tree as the shots continued. They were cut off. There was no way they could make it to the cars now. Their only escape was down the hill.

With effort, Annie slipped Nicholas onto her shoulder. "Come on!"

They turned and started down the steep slope—half sliding, half falling on the dried grass and loose gravel. The edges of Nicholas's vision grew white, pulsing with each jarring movement. But he refused to pass out. They traveled fifty yards before they spotted the dirt road. They barely arrived before an SUV slid around the corner, honking—a familiar voice shouting from inside.

The vehicle skidded to a stop and Travis jumped from the driver's side. He raced toward them, yelling, "Let's go! Meter's running!"

He heaved Nicholas onto his shoulder and they headed to the vehicle. As they arrived, Nicholas's vision grew white-hot. His body no longer obeyed. He saw the two of them opening a door, felt himself jostled inside, heard their voices growing farther and farther away, until he saw and heard nothing at all.

CHAPTER 11

"**D**ADDY?"

Alpha looked down from the scaffolding and saw six-year-old Nyrah waving her good arm as she ran up the grassy slope toward him. As usual she was at least twenty steps ahead of her mother and baby brother.

"Daddy..."

He loved that name. It always made his heart swell. He waved back and shouted, "I'll be with you in a minute."

"Not too long," Saida, his wife, called. She raised a picnic basket. "Don't want these to get cold."

"What is it?"

"Nyrah made them. You'll have to wait till you get here."

"I'll be right there." He turned back to his lead foreman, a giant, sweating man with biceps nearly as big as Alpha's thighs. They stood ten lengths above the ground at the northeast corner of the Temple.

"I know it's what we discussed," Alpha said, gazing up at the slabs of white marble that rose an additional fifteen lengths above them. "But is there a way to round the edges, to make everything appear just a little ... softer?"

"Softer?" the big man questioned.

Alpha knew it was the wrong word. From the day they first began the structure, he had used terms like grand, powerful, majestic—words that best described his experience with Programmer. And for the most part the artisans had captured these qualities. You could see it in the towering building, in the dozens of brilliant white steps leading up to the imposing pillars and giant bronze doors. And you could see it inside the sanctuary, with its walls of green and black marble, its onyx, its gold inlays. Yet there was still something missing—the absolute centeredness mixed with a type of affection, the tenderness of a parent toward his child. This was what he'd heard in the voice, the essence he had never been able to fully describe, nor the workers capture.

"Daddy."

He looked down to see Nyrah staring up from the foot of the scaffolding. "Daddy, payment is going to begin; you don't want to miss payment."

"I'll be right there, sweetheart."

She pulled herself up on the first bar, trying to climb the scaffolding. It was difficult, with her right arm broken and in a sling—the results of an adventurous child with too many trees to climb—but she would have continued and succeeded if he hadn't stopped her.

"Nyrah, stay down. I'll be right there."

He turned back to the foreman, who was still frowning.

"When you say 'softer,' you don't mean weaker?"

"No, no, not weak. Not weak at all."

"Daddy?"

"It's more ..."

"Daddy?"

He looked back to his daughter. "Sweetheart, stay down." Then, to the foreman, "Do you think we can talk about this after lunch, after payment?"

"No problem. I'm always here."

Alpha smiled. "I know you are. And I want to thank you. The work you men are doing is terrific, just . . . terrific. Thank you."

The big man grinned. "It's not for you."

"I know." Alpha grinned back. "And I'm sure He's pleased too."

With that, he turned and started down the scaffolding. For seven seasons they had been working on the Temple, building it at the very spot where he had first heard Programmer. Originally, it had just been him. An act of gratitude. Of worship. But eventually one neighbor joined. And then another. And another. As he shared Programmer's Law, as they saw the joy and prosperity his family experienced by living it, word quickly spread. So did the converts.

He reached the lawn and his daughter grabbed his hand. "Hurry," she said, pulling him along.

He thought of picking her up and carrying her, but knew she'd have none of it. She was too independent, had been that way since her first breathglow. They crossed the grounds, greeting friends and other citizens who were also gathering —some with picnic lunches, others just to watch and relax, looking for an excuse to enjoy the warm spring day. At the steps of the Temple a small gathering of musicians had already started to play.

By the time they arrived, Saida had spread a blanket upon the grass and was setting out plates. Alpha dropped to his knees and gave his wife a kiss, playful at first, then growing in warmth. Seven seasons had passed and his compassion toward her had not dimmed. Granted it was not as fiery as in his youth. But over the course of time, as he obeyed Programmer, as he treated his wife with the same respect he felt toward Programmer, their love grew richer, far deeper than he could have imagined.

"So, what's for lunch?" he asked as he scooped Orib into his arms. He lifted the baby's shirt and blew against his tummy, making the infant laugh.

"Daddy." Nyrah glanced around, embarrassed at the noise.

He did it again, just to make her giggle.

"Marinated life units, coated in crumbs and deep-fried," Saida answered. "Nyrah made them all by herself. Her very first time."

"But I ruined them." Nyrah gave a grown-up sigh. "They're all burnt."

"No, they're not," Saida said. "Well, not all of them."

"Enough of them." Nyrah sulked.

Alpha tousled her hair and lay on his back. He set Orib on his chest and closed his eyes in the warm sun. "If you fixed them, I'm sure they're perfect."

"So who is making payment today?" Saida asked as she continued setting the plates.

"Atrim," he said with a sigh.

"Again?"

"He insists upon ignoring the Greeting."

"Despite the Law?"

"He says there are other ways to honor citizens."

Saida clicked her tongue. "You devote so much of your time to dissecting Programmer's Law, applying it to our lives. And then men like Atrim just trample all over your work."

"He's not a bad man," Alpha said. "Remember last season when he helped with our roof?"

Saida shrugged. "Nevertheless, there are certain—"

"There he is now, Daddy!" Nyrah interrupted. "There he is!" Alpha sat up, shading his eyes from the sun.

"Can we go down and watch?" Nyrah asked. "Can we?"

"Sweetheart, your mother's gone to all this trouble

bringing us lunch."

The girl turned to Saida. "Can we, Mama? Please, can we?"

The woman hesitated.

"Pleeeease?"

"All right." The girl leaped to her feet and started tugging on Alpha's hand.

He turned to Saida. "You're sure?"

"It's already getting cold. A little colder won't make any difference."

Nyrah continued pulling. Alpha held back long enough to give his wife another kiss, making sure she wasn't angry.

"Go, go," she insisted. "But don't take all day."

"Come on." Nyrah tugged harder until he rose. "They're already tying him to the Grid."

"But don't expect Orib and me to wait," Saida called after them.

He gave a nod and Nyrah pulled him through the gathering crowd. They approached the Grid, where Atrim, a balding man just a little older than Alpha, was about to make payment. The priests had bound his legs to the iron mesh. Now they were tying his hands as one of the Council Members read the charges from the platform. It wouldn't be much—by Alpha's own decree, less than a season. Nothing too violent for Nyrah to witness, yet enough to impress her of the penalties for being a Law Breaker.

They found a clear view just as the Council Member finished reading the sentence. ". . . guilty of disrespect to Programmer and your fellow citizens by refusing to give the required Greeting in His name. For that you are sentenced to lose one half season."

"I did not remember," Atrim shouted to the crowd. It was an obvious lie, but his only defense. "I've had so much on my mind, I—"

The rest of his speech was lost as one of the assistants placed the leather pouch between his teeth. Then, stepping back, he shouted, "Secure!"

A moment later there was a soft crackle and Atrim's body convulsed. But only for an instant before it relaxed. Applause rippled through the audience—men and women, grateful to see justice served, to see Programmer obeyed. Atrim opened his eyes, blinking in surprise as if nothing had happened. In some ways nothing had. Losing one half season was barely noticeable. But every payment, no matter how minor, was necessary for the good of the community. Granted, nearly every day there were new circumstances that forced Alpha to refine Programmers words, adding to them for clarity and application. But it was a small price to pay to honor Programmer and to maintain the peace.

* * *

THE FIRST THING Nicholas noticed was the pounding in his head. The second was his inability to open his eyes. "What..." His voice cracked, his mouth and throat were parched. "Where am I?"

"Well, look who's back."

With greater effort, he pried open his lids. Annie's blurry form walked toward him. He tried lifting his head, but the pounding stopped him. The pain in his thigh wasn't much better. Grudgingly, he lay back down.

"You put on a lot of mileage, bro."

He turned toward Travis's voice.

"Figured it was time to bring you in for your hundred-thousand-mile checkup."

His eyes focused on the bed rails beside him, then the IV tube leading into his arm. "A hospital?" He coughed. "You put me in a hospital?"

"A hospital bed," Travis corrected. "Big difference."

Annie arrived and handed him his glasses. "We're at the Surf and Sand Hotel."

"The penthouse, baby," Travis said. "Courtesy of one Mr. Phil Dixon."

Nicholas put on his glasses and scowled, trying to think through the throbbing in his head. "Phillip Dixon, the computer guru?

"And bazillionare, you got it."

"He's who we're working for?"

"He's who I'm working for," Travis replied. "You're just a volunteer, remember."

Annie reached for a stainless steel pitcher on the rollaway table beside Nicholas's bed. Pouring him a glass of water, she asked, "Can I get you anything?"

Without answering, he took the glass and began drinking as he surveyed his surroundings. His bed was in the living room—a large two-story affair with glass furniture, white carpeting, and a staircase swooping down from the right. To his left was an outdoor balcony with an ocean view that didn't quit.

Travis sat on the edge of a nearby desk that supported a computer and large monitor. Pulling his cell phone from its charger, he asked, "Feel like chatting with him?"

"Who?"

"Phillip."

"Travis," Annie protested, "give him a little time before you start—"

"Time?" Travis interrupted. "He's had like eighteen hours." He began punching in a phone number. The boss wants a little virtual F2F, that's all."

Nicholas glanced to Annie.

"Face-to-face," she explained.

Travis continued. "Seems our little project's had a major

137

wrinkle and—" He stopped and spoke into his cell. "Hey, Shannon, Travis here." He frowned. "Travis Mackenzie." Brightening, he nodded. "Right, right. Tell Mr. Dixon we're all set."

Nicholas turned back to Annie. "Eighteen hours? Where's your son, where's Rusty?"

She pushed back her hair. "With the babysitter... I hope."

"You hope?"

She pursed her lips, obviously trying to stay calm. "They won't let me leave. I can't even call out."

Travis continued speaking into the phone. "Cool. We'll be hangin' right here." He hit the disconnect button and grinned. "Phil's gonna call us back. Guess he's got—"

Nicholas interrupted, "This woman has not been allowed to see her child for nearly a day!"

"I know, I know. Major downer."

"The boy's five years old!"

"Right, right." He turned to Annie. "We'll make it up to you, I swear. Just as soon as we fix this little migraine-maker of a problem." He turned back to Nicholas. "And when we do, well, let's just say Phillip Dixon doesn't forget his friends, if you know what I mean."

"No," Nicholas snapped, "I don't know what you mean. And what problem are you talking about? What's going on?"

Travis popped another mint into his mouth. "The good news is, they never got into either of the labs."

"They?"

"I told you, these big-time corp boys play for keeps."

"They're the ones who attacked us?"

Travis nodded. "But with zero penetration. Like I said, our guys are good. From what I hear, they didn't leave a man standing."

"Dead?"

"Yeah. Bad scene."

"What about Hugh? The girl?"

His brother glanced out to the ocean, then slowly shook his head.

Nicholas could only stare.

Travis turned back to him, "Course, they weren't exactly innocent victims, if you know what I mean."

"No, I don't know what you mean, and stop using that phrase. What about the program ... what about Alpha?"

"Hold your horses, I'm getting to it." He bit into his mint and began crunching. "Course, we had to do a little scorched-earth policy—you know, make 'em think the labs were destroyed and all."

"Think?" Nicholas asked.

"You saw the fortifications, man. No way could they damage them. But they don't know it. That's why Annie has to stay with us. Can't go spilling the beans and bring an encore performance, not while we're still running the thing."

"Running what thing?"

"The program."

"It's still operating?"

"And growing worse."

"What do you mean, how is it growing worse?"

Without a word, Travis rose and scooped up the open laptop computer from his desk. He approached Nicholas and set it on the rollaway table, scooting it so close Nicholas stiffened, trying not to recoil.

"Travis," Annie admonished.

"Relax, man, it ain't going to bite." He turned and strolled back to his own computer. "Alpha and the community, they've been compromised. Someone's broken into the program."

"You said it was protected."

"It was. But we left a little back door open."

"A what?"

"We insisted on giving them free will."

Nicholas nodded. "That's correct. We agreed they had to have free will or—"

"They'd be nothing but robots. Yeah, I know."

"How is that a problem?"

Travis sat at his desk and began working his own computer. "This is a playback from ten hours ago. When the virus was introduced."

"Virus?"

"Yeah. And it's not good, compadre. Not good at all." He entered a final set of keystrokes and the Temple area appeared on the laptop in front of Nicholas. The screen showed citizens working, talking, going about their daily routines. As far as Nicholas could see, there was nothing unusual.

Travis zoomed in the picture to a middle-aged woman. She was heading down the Temple steps with a package under her arm.

"That's Saida," Annie explained. "Alphas wife. She's just picked up her family's life units for the week."

"Why is she so old?" Nicholas asked. "You said we've only been gone, what, eighteen hours?"

"Eighteen hours, our time, Travis said. "That's years for them."

They watched as Saida continued down the steps, nodding and smiling to those she passed.

"I don't see a problem," Nicholas said. "Everything appears—"

"Shh." Travis motioned for silence. "Here it comes."

The woman reached the bottom of the steps and started crossing the Temple grounds when a young female voice spoke:

Saida ...

She gave a start, then looked around. As far as she could see, no one had spoken.

Saida ...

She adjusted her scarf and picked up her pace. "What do you want this time?" she whispered.

Am I a nuisance? I'll leave if you want.

She gave no answer.

Where's your husband, where's Alpha?

"You know where he is."

Yes, always at work, always refining Programmer's Law. Seems he never has time for you.

"We've been through all that. I told you there are many interpretations to be made."

Of course. So many interpretations.

Nicholas called over to Travis, "That voice, the woman, it sounds like—"

"Shh."

Don't you ever grow tired of them? The interpretations, I mean. All this talk about Programmers Law?

"Tired of them?"

Don't you find them just a little... restrictive?

Saida glanced nervously around, then whispered, "They're for our good. If Programmer says something, we do it, plain and simple."

But wouldn't you like to know why he says it? You do have a brain. Wouldn't you like to decide for yourself instead of always being told?

"Don't be ridiculous."

Saida...

The woman said nothing and walked in silence.

Saida...

Finally she answered. "Look, even if I wanted to know, there's no way."

Why not?

"It's just not possible."

Oh, but it is.

Saida adjusted the package under her arm, then scornfully replied, "How could a person know such things?"

There was no answer.

"Hello?"

More silence.

Saida glanced about. "Are you still there?"

At last, the voice replied. *Come... let me show you.*

"Come where?"

To the back of the Temple.

"The back?"

Yes.

Saida hesitated.

You won't be sorry. I promise.

She was still unsure.

Come. It's perfectly safe. Come.

Finally, with a sigh, Saida relented, "All right." She changed course and headed toward the Temple. "But only for a moment."

Of course.

"That voice," Nicholas repeated, "is it—"

"Rebecca? Yeah," Travis said.

"She's alive?"

"Hard to know. They could have dropped the virus in and scheduled its release anytime."

"They?"

"She's smart, but not that smart. Hugh's the computer brain." Travis chewed up the remainder of his mint. "Good ol' Hugh."

Nicholas turned back to his screen as Saida rounded the Temple. The rear of the structure had none of the steps, columns, or impressive doors, but its broad, flat simplicity still displayed grandeur.

Here we go, the voice said.

"Where?" Saida asked.

Turn around, silly.

Saida obeyed and turned to face the back wall. Suddenly images flickered upon it—bars and rectangles with colored writing and photographs.

"What are you doing?" Saida cried in surprise.

What would you like to know? the voice asked.

Saida frowned. "What would I like to know about what?"

Anything. Good, evil. All the knowledge you could ever want is right here. What would you like?

"I don't need to know anything."

Really? There's nothing you're the slightest bit curious about?

She hesitated.

Anything, Saida. Anything at all.

The woman lowered her voice. "Well, maybe ..." She glanced around, making sure no one was near. "Maybe how I can ..."

Go ahead...

More softly still, she whispered, "How I can get Alpha to look at me like he used to? You know, when we were younger?"

Instantly the wall filled with another page of writing, a series of written topics: Sexy Thighs, Sexy Belly, Fit for Sex, Secrets to Sex, Sexy Body Workout. .. each followed by a description of two or three sentences.

What would you like to know? the voice repeated.

She stared at the wall, speechless.

Saida?

She hesitated, turned away embarrassed.

It's only knowledge, Saida. There's nothing wrong with knowledge.

Another moment passed before, finally, slowly, she turned back to the wall.

"Hold it," Nicholas interrupted. "I don't under—"

Annie spoke in quiet awe. "The Internet."

"Unlimited knowledge for any and all takers," Travis said. He hit a series of keys and the image on the monitor fast-forwarded until another member of the community joined Saida, then another, and another. Soon, day and night, crowds of folks were gathered at the wall. Coming and going.

Nicholas turned to Travis. "The rest of the community was drawn to this?"

"Like moths to a flame."

He pushed up his glasses and scowled. "Our instructions weren't good enough for them."

Travis shook his head. "Now everybody wants to know why. Why they have to follow authority, why they have to treat each other as sacred, why not this way, why not that way. Now they all want to experiment on their own, to do it their own way.

Annie softly quoted, "'Each doing whatever is right in their own eyes.'"

"Regardless of the long-term consequences?" Nicholas asked.

"That's right."

"So, we've come full circle."

"Short-term gratification equals selfish ambition equals self- destruction," Travis said. "Just like old times."

Nicholas turned to him. "There must be somebody following our instruction."

"Oh, yeah," Travis replied, giving a sad, lopsided grin, "there are plenty."

"You make that sound like a problem."

"Hang on, I'll bring you up to present time, and you tell me."

CHAPTER 12

NYRAH STOOD WEARILY before the bathroom mirror, her silk burgundy robe hanging open. She straightened and turned to look at herself in profile. It was a good body—a little paunch in the belly, but still mostly young and firm—just what men liked.

It had served her well and she figured if she took care of it, it would continue to do so for several more seasons— before they stopped showing interest, before they stopped paying. And by then, who knows, maybe she'd find a husband and settle down, raise a family like her parents.

Her parents. She scoffed at the idea and leaned toward the mirror to check her breathglow. It made no difference how many life units she charged, it always seemed a little fainter after she finished. She never understood why, unless it was because the units were secondhand. As a Breaker she was no longer allowed on Temple grounds to directly secure them. Instead she had to steal, beg, or, in her case, find a service to trade for them.

Tonight her client had been a sweaty, big-gutted man. One of the elders. She'd seen him in the park with his kids, stealing looks at her for weeks. All it took was a little eye contact to build his courage, and a casual comment or two to reel him in. Of course, her reputation didn't hurt. Like so many others, he found her family tree more than a little exciting.

"So, you're really Alpha's daughter?" he had asked, unable to hide his awe as they prepared for bed.

"That's right." She turned her back to him, untied her robe and let it slide to the floor.

He stood on the other side of the bed, his fat sausage fingers fumbling to loosen his tunic. "The Law Giver's daughter."

Running her hands down her bare thigh to her calf, she began slowly unlacing her sandal. "His one and only."

"Wow." She heard his tunic drop to the ground. "So, why did— what I mean is, why do—"

"Why do I do this?" she asked.

"Well, yeah, I mean, you know. Yeah."

She removed her sandal and stretched catlike across the sheets, dropping it onto the floor at the foot of the bed. She was careful never to look at him. She tried never to look at them.

"Let's just say I enjoy being naughty."

"Yeah?" The bed groaned under his weight as he climbed in.

"Yeah." She lowered her voice, unlacing the other sandal. "Good can be so boring."

"Oh, yeah." She could feel him watching her every move. He was practically drooling. Men were such dogs.

"You wanna be bad with me?" She was on autopilot now. Reciting the same phrases she had used so many dozens of times before.

"Oh, yeah …"

His breath had reeked of wine and the decaying teeth of

old men. His white body had been slick with sweat. But his life units were as good as any other's.

Pushing aside the night's memory, Nyrah reached in and turned on the shower. The sooner she washed off his scent, the better. But there was something more, something deeper than his scent...

She had tried so hard to live her parents' life. But in one way or another, as far back as she could remember, the virus had always won. She had always failed. Her father pretended to understand, but there was no missing the pain in his eyes and the humiliation over her payments at the Grid. Until, finally, one day in her sixteenth season, she could no longer endure it. That was when she gave up. Let her brother, Orib, be the perfect one. If she was a bad seed, she was a bad seed, and there was nothing to be done about it.

Truth was, breaking free hadn't been all that painful. Actually, it was kind of liberating. She could finally be who she really was.

Nyrah stepped into the hot shower. It felt good letting the water pound against her body, scalding and cleansing it. But she knew she would never really be clean. Nor would she be free—not from her father's disappointment or her mother's tears. She lifted her head to the water, letting it pelt her face and mix with her own hot tears.

"ALL RIGHT, HANG ON," Travis said. "I'm transferring you now."

Nicholas was grateful when Nyrah's image flickered off his computer screen. Although she was only digital, it was difficult to watch someone who could have been his grand-daughter, trapped in such... circumstances. The fact that many of her features—her mouth, her nose, those high cheekbones—were similar to his wife's did not make it easier.

The image was replaced by a pudgy-looking man in his forties with a shaved head and a thick black unibrow—an icon Nicholas immediately recognized.

"Dr. Mackenzie. It's good to finally meet you."

Nicholas simply stared.

His brother motioned from the side. "Talk! Talk!"

Unsure where to look, he focused at the center of the screen. "Hello ... Mr. Dixon."

"Please, call me Phil."

Nicholas did not reply.

"I hear you've been helping your brother with our little project."

Nicholas pushed up his glasses. "A project, I'm told, that has taken human lives."

"Yes," Dixon agreed, "very unfortunate."

"Unfortunate?" Nicholas felt little need to hide his ire.

"Be nice!" Travis whispered.

"People are dead, Mr. Dixon. Several of them."

The image on the screen slowly nodded. "And I'm afraid if we continue, that may only be the beginning."

The phrase brought Nicholas up short.

Dixon continued, "As Travis has explained, many people would like to get their hands on this project."

Nicholas replied. "Capitalists such as yourself... whose interest is to only make money."

Travis dropped his head into his hands.

"You have no argument there," Dixon agreed. "Though, of course, it's not entirely about the money."

"Of course not," Nicholas scorned.

Dixon continued unperturbed. "Money's certainly a motivating factor, otherwise we would have no investors. But there are several other benefits as well."

Nicholas gave no expression.

"Besides predicting patterns in consumer goods and marketing, we were also hoping to study patterns of poverty, hunger, disease, the distribution of wealth …"

Nicholas remained silent, evaluating the man. He certainly appeared to be sincere. Then there was his sterling reputation as one of the world's great philanthropists.

"And finally, of course, there is the survival of our own civilization. If we can learn how to keep their civilization going, then perhaps—"

"Our own will survive," Nicholas interrupted. "Yes, I'm aware of the obvious."

"I supposed you were."

"Regardless, you are creating a program that apparently everyone, including the United States government, will stop at nothing to get their hands on."

"Actually, the government is the one organization that's on our side."

The information surprised Nicholas. "The FBI?" he asked. He glanced over to Annie but did not see her. "Homeland Security?"

"We send them detailed updates on a regular basis."

Nicholas scowled.

Dixon quickly added, "Although, I might point out your brother has been somewhat vague on where he's obtaining all the necessary computational power."

Grateful for an excuse to join the conversation, Travis crowded into the frame. "Which, like I said earlier, I'm already tapping to the max. Shooting straight here, Phil— with the addition of this virus, I don't know, we may need more power than even I can rustle up."

Dixon nodded. "Which is why we have to make a decision."

Nicholas shifted in his bed, continuing to listen.

"What I see is a project that has already led to violence and murder. One that is continuing to fail, even with the brightest minds such as yourself attached. And finally, according to Travis, it's a project that may have reached current computational limits. All reasons my board is reevaluating whether or not to continue."

"Except..." Travis prompted.

Dixon nodded. "Except there is one other approach. And, quite frankly, it may be our best and last." He turned to Travis.

"Would you mind explaining to your brother what we've been discussing?"

"No problemo." Travis cleared his throat, obviously pleased to take center stage. "First of all, there's no way of removing the virus, unless we like totally violate their free will."

"You can't remove it from the back of the Temple?" Nicholas asked.

"Old news, did it hours ago—or, in their case, years. No, I'm talking about how it infected them here"—he tapped his skull— "inside."

"You can't erase that?"

"Sure, but then we're back to messin' with free will."

"So what is this other approach?" Nicholas asked.

"What if one of us were to interact with the community? You know, explain why our way's the best way."

"We did that," Nicholas said, "when I spoke to Alpha."

"Right, I under—"

"If we speak to him on an ongoing basis, telling him every step to take, we return to the free will question."

"No, man, I don't mean talking to him in some 'cosmic voice.' I mean talking to him in person, mano a mano."

"And how do you propose we do that?"

"We create another member of their community. We

download one of our own personalities into it so we can talk to them face-to-face, show them how they're supposed to live."

"You're not serious?"

"Sure. That way, they still have free will. But instead of laying a bunch more rules on them, our guy talks to them in person. He stresses how important it is to resist the virus and follow our instructions. And—this is the kicker—he shows them how to live those instructions the way we originally intended."

"To give them Law was the right choice," Dixon said, "a stroke of genius. But as with all truth it can be misapplied."

"Like lawyers using the truth to tell lies."

"Or," Dixon added a bit more congenially, "Well-meaning people, who sometimes miss the forest for the trees."

Nicholas frowned, thinking.

Dixon continued, "It's impossible to adequately capture every nuance of truth with words. To convey the truths of life . . . you have to live that life."

"It's like the ultimate audiovisual aid," Travis said.

Nicholas's frown deepened. "How is this possible?"

"Remember the Reverse Engineering Lab we talked about?" Travis said. "How I used R.E. to add the more detailed traits to our program?"

"Yes."

"Well, that's old school. The team now has things refined to where we can download an entire personality—thoughts, emotions, memories—the whole enchilada. So we record all that information, download it into a new dude, and there you have him, live and in person."

"Whose personality?" Nicholas asked Travis. "Yours?"

Dixon cleared his throat. "Actually, no. Don't misunderstand me, Travis has a brilliant mind, but sometimes ... how do I put it..."

"I'm a fruitcake," Travis said. "Besides, there's no way I could think through all that philosophical junk like you can."

"Like I can?" Nicholas exclaimed. "You're not serious?"

"Why not? You're the one who finally got us on the right track. We're workin off your blueprint, bro."

Nicholas felt his mouth going dry. "You want me to enter into that-"

"No, no, no. Not you, man. A carbon copy of you. The real you would still be here in our world, all nice and cozy."

"The real me."

"Yeah."

"But you just said—"

"I said there's two of you." He pointed at Nicholas. "There's the you, you." Then he pointed at the laptop. "And there's the computer you."

Nicholas's thoughts spun.

"I always said you had enough ego for two people; now you'll prove it."

Nicholas turned to look at Annie, but he still couldn't find her. "Where's Annie?"

Travis scanned the room, then looked up the stairway to the balcony. "Annie?"

No answer.

"Hey, Annie!"

The brothers exchanged glances. Travis crossed back to his desk. "I'll give a call to the guards, make sure she's not trying to—" He came to a stop. "That's weird."

"What?" Nicholas asked.

"My cell phone. I put it right here in the charger." Again he looked around the room. "Annie!" Without waiting for a reply, he headed back to Nicholas's side and spoke into the laptop. "Listen, Phil, we're gonna have to call you back."

"Actually," Dixon said, "I think we've covered all that's necessary."

"And if I decide not to go through with this R.E?" Nicholas asked.

Dixon nodded in understanding. "I've been briefed on your fear of technology, Doctor. Let me assure you there is absolutely no danger. It is merely a matter of recording your brain functions. Nothing more."

"But if I refuse?"

Dixon's response was slow and deliberate. "Then, as I said, the board will have to seriously evaluate whether or not to continue the program."

"And the characters?" Nicholas turned to Travis. "The ones you've invested so much time creating?"

Travis shrugged, then looked away.

Dixon answered, "All elements of the program would have to be destroyed. Their world, their community, and all of the characters with it."

* * *

IT HADN'T BEEN difficult to escape from the hotel. While Travis and Nicholas were mesmerized by the great Phil Dixon, Annie had gone over to Travis's desk, taken his cell, and slipped up the stairs to her room. The hard part was remembering the babysitter's home number. Fran's cell service had been disconnected months ago for lack of payment. It took three tries and almost that many prayers until she got it right. Even then the results weren't exactly what she'd hoped for.

"This is Fran. I'm out. You're on."

After the beep, she left what she hoped was a calm and coherent message. "Fran, this is Annie. Where are you guys? I'm sorry about not picking up Rusty. Will you call me back at . . ." she pulled the cell from her face and searched for the number. Having no clue where to look, she resumed, "Never mind, I'll call you back. But stay at home. I'll be there just as soon as—"

The answering machine beeped. Apparently Fran expected her friends to be less chatty. In any case, it was time for the second part of Annie's plan—the ever-trusty escape through the ventilator shaft. She climbed on the bed to reach the grille, then rifled through her keys, looking for one with the best tip to act as a screwdriver. When she found it, she removed the screws, pulled off the grille, and dropped it onto the bed. But instead of climbing inside, she headed to the closet and waited for Travis's arrival.

He was there within minutes.

"Annie?" He knocked on the door. "Annie?"

She remained silent, listening intently. The bedroom door opened.

"Hey," his voice called, "are you—" He came to a stop and swore, no doubt spotting the grille. And, just as she hoped, he'd seen enough low-budget movies to make the obvious assumption. She heard the bed creak as he climbed onto it.

"Annie ..." His voice sounded hollow as he shouted into the shaft. "Annie ..."

He climbed off the bed and ran out of the room, to alert the guards, she hoped. She waited for what seemed forever until more footsteps returned. She heard the bed creak and then an unusual amount of muttering and grunting as Travis pulled himself into the shaft and started wiggling his way through it.

Once the room was silent, she stepped from the closet and peeked out the bedroom door. No one could be seen along the upper balcony of rooms or down below in the living area. Even Nicholas's hospital bed was empty. She stepped out and moved quietly along the balcony, then down the stairway. Once on the main floor, she headed for the private elevator at the far end.

"Are you okay?"

She gave a start and turned to see Nicholas in a white hotel robe. He was bracing himself against the sliding door that led to the outside balcony.

"Yeah," she said. "Shouldn't you be in bed?"

"Shouldn't you be acting responsibly? They have guns, remember?"

"He's my son. I need to get back to him."

They heard distant shouts from the stairwell next to the elevator.

Nicolas nodded. "Then I suggest you get a move-on."

The shouts grew closer.

He motioned toward the elevator. "Go."

She headed to the doors and pressed the button. She turned to ask how the meeting with Dixon went, but saw Nicholas had already hobbled out onto the balcony. She turned and hit the button again, then again. Finally the elevator doors slid open and she stepped inside. She pressed Close Door several more times, before it finally began to shut. But it was too late. She heard the stairwell door fly open and saw two armed men storm into the room. All they had to do was turn to see her.

But Nicholas had other plans.

"Up there!" He stood on the balcony, pointing to the roof. "I saw her up there!"

The guards moved into action, not bothering to turn, as the elevator doors silently shut. She took a breath and blew it out. Then another. Remembering she had Hostetler's business card, she reached into her pocket and pulled it out. Still clutching Travis's cell, she entered the agent's number and waited. Matthew Hostetler picked up on the second ring.

CHAPTER 13

ALPHA LEFT THE Temple early, hoping the walk would clear his head. The trees along the lane glowed in ambers and reds, their leaves clattering in the breeze. High above, he heard the call of geese. He closed his eyes to savor the moment and to rest his mind. But no matter how he tried, the Law Giver could not ignore the weight of his responsibilities. Every day there were new problems to discuss, new decisions to be made. This morning's debate was no different from the hundreds of others he had listened to.

"We cannot sit back and let the heretics run wild." Orib had stood in his box before the other Council Members. His voice rang loud and strong in the marble chamber.

Other Council Members agreed, some verbally, some in sympathetic nods.

"He's right," said Learis, a white-bearded Member and one of the oldest. "Why, I saw a good citizen of ours practically run over by one of these ... these ..."

"Bicycles," a younger Member helped out.

"Yes, bicycles," Learis said.

"They are a clear violation of Programmer's Law!" another shouted.

Orib agreed. "Exactly. And the Law is the Law."

Others nodded, repeating, "The Law is the Law, the Law is the Law."

Orib continued, "And the users should be appropriately fined." Alpha watched quietly from his box in the oval auditorium. As always, he was impressed with his son's zeal. Few loved Programmer as Orib did. Fewer still had his commitment to enforce the Law. And, though the office of Law Giver had become more symbolic than anything else, there was little doubt who would someday fill it.

"And how do you suggest we remove this plague?" another Council Member asked.

"Nip it in the bud!" Learis cried.

"But our Enforcers are already overworked," someone shouted. "They can barely keep the Law Breakers in line as is."

"Then we hire more."

"With what for salary? Our life units are dangerously low."

"We increase the cost of payment," Learis argued. "Adjust the Grid to extract more seasons."

"For what infractions?"

"For them all."

This brought a storm of reaction. Some agreeing, some disagreeing.

Orib raised his voice over the din. "It's been nearly two seasons since we raised payment."

"That's right," another said. "Is it any wonder our youth are so rebellious?"

Alpha looked on silently. In the old days, as people made payment, the Temple had more life units than it could disperse. But over time, as agency after agency was formed to combat the virus, as the details of the Law were more clearly defined, the need to support its enforcement rose. Of course, the answer had always been to increase the amount of payment—with the understanding that more Law meant greater obedience. And greater obedience aligned the citizens more closely to Programmer's wishes. But how much was too much?

The debate would continue for several more days (they always did) while every possibility was weighed, dissected, and weighed again. It had been that way from the first season Alpha heard Programmer speak. And it would continue long after Alpha was gone.

He rounded the final corner of the lane and approached his house—a single-story, thatch-roofed home with picket fence. It was modest by any standard, but since the children had gone, it always felt just a little too big.

The children . . . Orib with his love and dedication to Programmer, and Nyrah with...

He let his eyes shift to the cherry tree just beyond the porch. The one he and Nyrah had planted when she was barely five.

"And this is our tree, right, Daddy?" she had asked, trying to wipe the mud from her face but only smearing it.

"That's right," he had said.

"Always and forever, right?" She looked up to him, beaming ... and his heart swelled until it nearly burst.

"That's right." He smiled. "Just yours and mine."

And it was. When it was small, the two of them decorated it for the festivals. Later, when it grew stronger, they hung a swing from it. But one afternoon, when she was only eleven or twelve, he caught her digging into it with a knife.

"Nyrah!" He had stormed toward her. "What are you doing?"

"Nothing," she lied, hiding the knife behind her back.

He held out his hand. "Give that to me."

"I was just—"

"Now! Give me the knife, Nyrah."

Tears sprang to her eyes.

"Now!"

Finally, she obeyed, then spun around and ran into the house.

"Nyrah," he shouted. "Come back here! Nyrah!"

But she did not come back. Nor did she answer. And when he stepped around the tree to assess the damage, he caught his breath. There, cut into the bark with painstaking neatness, were the words:

DADDY + ME

It choked him up the first time he saw it, and if he let it, it still did to this day. If he let it.

Alpha arrived at the little gate and opened it. Behind him, the Temple loomed above the treetops, white and majestic. Nearly every season someone wanted to build an addition— as an act of contrition or commitment. And who was he to prevent them? As a result, the structure was nearly twice the size of what they'd first built... and it continued growing.

He stepped through the gate and closed it behind him. Seeing the newspaper at his feet, he stooped to pick it up. The headlines read "East Amasses Troops."

He rose with a slight groan, as much from his age as from the information. The Easterners had been part of the community until a dispute over the Law broke out. Originally, it had been a minor disagreement, but that didn't stop it from festering until a splinter group formed. Refusing to accept the Council's interpretations, they moved to another location and started their own community. A community that had grown and, according to rumors, was preparing to return and seize the Temple by force.

Alpha tucked the paper under his arm and wearily headed

toward the porch. Only as he climbed it did he hear female voices. Saida and another. He opened the door and they stopped.

Saida, who sat at the kitchen table facing him, stiffened. "Alpha, you're home early."

He knew the other woman before she even turned.

"Dad ..." Her face was gaunt. There were dark circles under her eyes.

His throat tightened. With so many conflicting emotions it was difficult to breathe.

She forced a smile. "It's been a while."

"What—" His voice clogged. "What are you doing here?"

"Alpha ..." Saida cautioned.

"I was—" Nyrah coughed and turned in her chair to better face him. "I was in the area."

"Get out." His voice trembled. Not with anger but with the battle raging inside him ... loving father against Law Giver, impossible love against absolute justice.

He stepped toward her and Saida rose to her feet. "Alpha—"

"I said get out."

"Alpha, how can you—"

Nyrah reached for her hand. "It's okay, Mama."

"No, it's not okay," Saida said. "You're my daughter. Our daughter. And I will not let—"

"Leave. Now."

"Nyrah placed her hands on the table and with effort pushed herself to her feet.

"She's not well," Saida cried. "She needs our help. She needs life units from the Temple."

"You are willing to go to the Grid," he asked, "to make payment?"

"The Grid will kill her!" Saida protested. "Can't you see how weak she is?"

Alpha closed his eyes. He'd heard this argument more times than he could count. From more people than he knew. And his response could not be, must not be any different. "The Law is the Law," he said. "Justice must be served."

"I've broken too much Law," Nyrah answered. "I would have nothing left to give."

The words came before he could stop them. "And who made that choice?"

"Alpha, how can you say that?"

"It's okay, Mama. We knew that would be his answer."

"So this is my fault?" he said. "I'm the one who is guilty?"

Nyrah shook her head. "No, you're right, it's not you. It's me. I'm the one at fault, not you, Daddy."

The name struck him like a punch to his stomach.

In the distance there was an approaching bell. Saida's eyes filled with fear. "Enforcers. A neighbor has seen you. You have to go."

Alpha watched as Saida helped Nyrah gather her things and head for the door. When she passed him, Nyrah slowed, but Alpha did not look.

The bell grew louder.

"Hurry," Saida insisted. "They're nearly here." They headed out the door and down the porch steps.

Alpha's heart pounded as he heard the latch of the gate open, then close, and the footsteps fade away. He slowly shuffled toward the table. He'd done the right thing, the only thing. The Law is the Law. Payment must be made.

The room seemed to shift and he leaned on the table for support. It shifted again. Her name came to his lips in a choked whisper: "Nyrah." Tears sprang to his eyes, blurring his vision. "Nyrah..."

* * *

"THIS IS FRAN. I'm out. You're on."

Annie flipped Travis's cell phone shut and sighed.

Matthew Hostetler turned toward her from behind the wheel of his late-model Camry. "Still no answer?"

"Nothing." She tapped the phone nervously. "Where can they be?"

"We'll find them," he said. "Don't worry."

She nodded and looked out her window, then began chewing on a thumbnail.

"I can't believe you don't want to file charges," he said.

"Right now I just want my son."

"I understand, but—"

"Look." She turned to him. "We're talking about Phil Dixon here. I saw him, okay? He's like a world-class humanitarian, a national treasure."

"Whose guards just happened to have a bloody shoot-out with some organization that attacked and destroyed his compound."

"It was self-defense."

"This is not the Wild West. We have laws. People were murdered. Property destroyed."

Annie pushed the hair behind her ears and looked back out the window.

"And if they held you against your will, that's kidnapping, and that's a federal—"

"I get it, all right? But they've got some very bad guys trying to—

"If they can't play by the law, maybe they're the bad guys."

She turned back to him a moment. This was definitely not the bungling man she'd seen the day before. Now he was all business and backbone. Maybe he was right. Then again, maybe he wasn't. Either way, she made her decision. She would tell him nothing more about Dixon's project. Not until she was reunited with her son. Then maybe they could have the luxury to discuss the nuances of the law, the pros and cons of situational ethics. Maybe even over a nice dinner. But not until she got her boy.

She opened Travis's cell again and hit redial. "Left." She pointed. "Turn left, here."

"This is your street."

"She lives six blocks down from me."

He took the corner.

"This is Fran. I'm out. You're—"

She flipped the phone shut. "It's the beige house with the black mailbox."

"Got it."

But even as Annie spoke, her heart sank. "Great..."

"What?"

"No car."

"Maybe it's in the garage."

She shook her head. "Her place is like a Radio Shack gone berserk. The garage is even worse."

Suddenly his hand was on her back, pushing her forward. "Down!"

"What? What, are you—"

"Get down!" His strength surprised her and she was suddenly bent over.

"What's going on?"

"Stakeout. Someone's watching her place."

Annie tried to rise, but his hand remained firmly on her back. "How do you know?" she asked.

"Nondescript van, tinted windows, two men sitting in the front seat."

Her pulse quickened. "Rusty? They're waiting for Rusty?"

"I doubt that."

"Then who?" She glanced up to him and had her answer before he gave it. "Me? Why would they want to—"

He gave her a look and again she had the answer. He

continued past them, keeping his eyes forward, until he could watch them in the rearview mirror.

"Can't you arrest them?"

"For what, parking on the street?"

He finally removed his hand and she rose, turning to look out the back. By now they were a half block away. "You can question them or something."

"Not with you in the car, not until I know what I'm up against." He pulled his cell from his pocket. "I'll run the plates, call my partner to check them out."

"And Rusty?"

"We'll find him, don't you worry."

He spoke with such assurance that Annie almost believed him. And when he turned those sad, earnest eyes on her, her doubts nearly disappeared. Nearly.

"Right now we need to get you someplace safe," he said.

"My house is just up the—" Once again she stopped, realizing her foolishness.

"We'll find you a place and we'll find your boy. You have my word on that. Don't worry."

She nodded and looked out the window, silently praying he would be right.

* * *

IT WAS THE LOGICAL CHOICE. That and nothing more.

If there was a way to continue his brother's work, to help him break ground in areas never before explored, why not? And the intellectual stimulation. It had been a long time since he had enjoyed such challenges. Challenges that, if overcome, would lead to the praise of peers, both now and in the future. There was also the sociological aspect. As Phillip Dixon had mentioned, if they couldn't save a computer model based upon their civilization, what hope did they have for their own civilization? Last, and most definitely least, there was Alpha. Not because of any false or illusory feeling of kinship, but out of simple curiosity—mere interest regarding how a computer-simulated program based upon his child (and now his grandchildren) would respond in various situations.

He leaned against a counter in the R.E. Lab, sipping his tea and staring at the caged chimpanzee. A smell drifted from the animal similar to human body odor. He wondered if it had anything to do with the DNA makeup of chimps and humans being so similar. Given the procedure about to take place, he hoped that wasn't their only similarity.

Earlier, he and Travis had returned to the compound and waded through the charred remains of the house on the side of the hill. It wasn't easy for Nicholas with his bad leg, but using an aluminum dawfoot cane, he kept up with his brother.

"I find it difficult to believe that you have no one stationed here," he had argued, "that you have no guards."

"Guards would let people know there's something to guard."

Nicholas frowned. "But the truth of the situation is—"

"There was plenty of action around here," Travis assured him, "back when you were getting your beauty sleep. But we leaked word that the entire compound was destroyed. The labs and all data were moved to a backup location in San Diego."

"And they believed you?"

"Rebecca's people aren't the only ones who have moles. Dixon knows a little about corporate espionage himself."

Nicholas shook his head, once again musing at how big corporations had become today's warring nations. Then again, as Travis had mentioned, the money from this single operation could exceed the net worth of several nations.

"Here," Travis said, "give me a hand."

They had arrived at the base of the hill where the lab door had been. It was carefully covered in several feet of charred wood, timbers, and broken cinderblock. It took the two of them twenty minutes to clear it. Even at that it was so camouflaged, so scorched and blackened by fire (or spray paint), that it was nearly impossible to see. Once inside, Nicholas noted that everything was exactly as it had been—including Rebecca's half-empty mug of coffee, heavy on creamer, and the remains of Hugh's fortune cookies. Eerie testaments to how transient life can be.

His brother fired up the screens and prepared to enter new data.

"How long will this take?" Nicholas asked.

"Not long. In the meantime, pull up a chair and breeze through what you've missed. Oh, and if you get the time, check out some of their biographies. We keep one on each of the little guys."

Nicholas looked with trepidation at the control board.

Eyeing him, Travis sighed. "Right, twenty-first century phobia—what was I thinking? All right, let's just stay with Alpha." He rolled his chair next to Nicholas, who remained standing, and began typing away. "This will bring up Alpha's Greatest Hits." Once he finished, he pointed to a key on the computer. "Just hold this down whenever you want to skip stuff and fast-forward."

Nicholas reluctantly took a seat. Even more reluctantly, he reached out and touched the controls.

"Go ahead, man, they're not poison."

Eventually, against his will, he began using the key to watch their past scenes. He was saddened but not surprised at the division growing within the community. The bigotry, the hatred, the intolerance—all because he had given them simple rules to follow, all because he had given them Law.

No wonder he hated religion. It was all he could do not to be moved with anger, sorrow... and pity.

It took Travis nearly two hours to complete his own task — creating a body for the computer-generated Nicholas. At one point Nicholas looked up to see his brother taping him with a video camera. Eventually the computer genius pushed his chair away from the console and stretched loudly.

"Have you finished?" Nicholas asked.

"Check it out." Travis nodded to the main monitor while unwrapping a stick of Juicy Fruit.

The screen showed a blurred figure wearing a jade-green robe in the style of the other members of the community. An ivory sash was around his waist, and he wore sandals with leather laces crisscrossing up to his bony knees.

Nicholas peered at the monitor. "Is that . . . supposed to be me?"

"Hang on." Travis shoved the gum into his mouth and entered a few more keystrokes.

The image sharpened with greater details until Nicholas was soon looking at a detailed, high-definition photograph of himself.

"So, what do you think?" Travis beamed.

Nicholas rose to his feet and leaned in for a closer look. "It's not terrible."

"Not terrible?" Travis entered another flurry of keystrokes, causing the image to rotate 360 degrees. "It's flippin outrageous!"

"Does he have to wear glasses?" Nicholas asked. "Can't you give him twenty/twenty vision?"

"Sorry, dude, the closer you two are physically, the easier it will be for you to adjust."

"Me?"

"You, him, it's all the same."

Nicholas wasn't crazy about the comment.

"Hey, at least I didn't give him your gimpy leg."

Still looking, Nicholas dropped his hands to his stomach, wondering if it was the character's robe or if he really had gotten so thick around the middle.

"So, we're all set." Travis returned to his keyboard. "I'm transferring him next door, where we'll join the R.E. team."

"They're here?" Nicholas asked. "When did they return?"

"A few minutes after us. I convinced them to postpone their R&R and come back to help me prep."

Nicholas shook his head. There was little his brother couldn't con someone into doing.

"Hey, they owe me—big time. After all, I'm gonna make them stars. Course, our pal Mr. Dixon may have sweetened the pot with a little bonus. Who knows? Anyway"—Travis rose, unwrapping another piece of gum—"we better get our butts over there, 'cause they ain't gonna wait forever."

Once they entered the R.E. Lab, which had been as elaborately camouflaged as theirs, Nicholas met the team leader, a middle-aged Eastern European by the name of Agapoff, and her young female assistant. Only then did he discover that less than half of the preparations had been made. Travis had entered all of his physical characteristics—now it was time to enter the mental ones...

First they had to shave his head. Although the assistant was careful, it didn't stop Nicholas from grousing and complaining— or the girl from nicking his scalp. Twice. His protests only increased when they began smearing his head with a viscous, medicinal-smelling gel.

"To reduce the signal interference," Agapoff explained.

Nicholas scowled. "Signal from ..."

"The nanobots we're about to introduce."

"Hold it!" He raised his hand. "Nanobots?"

"That is correct."

He turned toward Travis, who was immediately at his

side. "It's a fancy word for that serum over there." He motioned to a hypodermic needle lying on a silver tray. "It's like a vaccine man, only safer. Way safer."

Nicholas stared at the syringe. "How... safer?"

"It'll completely dissolve and pass through your system in, what"— he turned to Agapoff—"like a day or something?"

She replied, "In the time it takes for a normal blood cell to dissolve, it will be gone."

"See, man? Totally organic. Just think of it as a mini blood transfusion."

"And what will I feel?"

"Nothing. Like I said, just think blood transfusion, you'll feel nothing."

Nicholas eyed his brother

"I swear man, you'll be perfectly safe."

Nicholas turned to Agapoff. "Is he telling the truth?"

"Yes, Dr. Mackenzie. It is perfectly safe."

Still not entirely convinced, but knowing Travis would never purposely endanger him, Nicholas agreed... but not before making everyone understand how little he appreciated the process.

Finally, there was the headpiece—a flexible wire-mesh covering. It was like a swim cap that fit snuggly over his skull. From the back, a thick ponytail of wires ran to the floor and over to the computer.

"It is the receiving unit," Agapoff explained. "There are eleven hundred and twenty separate receivers. They will pick up the signals from your brain and send them into Travis's program."

Nicholas turned to his brother. "Is there anything else?" he growled. "Any further surprises you failed to mention?"

Travis flashed his lopsided grin. "Sorry, man, I thought you knew. But that's it. I swear."

Nicholas took a breath. Then another. He tried to ignore the cold dampness breaking out on his face and chest.

"You look a little pale," Travis said.

"I wonder why."

"There is nothing to be nervous about," Agapoff assured him.

"Can you give him like a sedative or something?" Travis asked. "Technology's not his thing."

Agapoff shook her head as she tied off his arm and looked for a nice, plump vein. "His consciousness needs to be fully functional if we are to make an accurate recording." She turned back to Nicholas. "You are sure you will be okay?"

"Yes, I'm sure. Of course I'm sure. Don't I look sure? Let's get on with it."

She nodded and picked up the syringe. Nicholas watched as the needle pierced his skin and the milky contents emptied into his body. He felt a wave of nausea, which he tried to swallow back.

The woman called across the laboratory to the girl. "What is our status?"

The girl hunched over her computer. "Online and waiting."

The nausea began to recede as the woman untied his arm and walked away.

"Is there a problem?" he asked. "Why have we stopped?"

She turned to him. "Stopped? Why, Professor, we have barely begun."

That had been four and a half hours ago. And now, staring into the chimpanzee cage and sipping his tea, he waited, assured his job was complete. So was Agapoff's. The ball was back in Travis's court. Even as they waited, the woman and her assistant prepared to leave the compound.

"Hey, bro?"

Nicholas turned from the cage to Travis, who now sat at the computer terminal.

"Come on over, check it out."

Nicholas grabbed his cane and rose. The young assistant moved to help, but he refused her offer and limped to his brother. Up on the screen before them was an even more detailed facsimile of himself, in all its unflattering detail.

"Care to say a few words?" Travis asked. Nicholas could only stare. The resemblance was uncanny, absolutely lifelike now that it was breathing and blinking and looking about.

"All right, then," Travis said. "Let me do the honors." He turned back to the keyboard and spoke the words as he typed: "Dr. Nicholas Mackenzie, meet Dr. Nicholas Mackenzie."

Both Nicholases scowled. Then, after a moment's hesitation and in perfect unison, Nicholas and his computer double raised their hands and pushed up their glasses.

PART III

CHAPTER 14

THE FIRST THING Nicholas noticed was the light. It was as real as his world's, but more vivid—like the light of southern France the Impressionists had been so fond of painting. It had a luminescent quality, as if coming from two directions—like standing on a pier with light striking you from the sun above and its reflection off the water below. Colors were just a little brighter, the edges a little clearer, the shadows a little darker.

He took a breath, smelling the coolness of approaching evening, the sweet, roasted-oat smell of cut hay.

What do you think, bro? Pretty amazing, huh?

It was barely a thought, hardly discernible over all the other input flooding his senses. But he immediately recognized its source. Without answering, he looked down at the muddy road where he stood. He knelt, grateful the pain in his leg was gone. He scooped up a handful of mud and raised it to his nose. It had a slight fetid smell from decayed leaves and vegetation.

Finally, he whispered, "Impressive."

Of course, what'd you expect?

He rose back to his feet and looked at the folks passing him along the road. He caught two older women staring, then glancing away and trading whispers. A mother spotted him and held her child's hand tighter. Only then did he notice the drabness of their clothes. Instead of the bright green coloring of his robe, these people wore shades of gray and black and charcoal. But it wasn't just their clothes. The same could be said about their expressions. There was a dull lifelessness to them. And their breath. As far as he could tell, the soft glow that once surrounded their mouths and noses had all but disappeared.

"You must be an Easterner."

He turned to see Nyrah approaching, and for a moment he couldn't breathe. She was so real. She was no longer some high- definition image. Now she was completely three-dimensional and as real as . . . well, as real as he was. Unlike the other members of the community, her robe was orange, so bright it was nearly clownish—and its neckline plunged beyond most definitions of modesty. She appeared to be pregnant, but was more frail and gaunt than he remembered. Still, it was her eyes that drew him in. Once sparkling with the life of a rambunctious little girl, they were now heavy and worn, outlined in thick mascara.

"I'm not—" He cleared his throat. "I'm not from around here, if that's what you mean."

She forced a smile that never made it to her eyes. "If you need a place to stay, we'll be happy to give you one."

"We?"

She motioned to a small group approaching them. Like Nyrah, they were dressed in brighter, garish colors—reds, blues, pinks—far different from the others in the community, though their expressions were no less worn and the glow from their breath no more present.

"Actually," Nicholas explained, "I was hoping to go to the Temple."

"Temple?" Nyrah gave a snicker that broke into a hacking cough.

Nicholas looked on, troubled by what he saw.

When she caught her breath she continued. "No way will they let you on the grounds like that. Not with all that color."

He glanced down at his robe, then looked up as the group began to circle them. A gray, wiry-haired man with a pinched weasel-like face approached.

"Well, well, well, what have we got here?" His eyes were watery with a mischievous twinkle. His breath stank of alcohol and he needed a bath.

"You're not a citizen." A younger girl with rainbow hair approached. She was no more than fifteen. "Not in that getup." Her smile included a broken tooth blackening with decay. She stepped closer, her breath no better than the man's. "But I bet you got units, don't you?"

Nyrah moved in, blocking her path. "She right?" She coughed briefly. "You got life units?"

Once again he was drawn to her eyes. So worn and empty. She moved closer, pressing her body against his. "I bet you do." She lowered her voice to a throaty whisper. "You got plenty of units for the right girl, don't you?"

Her name leaped to his lips before he could stop it. "Nyrah..." She stiffened as if slapped. "What?"

He searched her face, looking for any remaining trace of the child.

"What did you call me?"

"Where is your father, Nyrah? Where is Alpha?"

She opened her mouth but did not speak.

The wiry-haired man moved closer. "What did you say?"

Still holding her gaze, Nicholas asked, "Is he well?"

"You know my father?" she asked. "You know the Keeper?"

Emotions rose faster than he could stop them. Still, with effort, he managed to sound matter-of-fact. "I observed you on the Temple grounds with your family . . . years ago. The two of you were watching a payment being made."

"We watched lots of payments."

"Your arm was fractured. And you'd prepared your first meal—life units coated in bread crumbs. You were upset because you burned them."

She frowned, staring at him, until the memory surfaced. Her eyes narrowed. "That was a long time ago."

Nicholas nodded. "Before you started selling yourself."

Nyrah raised her chin. Swallowed.

"Do we got a problem?" the older man asked.

Nicholas turned to him. Saw his hand resting on a long knife strapped to his side. He'd seen this man earlier on one of the screens in Travis's lab but had paid no attention. Now he wished he had. He frowned, wondering exactly who he was.

Suddenly there was a flicker, a hiccup of his surroundings. And instantly Nicholas knew. He'd been clueless about the man a moment before, but now he knew everything—his life, his schooling, his ambitions, and his failures. Travis had obviously found a way to instantly download the information into him.

Without hesitation, Nicholas acted upon it. "No, Kallab," he said, "we're fine."

The twinkle in the man's eyes faded. He traded looks with Nyrah, then broke into another grin. "So you're a spy. Working for the Temple?"

"I work for nobody. And certainly not the Temple."

The girl with rainbow hair snickered. "Not in those clothes you don't."

"So what are you?" Kallab asked. "A trickster, a magician?"

"I like tricksters," the rainbow girl cooed, moving in closer. "So nasty and naughty."

"Yeah," Kallab agreed. "And they owe as much payment as child-whores and man-killers." The girl turned to him. His sly grin became a sneer, forcing her to look away, wilting under the accusation.

Nicholas stared. She was no more than a child. What could she possibly have done to—

* * *

"Stop program."

Travis turned from the console to his brother. "Again?"

Nicholas continued looking at the image of the girl beside the computer-generated image of himself. "What's her name?"

With a sigh, Travis reached back to his keyboard and entered the same command he had typed moments before when reviewing Kallab's biography. All images on the computer screens froze. With additional keystrokes he enlarged the girl's face, rotated it 360 degrees, and ran a quick facial recognition program on her.

She appeared on several of the smaller screens surrounding the main one. Each image was from an excerpt of her life—a preschooler, an older child, a preteen eating in what looked like a school cafeteria. Travis shuttled the latter image forward until she was sitting in a classroom, waiting as a teacher strolled between benches passing back papers. When she received hers, Travis froze the picture and zoomed in to the name at the top. The writing was fuzzy until he hit another series of keys and it came into focus revealing the letters:

D O R T H A.

"Dortha," Travis read. "Her name is Dortha."

But Nicholas barely nodded. His attention had been drawn to another screen. On it she was eleven or twelve years old and awkwardly enduring the groping and hungry kisses of a much older man.

Nicholas looked on with concern. "What's that?" he asked.

"Come on, bro," Travis complained, "time's a-wastin?"

"Bring up her biography. What's happening there?"

Travis made no attempt to hide his impatience as he turned back to the keyboard.

Nicholas explained. "If I am to effectively communicate with them, I need to learn their backgrounds. Just as I learned Kallab's."

Instead of bringing the document up onto the screen as he had Kallab's, Travis simply read from a smaller preview monitor: "Fifteen, good parents, good grades, blah, blah, blah ..."

Nicholas motioned back to the image of the girl being groped. "And that?"

"Hang on. Here we go. Her uncle started having sex with her ... until she killed him."

"She what?"

"That's what it says."

"How old was she?"

Travis hesitated.

"How old?"

"It started at twelve, she offed him at fourteen."

Nicholas shook his head, quietly muttering, "The things we do to each other."

Travis continued, "She ran away when they tried making her pay on the Grid. Ever since, she's been living with whoever gives her life units."

Nicholas motioned to the main screen, where the image

of himself and the girl were still frozen. "Go ahead and tell him that. Let him know."

This time Travis gave no argument as he worked the keys. "Transferring her bio to him now."

When he'd finished, he hit another key, bringing the original scene back to life.

* * *

NICHOLAS BLINKED. With his sudden information, he addressed the girl. "You were just a child, Dortha. It was not your fault." Her eyes widened, then squinted suspiciously. "How do you know me?"

"I know it was your uncle who was responsible. Not you."

She stared, poker-faced, except for the twitching under her left eye.

"You did the only thing you could. You removed yourself the only way you knew how."

Her face remained stoic, though her eyes grew shiny with moisture.

Nyrah stepped in. "Who are you?"

Nicholas turned back to Alpha's daughter. But before he could answer, a big man in red hair and a moth-eaten goatee pointed up the road. "Enforcers!"

Nicholas shaded his eyes. In the distance he saw a fist of dust rising from what looked like approaching horsemen. Suddenly the group surrounding him moved into action, quickly dispersing in all directions.

"Hey!"

He turned to see Nyrah stopping at the edge of the road.

"You just going to stand there?" she shouted.

"I have broken no law."

"Yeah." She headed back to him and grabbed his arm. "Come on, hurry!"

"Why? I have done nothing wrong."

She pulled him off the road and into the countryside. "Right."

"It's true."

She shook her head. "For being so smart, you sure are dumb!"

CHAPTER 15

"SO WHAT DO you think?" Travis asked.

Nicholas stared at the screen, unsure how to respond.

"Kinda freaky watching yourself?"

"Yes," he answered. "Kind of freaky. And now?"

"Now I guess we just sit back and let you do your thing."

"Let him do his thing," Nicholas corrected.

"Whatever." Travis looked back to the screen and began popping his knuckles, one after another. Finally, unable to endure any silence for too long, he said, "I suppose we could talk to him, though. You know, check in and see what he's thinking."

"I know what he's thinking."

"Yeah." Travis chuckled. "I guess you would." Another moment passed before he leaned forward and began typing.

"What are you doing?"

"Pushing the program. "Fast-forwarding till we see something of interest."

Nicholas watched as the images increased speed, then broke up as the digital readout below raced forward. He sat back in his chair and tried to relax. The ordeal had been more exhausting than he had anticipated. And, though he was watching an exact duplication of himself, he had noticed something different. The reaction to Nyrah. It was not the same as he would have responded. It was close, but not identical. His computerized double had been just a bit more gentle, a bit more taken by her presence.

"Ah, here we go." Travis hit a few more keystrokes. "This looks like something."

Nicholas turned back to the screen and pushed up his glasses.

* * *

"Look out!" the redhead with the goatee cried. "Move it!"

Nicholas glanced up from his conversation with the group and saw the big man wobbling on a bicycle. He was trying to keep his balance in the thick mud . . . while swerving wildly to avoid hitting a spindly old lady.

"Look out!"

Despite her attempts, and his, the lady kept getting in the way. When she was finally clear, the bike swerved and put her in jeopardy all over again. It was quite a show, and in spite of himself Nicholas chuckled with the others. The old lady saw no humor and let them know in language Nicholas had not heard since his Marine Corps days. An outburst that made the small group sitting around the fire laugh all the harder.

"Didn't know the ol' gal had it in her," Kallab hooted. "Go, Big Red! Go!"

"Run, Mrs. Sareym!" Dortha shouted. "Run!"

Mrs. Sareym made a hand gesture Nicholas didn't recognize, but that sent the others into more fits of laughter. Their response wasn't mean-spirited, not exactly. But this and the plum wine seemed about their only entertainment, an escape from a hard, difficult life. Eventually, the show disappeared behind the shacks and lean-to shelters, though you could still hear his occasional shouts and her frantic screams.

Kallab shook his head in amusement. "Some invention. Wonder the Council ain't outlawed them."

"Oh, they will," Nyrah said, "just give them time."

He nodded, continuing to muse.

Nicholas had been in camp nearly three hours, at least by this world's time. He had no idea how long that was in actual time. Darkness was settling in and small fires had cropped up in front of the various shelters. Because of a recent rain, the flames smoked and smoldered, covering the camp in a thick steel-blue haze. It made the air sharp and it burned the back of his throat, but it was a welcome relief from the smell of raw sewage.

Because the camp was on a hillside, the residents had taken advantage of the slope and dug a shallow trench all the way down—which explained why the top of the hill was prime real estate and the bottom was ... well, not so prime.

Turning to the small group, Nicholas said, "I'm surprised they don't bother you here. The Enforcers."

"They would if they could," Kallab said. He reached for the clay jar of wine and poured himself another bowl.

"Right now all their focus is on the Easterners," Nyrah explained.

"Which"—Dortha, the rainbow-haired girl, leaned toward him—"you sure you ain't one?"

"Aren't one," Nyrah corrected.

Dortha ignored her. "Or a Member? You sure you ain't from the Council?"

"No," Nicholas said. "I am neither."

"But our wine you don't drink," Kallab said. "And your history you don't give."

Nicholas nodded. "That's true," and he left it at that.

A moment of silence fell over the group. Despite his attempts to remain clinical and objective, Nicholas's feelings toward Nyrah and the others continued to grow. Earlier he'd attributed it to his greater understanding, the result of the additional background information Travis was feeding him. To an extent that was true.

But the continual interaction, his constant immediacy with these people, was taking its toll. And, try as he might, he could feel barriers slowly eroding.

He leaned forward to warm his hands over the fire. When he looked up, he asked a question he'd been contemplating since they'd met. "Tell me…why don't you go to the Temple and make payment like the others?"

The group snickered.

"I'm serious." He looked into their tired and worn faces. "Wouldn't that allow you to rejoin the community and live a normal life?"

"Would you let someone suck out all your life on the Grid?" Nyrah asked.

Kallab raised his bowl. "And for us, she does mean all."

Nicholas had no answer.

"Besides"—Dortha giggled—"breaking Law can be fun." She grinned to the others. "Ain't that right, guys?"

Nyrah glanced away, giving no response. Kallab let his eyes drift to the fire.

"Well, it sure is for me," Dortha said. She reached for the wine and refilled her bowl. "I have plenty of fun."

Nicholas turned to Kallab. "You were studying to become a Council Member. All your life that's what you wanted to be."

The man stiffened.

"No way," Dortha scoffed.

Nyrah turned to him. "Is that true?"

He threw Nicholas a look. "That's some trickery you do."

But, of course, it wasn't trickery. From the burst of insight Nicholas had received on the road, he knew there was far more to this man than he let on. "Why did you quit?" he asked. "Were you afraid you couldn't measure up?"

"Measure up?" Kallab snorted. "Nobody can."

"You got that right," Dortha agreed, taking another sip of wine.

Nicholas held his gaze and repeated, "Why did you quit?"

Kallab sat in silence, then reached for the jar of wine. But it was no sooner in his hands before he slowed, then stopped. He sat another moment, staring at the jar.

Nicholas waited with the others.

Finally he answered, "These thoughts, in here." He motioned to his head. "They were always so ... wrong."

"But you never gave in to them," Nicholas said. "In your younger days you had no record as a Law Breaker."

The man eyed him, then poured the wine. "Not the way people could see. But inside, the virus, it was always nagging at me. Always eating away."

"We all have thoughts," Nyrah said.

Kallab looked at his bowl. "I couldn't stop them, no matter how I tried." Finally, he shrugged. "So I quit the fight and here I am." He tilted back his head and downed the drink. Then, with his trademark twinkle, he added, "In all of my Breaker glory."

"Here, here," Nyrah said, raising her bowl. "Up with all Breakers."

Dortha added, "And down with all Members."

They clicked their bowls and drank.

Kallab belched. "That ain't sayin every Member's a stinker." He looked over to Nyrah. "Like your old man. He's a saint."

"No argument there," Nyrah said.

"They don't make them any finer."

She nodded and finished her drink.

The praise gave Nicholas a certain satisfaction . . . and the opportunity he'd been waiting for. "Do you think it would be possible for me to meet him?"

"The Law Giver?" Dortha asked incredulously.

Nicholas nodded.

Nyrah looked over to Kallab.

He gave another shrug. "It could be risky, getting so close to the Temple grounds." He looked back to Nyrah, his mischievous grin returning. "But I suppose we could survive."

Nyrah smiled back and motioned for more wine. "That's one thing we're good at—surviving."

"That's right," Dortha said. She raised her drink. "To survivors."

The others lifted their bowls and joined the toast: "To survivors."

They drank, then slowly, inevitably fell back into silence. Nicholas continued to watch ... struggling against emotions he could not entirely define, as smoke and darkness gradually engulfed the camp.

* * *

THE EDGEWATER INN lay just north of the Santa Barbara pier, overlooking the beach and marina. Annie had seen it for years, even had a dinner or two in its posh restaurant downstairs—but only when someone else was buying. And she'd never been up to its rooms. Not until now.

"This is pretty expensive," she said as they entered the suite. "You sure the Bureau can afford it?"

"I'll have to do a little explaining. But with all we've put you through, I think it's the least we can do." As he spoke,

Matthew slid open the mirrored door of the hall closet to check inside. Satisfied, he turned and headed into the bathroom.

She followed him to the doorway. "What are you doing?"

He opened the shower stall to take a peek. Then, turning, he smiled, a trace of embarrassment. "Sorry, force of habit." He headed back to the hallway, their bodies brushing slightly. "Sorry."

She followed as he walked into the bedroom and crossed over to the balcony. "Why don't you try your babysitter again?"

Annie nodded, pulled out Travis's phone, and hit redial. The recorded message began and she flipped it shut.

Matthew opened the sliding glass door and checked the balcony.

"So, how long do I have to stay here?" she asked.

He scanned above, then below, before stepping back inside and locking the door. "We've posted an Amber Alert. The highway patrol, the police, even the media have her car and license number."

Annie's stomach tightened. "You don't think she'd ... I mean, Fran wouldn't—" And then it happened, she started to tremble. She looked away, trying to stop, but it only grew worse. It was embarrassing, but the day, the demands, the fears ...

Matthew moved to her side.

"I'm sorry." She angrily swiped at her tears.

"Are you okay?"

"Yeah, I'm..." It grew difficult to stand. She turned to the bed, but it was too far away. Suddenly her knees became rubbery.

"Hey…"

She staggered and Matthew caught her. Her body

convulsed— a deep, gut-wrenching sob she could not control. And then another. "I'm sorry." She gulped.

"It's okay," he whispered.

Tears began streaming down her face. Another sob escaped.

"It's all right."

She had no idea how long they stood like that, him holding her. But at last she was able to catch her breath and pull away. She wiped her face and again repeated, "Sorry."

"No, that's okay," he said. "I understand." She could feel him watching her as she gathered herself, too embarrassed to look up.

"You sure you're all right?"

She nodded and gave her eyes one last wipe. Changing gears, she took a breath and returned to the topic. "They, uh, they let you do that... post an Amber Alert, I mean—for something like this?"

"Let's just say this fancy hotel isn't the only thing I'll be answering for."

She looked to him and he gave her a little smile, a nod of assurance, before resuming his task. He crossed to the bed, kicked the wooden pedestal underneath, and stooped down to make sure there was no place to hide. Annie continued watching, once again moved by his strength and sensitivity.

He was heading to the other side of the bed when his cell phone chirped, and he pulled it from his pocket to answer. "Hostetler." His face momentarily clouded. "Are you sure?" He looked up at Annie, then shook his head, indicating there was no problem.

She didn't entirely believe him.

"Right. I'm on my way." He closed the phone.

"What's wrong?" she asked. "Was that about Rusty?"

"No, no." He said. "It's my daughter." He returned the

phone to his pocket. "I was supposed to pick her up from karate."

Relief filled Annie and she nodded.

He started for the door. "I guess time got away from me." Then, stopping, he turned back to her. "You don't mind, do you? It will only take a few minutes."

"Sure." She started to follow. "It's not like I have any pressing engage—"

"No." He paused at the door. "It's best you stay here."

"Oh." She came to a stop.

"You're perfectly safe, trust me. No one knows you're here."

She nodded, forcing back the uneasiness.

He opened the door. "Just keep this locked. Don't open it for anyone. You're four floors off the ground, no one can get inside."

"When will you be back?"

"It won't be long, I promise." Sensing her concern, he added, "You're in good hands, Dr. Brooks. I won't let anything happen to you or to your son." Once again those earnest eyes locked onto hers. "You have my word."

She brushed her hair behind her ear and nodded.

"I'll be right back," he repeated. "Everything will be fine."

* * *

THE TEMPLE ROSE BEHIND THEM, brilliant as hammered gold in the noonday sun. A small entourage of Council Members walked along the grounds with Alpha. They were taking a break from another heated discussion. Though in reality they were also campaigning, hoping that with Orib's help they could sway his father to their viewpoint. True, the Law Giver was simply a figurehead, but he was a figurehead everyone looked up to. Of course, none of this was news to Alpha. People were always trying to gain his ear. And, as Law Giver, he felt it was his responsibility to lend it.

"The Easterners grow stronger every day," Orib said. "Every day their troops increase in number while ours remain the same."

"We must follow suit," another exclaimed. "We must hire more Enforcers."

"Which means increasing payment," a third insisted.

"I understand the concern," Alpha said. "But why does every problem seem to involve increasing Grid payment?"

Learis, the senior member, spoke from beside him. "I ask you, my brother, which is the greater evil—to increase Grid payment or to be overrun by heretics?"

Others nodded, voicing their agreement.

They approached the Temple perimeter and were about to turn back when Alpha heard a voice that stole his breath.

"Dad?"

He looked up to see her standing on the edge of the grounds with a handful of others, all wearing their bright, illegal colors. She was far too thin, though she proudly displayed the bulge of her pregnant belly, no doubt a testimony to her father's failure. Still, in spite of himself, he slowed. After so much time, after all she'd done. When it came to Nyrah, his heart still betrayed him.

Orib quickly stepped between them. "What are you doing here?"

"I've come to speak to our father."

"How dare you?" Orib bristled. "How dare the dead address the living?"

She did not answer her brother. Had no answer to give.

Taking his arm, Orib turned Alpha, and they started back toward the Temple.

She called again. "Dad..."

Alpha's legs stiffened, seeming to have minds of their own.

"There's somebody who wants to meet you."

He hesitated and, despite Orib's attempts, slowed to a stop. He could not look at her, but he could not walk away either.

And then another spoke. "Alpha?"

The voice was startlingly familiar. He turned and saw an older man, perhaps her husband ... or last night's client.

The stranger took a step closer. "It's been a long time," he said.

Alpha frowned. He could not remember meeting him. But the voice, there was something so immediate about it, something that resonated so deeply inside.

Orib's grip tightened on his arm. "Come, Father."

He nodded and they turned.

"Alpha 11?"

He stopped. No one ever used that name anymore. Not since Programmer.

"How is Saida?"

He turned back to confront the stranger. But there was no mockery in the man's eyes.

Alpha cleared his throat. "Do I know you?"

"From a long time ago." He searched the man's face, trying to remember.

"We spoke for the first time, right over there." The stranger motioned toward the Temple. "When your firstborn son had died."

Alpha frowned, confused.

"When the rats were attacking Saida. When I ordered you to take authority."

Confusion gave way to astonishment. No one knew those details. Yes, he had been faithful in proclaiming Programmer's Law to the rest of the community. But he had never once spoken of Saida's humiliation, of how she had given up and allowed the rats to overrun her.

The stranger smiled warmly, sensing his confusion.

"Who ... who are you?" Alpha asked.

"You know me." He nodded toward the Temple. "As an act of reverence you built that structure."

Alpha could only stare.

"Father?" Orib asked. "Father, are you all right?"

He turned to his son, his mind reeling with impossibilities.

"Father?"

He tried to speak, but could not.

Orib wrapped a concerned arm around his shoulders and gently turned him. "Come, Father, we'll be late. Come." They headed back toward the Temple with the rest of the group, Alpha's feet wooden and unsteady.

The stranger called after him. "Alpha?"

"You have no business here," Learis shouted over his shoulder. "If you do not disperse, we will call the Enforcers."

But the man wouldn't be put off. "Alpha?"

"Don't listen to him." Orib spoke gently to his father. "He's simply another Law Breaker practicing his mischief."

Alpha nodded, his thoughts swirling, as they continued toward the Temple.

* * *

TRAVIS TURNED from the console to Nicholas. "You okay?"

Nicholas continued scowling at the scene before them.

"Bro?"

"Look at him."

"What?"

"His face," Nicholas growled. "Look at his eyes."

Travis turned back to the console. "Hang on, let me zoom in."

This was his double's second day in the community—mere minutes for Travis and Nicholas, since Travis insisted on skipping the boring, mundane times. But it was the boring, mundane times that caused Nicholas the greatest concern. These were the times when his duplicate ate with the group, when he talked idly with them, when he seemed to be growing more and more attached to them.

"Here we go," Travis said.

Nicholas glanced up as the picture zoomed into a close shot of the digital Nicholas looking after Alpha and his party. Travis hit another key and the image focused in on his eyes. They were filled with moisture.

Travis turned back to him in surprise. "Are those ... tears?"

Nicholas berated himself as he continued to watch. He should have seen this coming. "We have to talk to him."

"No problemo." Travis turned back to the console and entered another set of commands.

Nicholas stepped closer.

Travis finished, then leaned toward the mic. "Hey, bro, how's it going?"

The image on the screen looked up, startled.

"We gotta talk, dude."

The image nodded, almost imperceptibly.

Nyrah turned from the group, which had started off, and called, "You coming?"

"Go ahead," the digital Nicholas answered. "I'll, uh, catch up."

"Sorry it didn't work out," she said. "But I've got connections. We'll find a way, don't worry."

He tried to smile.

Once the group was a healthy distance away, the duplicate Nicholas quietly spoke. "That was . . ." he discreetly pressed the moisture from his eyes. "Remarkable."

"Yes," Nicholas spoke into the mic, "a bit too remarkable."

Of course, his double knew exactly what Nicholas was talking about. Still, he tried to explain. "It's different than I thought." He turned back to look after Alpha and his party as they disappeared down the walk. "I could have reached out and touched him."

But Nicholas refused to be drawn in. "He's not real."

"Did you see his eyes? They were Stephanie's. And the skateboard scar, traces of it are still there." His double swallowed. "And his personality. Did you hear the sensitivity in his voice?"

"He's not real."

His double barely heard. "He was in front of me. All grown up and in front of me."

Nicholas held his ground. "He was generated by a computer."

"You'd have to be here."

"He's a digital representation."

"I'm a digital representation."

Nicholas closed his eyes. No wonder people called him bullheaded. He tried again. "This is not reality."

"You're wrong. This is my reality. And Alpha is my . . ." He trailed off, having the good sense not to continue.

Nicholas let the silence hang, making sure his double saw the irrationality of his statement. Finally he spoke. "It's a dangerous path."

"I know." Nicholas sighed heavily. "But if we want them to trust me, I have to build relationships."

"Building relationships is one thing, but allowing yourself to—"

"Listen, fellas," Travis interrupted. "I hate to break up

your little party of schizophrenics, but where are we going with this?"

The digital Nicholas answered, "Our objectives have not changed."

Nicholas nodded. "To stress the importance of resisting the virus, and to clarify the truths behind the Law."

"Precisely," his double agreed. "We are in full agreement."

"I hope so," Nicholas said, making sure the concern registered in his voice. "I sincerely hope so."

CHAPTER 16

"SO YOU'RE SAYING the Law no longer counts?" Nyrah asked. She spoke loud enough for the rest of the crowd to hear. "That it's no longer true?"

"No." Nicholas shook his head. "I'm not saying that at all."

"Then what exactly are you—"

"The Law is still true. Following it is the best way to keep the virus in check and stop it from spreading. But following it is not enough."

The crowd, mostly Law Breakers, groaned and shook their heads. A handful turned and started walking back down the muddy slope to their shelters.

Nicholas raised his voice. "What I'm saying is that there is something greater than the Law, something more real."

"More real than the Law?" Dortha asked.

Nicholas nodded. He was barely able to see their faces in the flickering fires. Evening had settled over the camp, which meant another night of hospitality in Big Red's lean-to. Nicholas didn't mind, though the thin pile of straw on the hard-packed earth didn't help his back. Nor did the ravenous fleas help his disposition. (He'd have to ask Travis why such

198

details were necessary.) Still, Big Red had a big heart. And in their own way, so did many of the Breakers. Honor among thieves? Maybe. Though Nicholas suspected it had more to do with the suffering of outcasts.

He'd given considerable thought to the noonday discussion with Travis and his in-lab counterpart. He knew the dangers of his feelings. If he wasn't careful, they could cloud and distort his logic. And yet, the emotions he felt rising up inside . . . was it possible they were part of an even deeper logic? For a species to continue, wasn't it imperative that the parent love his child? His family? Of course. And because his son served as Alpha's prototype, and in turn that of the rest of the community, wasn't Nicholas, in a sense, surrounded by family? Dangerous thinking, he knew. But it didn't interfere with the overall objective. If anything, it gave him even greater motivation to reach the community. And to have further discussion with Alpha. Because if he could explain the truths to their leader, and the leader passed those truths down, the mission would be a success.

Granted, the first encounter with Alpha had been a failure. But Nyrah had assured him there would be others. In the meantime, the people here at the camp seemed willing to listen. Well, some of them. He wasn't fooling himself. He knew most of their attention came from simply being bored. And, of course, he would have preferred a more intellectual crowd. But there was something so raw and true about them. Something so honest in their need.

"You didn't answer the question," Kallab called to him from the back. "What's more real than the Law?"

"What's more real than the Law?" Nicholas repeated.

Kallab folded his arms and waited.

"The thinking behind the Law."

"Whose thinking?" another shouted.

Nicholas hesitated. He knew they weren't prepared to

hear about all the philosophical giants he'd studied throughout his life.

Nor would they be interested in the voluminous amount of teachings he'd reduced into the simple instructions he'd originally given Alpha. So instead he gave the only answer they would understand that would still be truth.

"It was our thinking," he said.

"Whose?" Kallab demanded.

"Programmers."

The crowd looked to one another as if they'd misheard. Some began to murmur.

Nicholas pressed on. "The thoughts behind the Law are more real because it was those thoughts that spoke the Law into existence."

The clarification didn't seem to help.

He tried another approach. "The Law is like..." He pushed up his glasses. "The Law is like a child's dot-to-dot picture. You can connect the dots, but that doesn't help in ..."

Their blank expressions brought him to a stop.

"A dot-to-dot picture?" he repeated.

More baffled looks.

He picked up a nearby branch and began making several indentations in the mud. "The Law is like these dots."

He continued until he made three sets of over a dozen little holes. Then he began connecting them.

"There is nothing false or wrong with them. But they are not the whole picture."

He connected the first set of dots, making a crude circle. Next he drew a straight line through the mud to the second set.

"You think by focusing on these, by connecting them, that you have a complete picture."

He connected the second group of dots, creating a crude pair of arms. He continued the straight line a little farther until he connected the third set, making a pair of legs. Now he had a figure of a stick man.

"But you still don't see the real picture. You have only an approximation. The roughest of concepts."

He stepped back and tapped the figure with the branch. "These dots are nowhere close to the complete picture of a man."

"So what good is it?" Dortha asked. "The Law, I mean. Why do we even need it?"

"It holds back the virus," someone shouted. "It keeps us safe."

"It keeps us in a cage," Nyrah countered.

"She's right." Kallab motioned to the drawing. "Those aren't dots, my friends. Those are bars." He motioned over his shoulder toward the Temple, which rose in the distance. "And that's our prison."

Others agreed.

Nicholas shook his head. "No." He pointed back to the figure and the indentations. "These present an accurate outline for life. But they are not life. Can't you see the difference?"

Most could not. He tried again.

"This is the rule book, not the game."

"What game?" Big Red called out. "Whose game?"

"Yours," Nicholas answered. "The one Programmer wants you to live and enjoy."

"Programmer?" a voice in the back shouted. "Stop all this drivel about Programmer!"

The crowd turned and Nicholas caught sight of a balding, middle-aged man.

"If Programmer cares so much about our lives, why did he do this?"

As the people parted, Nicholas saw the man was holding the hand of a six-year-old boy. The child was barely older than Annie's son. But instead of the bright fresh face of a child, the right side sagged, drooping like melted wax. His cheekbone was either missing or caved in. His eye socket was no longer visible through scar tissue that had healed into leather ridges of purple, brown and red.

Nicholas stepped forward. "What happened?"

"Thieves," the father spat. "They broke into our home when I was at Temple. It wasn't enough they killed my wife and stole our units—but when my boy tried to stop them, they beat him into ... this."

Nicholas continued toward him as the crowd separated.

"If Programmer cares so much about us," the father said, "why did He do this?"

Nicholas did not respond.

"Answer me," the father demanded. "Answer me!"

Nicholas arrived and stood before him. With growing compassion, he knelt down to the boy. The child took a half step behind his father.

Nicholas looked up to the man, his voice thick with emotion. "The virus did this. And the people who followed it. Not Programmer."

"He allowed it!"

Nicholas turned back to the boy, then sadly nodded in agreement.

The father had begun to tremble. "If He's so good, why didn't He stop them?"

Still looking at the child, Nicholas quietly answered, "They have free will."

"The thieves?"

"Everyone."

"What about my son? Shouldn't his free will give him the right to live a normal life?"

Nicholas rose back to his feet and faced the man. "What

would you have Programmer do? Turn the thieves into puppets? Dictate their every move?"

The father swallowed, clenching his jaw.

Nicholas turned to the crowd. "All of your lives you have demanded to be free, to live life your own way. By following the virus you've told Programmer to stay out of your affairs, refusing to be enslaved by his Law. And when he honors your wishes, when he steps back and allows you the freedom you demand, you complain he's not controlling and enslaving others. You cannot have it both ways, my friends."

Kallab stepped forward, motioning to the boy. "You're saying there is only the Law or this?"

Nicholas paused. It was a valid question. One he'd wrestled with even back at the lab. Granted, his objective was to encourage them to resist the virus and show them how to live the principles of the Law. But was that enough? He looked back to the stick figure. Even now, wasn't he simply spewing out words, presenting highbrow metaphors? Shouldn't there be more? He turned back to the boy, his emotions continuing to rise. As he stared, an idea began to form.

He knelt back down. Slowly, he raised his hand toward the child. The boy retreated farther behind his father. But Nicholas remained, his hand outstretched, the idea growing stronger, taking a more defined shape.

The boy looked up to his father, who continued to glower.

Nicholas waited, smiling to the child, giving a nod of encouragement.

The boy began to move. Slowly, tentatively, he took a step toward him.

Nicholas gave another nod.

He took another step.

Nicholas continued to smile and raised his other hand. Now both were stretched out to the child.

After another look to his father, the boy raised his own hand. Nicholas reached until their fingers touched. Then he gently wrapped his two hands around the child's. The boy fidgeted, but did not pull back. Instead, he eased closer.

Slowly, ever so gently, Nicholas removed his left hand from the child's and reached toward the boy's ruined face.

* * *

"ALL RIGHT, THAT'S ENOUGH," Travis said. He entered a set of keystrokes and the action froze.

Nicholas scowled. "What are you doing?"

"What are you doing?"

"It appears he's about to repair him."

"What?"

"He's going to heal the child's face."

"He can't do that!"

"He can't." Nicholas turned to his brother. "But you can."

"He's pushing me? Expecting me to play along?"

"Apparently."

"Why—so he can show off for his new pals, pretend he's Jesus Christ? In case you haven't noticed, this is getting creepy-close to some religious thing."

Nicholas had noticed and the thought gave him little comfort. But he understood it. He didn't like what was happening, but he understood.

Travis continued, "First we got ourselves a know-it-all prophet, now he's a miracle worker. What's next, walking on water?" Nicholas's scowl deepened.

"What's he trying to prove? Where's all this fancy logic of yours?"

Nicholas turned back to the screen. There was logic here, he could see it. It wasn't his brand, but there was logic.

"Well?"

"He has two valid points."

"I'm waiting."

"First . . . such action would underscore his authority. They would be more likely to listen to our message if they witnessed this type of power. Second ... it would prove that Programmer's ways are good, that we really do want what's best for them."

"And third," Travis added, "it's impossible."

"Why do you say that?"

"You can't go messin' with their reality."

"It's your program. You can do what you wish."

"No way. I just can't hit Delete and, poof!, the effects of following the virus suddenly disappear. Everything has to balance. One plus one has to equal two."

Nicholas nodded. "Otherwise the integrity of the program is ruined."

"Exactly."

"Then send the effects someplace within the program."

"Where?"

"What difference does it make?"

"It makes a ton of difference. I can't transfer it someplace where it doesn't have the same impact."

"Because?"

"What? You want me to send the kid's suffering into a rock?"

"All right."

"No, not all right." Travis was getting worked up. "What about the physical pain, the angst, the emotions?"

"Then send it to a person," Nicholas countered. "The thieves who attacked the boy."

"And kiss free will goodbye. Suddenly everyone is

obeying 'cause they're afraid of getting clobbered. Puppy dogs cowering in the corner."

Nicholas nodded, seeing his point. He looked back up to the screen, then frowned. Another idea began to surface. And, just as he wasn't fond of his double's logic, he wasn't pleased with the choice now emerging. Still, it made a type of sense. He took another moment, evaluated the options, and spoke. "Then send it to him."

"Oh, yeah, right."

"I'm serious. If everything has to balance, transfer the pain and suffering into him."

"You want your double going through what that kid went through?"

Nicholas shook his head. "No. But if it's a solution and if it doesn't violate the program's integrity, then he should at least know about it. He should at least be given the option to consider it."

"That's insane!"

"Of course it is. But it's also logical."

Travis blew out his breath. "And heartless."

Nicholas looked back to the monitor, steeling himself against any rising sentimentality. "No. If it's his choice, it is not heartless. If he understands all the facts and still makes the decision, it's a rational approach that he's chosen to follow."

Travis swore, running his hands through his hair.

Nicholas asked, "If he were to say yes, how long would it take to program the changes?"

There was no response.

"Travis?"

"Not long," his brother grumbled. "It's just transferring data."

Nicholas nodded. He took a breath and looked back to the screen. "All right, then. Let's tell him."

* * *

THE LOGIC FLASHED through Nicholas's mind in a millisecond. And it made perfect sense. Although there was one
additional aspect his in-lab double had not mentioned—the
deeper logic.

If he absorbed the child's injuries, the boy could live a
normal life, completely free of the infirmities. It was an
exciting thought, knowing he could make such a positive
impact upon one of them. Exciting and terrifying.

They'd never discussed anything close to this and he
wasn't sure how it would work. What would he feel? Would
there be pain? These were important questions they should
discuss and analyze. And would have ... if he had not looked
into the child's face and seen the answer.

He smiled, attempting to ease the boy's fear and disguise
his own. He cupped his hand and gently placed it against the
child's right cheek. Then, bracing himself, he whispered a
single word, inaudible to everyone but himself and those in
the lab.

"Yes."

There was another flicker. His palm grew hot. The heat
rose up his arms and into his face. His right eye began to
water. Suddenly there was a tightening, then a cramping of
his cheek, the muscles surrounding his eye and nose and jaw.
He heard cartilage snap, felt bone breaking and dissolving.
He cried out, grabbing his face, felt the flesh tightening and
twisting under his fingers.

More snapping. The pain was excruciating. His face was
on fire as he sank to his knees. He thought he'd pass out. He
hoped he would, but he didn't.

Soon the pain began to subside. Slowly. Along with the
heat. He wiped the tears from his eye, feeling the deformity
of the socket, the entire right side of his face. He pulled away

his fingers and looked up to the crowd. Saw their shocked expression, their hands rising to their mouths. He tried to smile, to assure them, but only the left side of his face worked. The right side hung limp and useless.

He turned back to the boy. The child's right eye and cheek were perfectly formed, his skin smooth and clear, save for a sprinkle of freckles across the bridge of his nose. Nicholas reached out to the boy, but the child recoiled in terror, ducking behind his father.

The father stammered, "What... have you done?"

Nicholas looked up.

The father stooped down to his son, felt his face in disbelief. "What have you done?"

Nicholas settled back onto his knees, exhausted. The pain had slowly given way to a deep, impossible-to-describe... satisfaction.

* * *

"Hello..." As a retired speech and drama teacher, Annie's mother always answered the phone as if she were in a musical.

"Hey, Mom."

"Hello, dear, how are you? Is everything all right?"

Annie sat on the hotel bed, wrapping the telephone cord around her finger. "Not great. Why do you ask?"

"You haven't been answering your phone."

"Yeah, I think I may have lost it."

"Lost it? Those things are expensive."

"Right, I-"

"You need to be more careful. With the economy the way it is and your salary, you should—"

Annie blew the hair out of her eyes. "Right, you're right."

"It's just an observation."

"Listen, you haven't talked to Rusty, have you?"

"Well, not exactly 'talked.'"

Annie's heart skipped. "What's that mean?"

"I received some sort of note from him on my telephone."

"A text message? Rusty sent you a text message?"

"Yes, at least that's what Sis called it. A text message, yes."

Annie was on her feet. "Where was he, what did he say?"

"Something about finding you."

"Finding me."

"I can't remember the exact words, but he was calling from someone's cell phone and—"

"Can you retrieve it? Can you read it to me?"

"Read what, dear?"

"The text message?"

"Are you sure you're okay? You sound a little—"

"I'm fine, Mother. Can you read me the message?"

"I'm really not sure how to do that, sweetheart. Your Aunt Myrtle was the one who—"

"Is she there?"

"No, she stepped out to get some dairy creamer. We're really having a wonderful time."

"Good, I'm glad. Listen, would you look at your phone for me? Would you look at the front of your phone?"

There was no answer.

"Mom? Mom, can you hear me? Mom?"

"Are you still there?" her mother asked.

"Yes, what—"

"I can't look at the phone and talk to you at the same time."

Annie rubbed her forehead. "Right. I'll talk louder. When you look at the phone, do you see the button with the word okay on it?"

No answer.

"Mom?

"Yes, it's this little silver one in the center."

"Great. Go ahead and press it."

"Hang on." There was a brief pause and she returned. "The screen lit up again."

"Perfect. Now on that screen do you see the word Messages?"

"Hang on."

Annie began to pace.

"There are lots of words, dear, but nothing that says Messages."

"Mom, we have the same phone. You should see the word—"

"There's a Message singular, but no Messages, plural.

"Message singular will work just fine. Now I want you to press the button immediately under that word."

Another pause. "Gracious me, there's an entirely different list."

"That's good. Now scroll down to the line that says—"

"'Scroll down?'"

"It's the button under the Okay button."

"Sweetheart, I'm afraid this is getting just a little too—"

"Mom, please, this is important!" Annie paused to rein in her frustration. "I want you to just keep hitting that button until it takes you to the words that say In Box."

"Hold on." There was another pause. "Yes, I'm there."

"Now hit the Okay key."

"Again? Are you certain?"

"Yes, Mother, I'm certain." She waited. "Did you hit it?"

"Now there's an entirely different list."

"Great. Scroll down, using that same little key under the Okay key, to the first number.

More silence.

"Mom? Mom?"

Her mother was farther from the receiver. "It looks like some sort of message."

"Great, will you read it?"

Her mother cleared her voice and read: " 'Gram, Mom's not answering. Fran's got this cool—' I guess that's cool, he's misspelled it with a k."

Go on.

"Fran's got this cool phone tracker and found Mom's cell phone. We're going up to get her."

Annie sucked in her breath.

"What does that mean, dear—'going up to get her'? Up where? Where are you?"

"I'll have to call you back, Mom."

"But how do I get this off of my—"

"Aunt Myrtle will show you. I gotta go. Goodbye, Mom."

Without waiting for a reply, Annie hung up, then suddenly cursed herself for her stupidity and redialed. Her mother's phone would have recorded the number Rusty had called from. But the line was busy. She hung up and tried again. Same result. And again. She slammed down the receiver and stewed. Then, pulling Matthew's card from her pocket, she dialed his number. The message kicked in after the fourth ring:

"Hello, this is Agent Matthew—"

She hung up and without a moment's hesitation headed for the door. She raced down the stairs and into the lobby, where she asked the concierge to ring up a taxi.

CHAPTER 17

TRAVIS AND NICHOLAS stared at the screen in astonishment. Once again Travis had pushed the program, fast-forwarding it. This time it was to find the next encounter between Alpha and Nicholas's double. Up on the monitor a large crowd had gathered. As planned, the digital Nicholas was reducing all of his philosophical knowledge into small digestible pieces so the people could better understand. But it wasn't the teaching that made both Travis's and Nicholas's jaws drop.

Travis could barely get out the words. "What... has he done?"

Nicholas pushed up his glasses and stepped closer to the screen.

"With that boy you gave him the ability to transfer power."

"Yeah, but not this. It was supposed to be a onetime thing. Not this ..."

* * *

THE AIR WAS crisp but not cold. With no breeze, the winter sun slowly soaked into Alpha's body. It had been his idea to come. He could not forget the tugging he felt inside when the stranger spoke. Nor could he ignore the reports of the man's deep and somewhat troubling teachings. Finally, there were the healings. All reasons enough to leave the Temple to see and hear for himself. Of course, Orib would not let him go without an entourage of Council Members. And, of course, they had to sit on an outcropping of rock to the left and above the proceedings so citizens and Breakers alike would know of their presence.

They had barely settled themselves before he saw Nyrah. He was certain she'd also seen him. Yet, sitting less than seventy lengths apart, both father and daughter pretended to ignore the other's presence. A task that, at least for Alpha, was nearly impossible.

"Look at them," Orib said scornfully. "They cling to every word, in spite of his gross deformities."

His son was right. The stranger was grotesque. Besides a monstrous face, which he supposedly acquired by healing a small boy, he had a gnarled left hand, a hunched back, and his right leg had shriveled into a stump. And, as late as this morning, it was reported he'd lost his sight to a man who had been blind.

Still the crowd grew. Although some came for the novelty, Learis and other Members insisted it was his clever spinning of words and perverting of the Law.

Perhaps. But as the stranger spoke, Alpha felt something much more.

"If you are poor in understanding Programmer's thoughts"— the man took a wheezing gasp—"then you are open to receive them."

His ragged breathing made it painful to listen. And his twisted mouth made him difficult to understand. Neverthe-

213

less, there was something about his words that was captivating.

"But if you think . .. you are rich in knowing our ways, then you are poor."

There it was again, the not-so-subtle claim that the stranger and Programmer were somehow related. Alpha closed his eyes against the blasphemy.

"If you are humble"—he gasped another breath—"you will inherit life as we designed it."

"If we're humble," someone shouted from the back, "we'll be destroyed."

Others agreed.

"No!" The stranger's shout sent him into a fit of coughing. The crowd grew silent, waiting. At last he continued. "You've lived upside down for so long, you don't know the difference."

Alpha leaned forward, listening intently.

"If you want to be a leader, you must serve. If you want wealth—" He coughed, then continued, "Give away false riches so your heart has room for real treasures."

Alpha caught himself quietly nodding. Amid the heresy there were great truths.

"If you're hungry for good, we will feed you."

"How?" a young mother cried from the center of the crowd.

The stranger turned to her voice. "By offering you real food."

"You offer nothing but words," a Breaker yelled.

"He's right!" another shouted. "If you really had something to offer, you'd give life units—not your fancy ideas."

Others in the crowd murmured in agreement.

"Good." Orib turned to his companions. "Someone has finally challenged him."

They nodded, but Alpha watched, not entirely convinced.

The stranger turned to Nyrah and those closest to him. It was impossible to hear what he said, but it was obvious his inner circle of followers were confused. Finally one of the Breakers stepped forward and stretched out his robe. The stranger motioned for another to pour the contents of a small basket into the robe. As he did, a dozen life units tumbled out.

The crowd buzzed in surprise. They reacted more loudly when the Breaker turned and began distributing the units to them. Meanwhile, another Breaker stretched out his robe. The same follower tilted the same basket and another pile of units poured out.

Orib rose to his feet as the second Breaker turned to the people and began distributing the life units.

The crowd grew louder as a third Breaker received his supply of units. And a fourth, his. And a fifth. All from the same basket and all being distributed to the people.

"This is not possible." Orib turned to his fellow Members. "He's a trickster! An illusionist!"

But it was a different illusion that caught Alphas attention. With every basket the stranger ordered to be poured out, he seemed to be getting a little weaker.

* * *

"He's transferring energy again?" Travis shouted. "Into life units now! When's this going to stop?"

Nicholas stared up at the screen. "I... don't know."

"What do you mean, you don't know? That's you up there!"

"Not anymore."

"Yes, it is. Down to the tiniest synapse!"

Nicholas shook his head. "He's different. Something's happening."

"To you?"

"To him. He's changing."

"He won't be winning any beauty pageants, if that's what you mean."

Nicholas looked back to the screen as the people hungrily received the life units—some in greed, others in gratitude, a few even with tears.

"We've got to stop this," Travis said, "or he'll die. He's got nothing left to give."

"There's no way to transfer additional energy into him?"

"Computational powers are maxed out. And there's no place left I can steal them from. I'll have to go inside the program itself. Redistribute from there."

"That's possible?"

"Sure. It won't be pretty, but it's possible. And once he's restored, we gotta have another talk. Make it clear to him. No more miracle-man stuff—no way, nohow."

Nicholas nodded and turned back to the screen, hoping they weren't too late. Hoping it was still possible to reach him.

ANNIE DIDN'T WAIT for change from the taxi driver. She threw him a twenty and scrambled out the door. He shouted something to her, but she didn't turn. She raced to the lobby door and yanked it open. Under the flickering of a bad fluorescent light, she headed for the elevator and hit the button over and over again. It wheezed and started its lumbering journey downward. But every second was a waste. She spotted the stairwell and dashed to it.

When she opened the door, she was hit by the smell of old urine. Careful where she stepped, but moving as quickly as possible, she ran up the stairs and arrived at the third floor.

She flung open the door and quickly strode down the hall toward the FBI office at the end of the corridor. There was no light on behind the door's old-fashioned ribbed glass. Still, when she arrived, she tried the knob. To her surprise, it turned and opened.

To her greater surprise, the reception desk was gone. As was the rest of the furniture.

"Hello?" She crossed the room to Special Agent Matthew Hostetler's door and opened it.

Like the reception area, it was empty.

* * *

ALPHA COULD NOT FORGET the stranger's words as he sat alone on the porch swing. He sat by himself a lot these days as Saida continued to drift; from him. She was a strong woman, always able to withstand the pressures of being the Law Giver's wife. But lately, day by day, he'd been slowly losing her to an impenetrable melancholy. And this evening's meal with Orib and his nervous young wife was no exception.

"Well, look what your mother has made," he had exclaimed earlier as Saida entered from the kitchen where she'd insisted on preparing the meal alone. She carried a large platter of shredded and broiled units. "What a cook she is!" He gave a wink to his daughter-in-law and added, "I hope you're taking notes."

"Shush," Saida said as she placed the platter on the table. "Hanaf's a fine cook."

"I have a lot to learn," the pretty blonde admitted. She took a self-conscious sip of her water.

"It's just a matter of practice," Saida assured her.

"But you've always been a great cook," Alpha insisted. He

reached to pull her closer, but she had stepped just out of his grasp. "It's one of your many not-so-hidden talents."

"Eat," Saida said scornfully as she slid into her place at the table, "before it gets cold."

"It would be good even cold."

"Eat."

Alpha grinned and reached out his hands to the others, who took them to say grace. Once he had finished, he dug into the meal with enthusiasm.

"Mm, this is great," he said. "Isn't this great, Orib?"

"Yes," his son agreed.

"Better than great," Alpha said. "Don't you agree, Hanaf?"

"Yes, it is very good."

Orib turned to his mother. "You'll have to give her your recipe."

"Yes." Hanaf nodded. "Please do."

Saida offered a practiced smile. Soon there was only the sound of scraping forks and the accidental clink of Hanaf's glass as she took another drink of water.

"So ..." Orib turned to his father. "You heard the Easterners took another outpost?"

Alpha nodded. "To the south this time."

"Yes."

"Hardly a concern."

"True."

"The Enforcers are down there."

"Agreed," Orib said, "but it does spread the northern flanks a little thin. And with the addition of this stranger—"

"Please," Saida interrupted. "May we talk about something else?"

The two men traded looks.

"I'm sorry," she said. "It's just, it seems we are always discussing your work." She retreated back into her silence.

"You're right, Mom," Orib said. "I'm sorry."

"Yes, you are right," Alpha agreed. "So, what shall we talk about?"

There was a brief pause. Hanaf cleared her throat. "You know my cousin Bernal?"

"She was in your wedding," Alpha said.

"That's right. One of my bridesmaids."

"Married the weekend before we were," Orib added.

"Yes," Hanaf said. "She told me just yesterday that she's with child."

"A baby? That's wonderful," Alpha said, stealing a quick look to his wife.

"And fast," Orib replied.

"But completely legal," Hanaf insisted. "I mean, they did everything according to the Law."

"Good for her," Alpha said. "That's very good."

"Yes, and she said if it's a boy they're going to name it after Orib.

"Really?" Orib said.

Hanaf reached over and rubbed his arm in pride. "Isn't that sweet? I think it's so sweet."

"Especially since I used to beat up her husband in school."

The group chuckled. All except Saida. She smiled tightly as she pushed back her chair, its legs scraping against the worn wooden floor.

"Are you all right?" Alpha asked.

"Yes, I, uh ..." She touched her face, her eyes. "I'm not feeling well. You'll have to excuse me."

Alpha started to rise.

"No, sit. I just need to lie down a bit."

"But-"

"Sit... sit." Without another word, she turned and headed for the bedroom.

"Saida?"

She gave a half wave, leaving the men to exchange glances and a confused Hanaf to reach for her glass of water.

Now, outside on the porch, Alpha stared up at the stars. He took a deep breath and slowly exhaled. But the tightness in his chest would not go away.

* * *

NICHOLAS AWOKE TO THE HEAT. The stump of his leg was on fire. The itching was intolerable. With it he felt a tingling sensation, then movement. The limb was growing, extending. Its end began shaping into a knee. It continued to lengthen into a shin and calf, then an ankle, a foot, toes. At the same time the heat crept up his back. He could literally hear the popping and cracking of vertebrae they straightened. The heat spread down his arm and into his withered hand, rose up his neck and into his face.

He sat up and whispered harshly, "Travis!" The heat spread into his eyes. Darkness was replaced by flittings and flashes of light. Images began to appear. Soon he saw the blurry form of Big Red's lean-to.

"Travis!"

He glanced over to the big man snoring on the floor beside his latest woman. He scrambled to his feet and carefully stepped over them. By the time he was outside, barefoot in the cold mud, the restoration was complete.

"What are you doing?" he demanded.

I'm saving your life! his brother replied. *What are you doing?*

"What do you mean?"

You know what I mean. You know exactly what I mean.

Nicholas slowed to a stop and bent over to catch his breath. Of course they knew, he couldn't fool them. He took another breath and rose. "What I'm seeing ... there's so much need here. I had no idea."

We see it too. It was his other voice, his lab voice.

"But you don't... feel it. Not like I do."

Travis answered, *Well, you better start feeling less and thinking more. Otherwise this whole little exercise is over.*

"But all the suffering . . . Everywhere you look there's this hunger, this ..."

You keep transferring your life into them, you'll be dead, bro! Then you'll do nobody any good.

Nicholas looked down at the mud around his feet. How could he explain what he was experiencing, the depth of his connection?

Listen, man, I'm all out of power here. No way can I revive you again.

He glanced at his healed leg, his hand. Both were perfect and intact. "You did a pretty good job here."

I stole it from our own program.

"You what?"

Look around you, dude. See how flat everything looks?

Nicholas paused to survey the camp—the hill, the shacks, the lean-tos. Everything was exactly the same. No. There was something missing. A certain reality.

His brother continued, *I had to pull power from the lighting. Your program's supposed to have four types of light. Now you got two.*

Nicholas stooped down to pick up a mud-coated stone. It looked and felt like a stone, but there was no glint of moisture, no brightness, no shadow. Although he could feel the textures, everything else about it appeared flat.

But I can't keep doing it.

Nicholas rose and turned toward the distant temple. The spires glowed brightly in the moonlight, but they seemed to have no depth, no definition. He tilted his head up to the moon. It was nearly full. And yes, there were blotches of dark and light, but it looked more like a painting than a three-dimensional object.

Do you hear me?

"I understand. But you have to understand the pain these people are undergoing, their loneliness, their...hopelessness."

His lab voice ignored him. *You're also creating another dilemma.*

"Which is ..."

The program will be useless for our purposes if you arbitrarily break the rules.

"There's nothing arbitrary with what I'm—"

By continuing to absorb the effects of the virus, you're eliminating any balance of cause and effect.

Travis stepped in. *We can't have any more magic, bro. Everything has to balance out and be rational. Otherwise the program becomes bogus.*

Nicholas understood. He'd even considered the problem earlier. "My reality must be run by the same logic as yours."

Precisely. Stick to the plan. Talk to them. Be an example.

"That's it?"

That was our objective. There is nothing more we can or should do.

Nicholas closed his eyes.

No more sideshows and special effects, all right?

He took a breath, exhaled, and slowly nodded. "I'll try my best."

You gotta do more than try, bro.

He took another breath. "Yes, I understand."

But even at that, even as he agreed, he knew there was something more. He'd briefly touched upon it—when he was experiencing the healings. It was just out of his reach, not possible to define, at least not yet. But he knew there was something more.

CHAPTER 18

ANNIE'S THOUGHTS RACED and tumbled over each other as she ran from the FBI office and down the stairs. It was an obvious front. But why? And who really was Special Agent Matthew Hostetler? By the time she reached the sidewalk she was shaking. To think she'd been attracted to the man—that boyish charm, those puppy dog eyes, and the "daughter." *Did you see my Barbie press-on nails commercial?* She *was* an actress. Everything was a scam. A show put on just for Annie.

She spotted a young man on Rollerblades across the street. Their eyes briefly met. Was he watching her? She gave a start as a bag lady suddenly rattled past her with a shopping cart. And what about the man text-messaging in the doorway of the adjacent building?

She turned and started down the sidewalk. She wasn't sure where she was going. It didn't matter as long as she was moving. What about Rusty? What happened to her son? How was he a part of this? And Phillip Dixon? With his money, there was nothing he couldn't do. So what *was* he doing? And what about Travis? And what about— She pushed the thought from her mind. No, she could trust Nicholas. That much she was sure of.

She reached into her coat and pulled out Travis's cell phone to call the police—then she stopped. Could they be trusted? If she couldn't trust the FBI, how could she— But it wasn't the FBI. Or was it? She heard the rumble of a city bus and looked up to see it stopping ahead. She picked up her pace, then broke into a run, chasing after it. It made no difference where it was heading.

Once inside and settled, she tried to slow her breathing. *Think*, she told herself. *For Rusty, think.*

We're going up to get her. That's what he'd texted her mom. But he didn't have a cell phone. Neither did Fran.

We're going UP to get her.

All right. That was her next step. But she had no car. And a taxi? What taxi would drive up into the mountains and search for-

Car rental! Of course. She'd rent a car and drive up to the compound herself.

It didn't take long to find a rental company; there was one near the pier. That was the easy part. Standing around after she gave her credit card info, that's when it got difficult. Even as they entered her information, she realized her mistake. Anyone could be tracing her—which made the clerk's endless speech about insurance coverage and special offers and did she want to fill up the tank before returning the car all the more unbearable. Fortunately, no one came bursting through the doors with blazing weapons.

Fifteen minutes later, she was finally on the road, safe and sound ... and heading for the mountains.

* * *

NICHOLAS SAT on Orib's sofa, anything but content. Nyrah

had pulled the strings she'd promised. He'd been told he'd finally meet Alpha. But when he arrived, the Law Giver was nowhere present. "Unavoidable emergency," they'd said. Of course, he knew better. Unless the emergency meant insulating their leader from Nicholas's "heresy," or to make a statement to the growing crowd outside that his teaching was still under suspicion. Not that it made much difference. As far as he could tell, no one was embracing what he was saying, anyway. His lab double and Travis could discuss the need for resisting the virus and how to live the Law all they wanted, but if no one was listening, what good did it do? Still, maybe that would change. He'd certainly gotten enough attention with the healings, not to mention his own "miraculous" recovery. Maybe the handful of Council Members in Orib's living room would finally see. Maybe those who worked and studied and handled the Law every day would at last understand the thinking behind it.

At the moment, Orib was speaking. And, though his point was no doubt important, it was difficult for Nicholas to give him his fullest attention. Just as there were clear resemblances between Nyrah and his ex-wife, he now saw similarities between himself and the young man who could have been his grandson. The nose just a little too large for his face, the sharp chin, and, of course, the eyes. Although they were more anxious for approval than he'd prefer, there was no missing their dark intensity.

"All I'm suggesting," Orib said, as he passed the platter of deep-fried units to him, "is if your powers really are from Programmer, then you will want to use them to stop the Easterners."

"Stop them?" Nicholas asked. He took a slice from the plate. It had the texture of toast and the smell of basil, along with other herbs he did not recognize.

Orib explained, "They have killed nearly thirty of our

people at the southern border. We were able to retaliate by destroying nearly that many ourselves, but we simply do not have enough resources."

The news brought Nicholas up short. "So much killing? Why?"

Learis, an elderly Member with a white beard, spoke up. "They want control of the Temple."

"Because of the life units?" Nicholas asked.

"Because they are heretics!"

Orib stepped in, more calmly. "At one time they were our brothers, but because of a dispute over the Law, they rose up in rebellion and we banished them."

"What type of dispute?" Nicholas bit into his unit. Despite the seasoning, it was dry and tasteless, much like the rye crackers at the university cafeteria.

"They insist upon worshipping Programmer on the ninth day of the week."

"The ninth day?"

"Yes."

"And how is that—"

Learis interrupted, "As you know, the Law clearly states Programmer is to be honored on the fifth day."

The information struck Nicholas hard. All that killing... simply over which day of the week to honor, what? Him? And yet how was it any different from, say, ostracizing the Breakers, or the other divisions he'd seen within the community... the separation of father from daughter, brother from sister? Wasn't it all because of the Law? And all the well-meaning nuances that had been added to it? Yes, he had expected Alpha would adjust and refine its principles. But how had it come to this?

Unable to finish the unit, he turned to Orib and asked, "What would you have me do?"

"Crush the Easterners," Learis said. "Destroy them."

"Why?"

"Why?" Learis looked to the others, perplexed. "To preserve Programmer's honor, of course."

"You don't believe Programmer can look out for his own honor?" Nicholas asked.

"To save His people," a younger Member explained.

"And who exactly are his people?"

Orib forced a gentle laugh and motioned about the room. "Why, you, me, we're all His people."

Nicholas looked back to him, recalling with sadness the bio Travis had downloaded during their first encounter. A young boy so desperate to live up to his father's reputation ... so anxious to please.

Orib felt his gaze and glanced away.

Nicholas turned to the others. "And we're his people because ..."

Learis's impatience was obvious. "Because we protect and keep His Law."

"And the others do not?"

"They break it continually."

Despite the growing tension, Nicholas pressed his point. "As opposed to you, who never break Law?"

Orib glanced about the group, chuckling, attempting to diffuse any conflict. "We try our best."

"I'm sorry," Nicholas replied, "I didn't know there was a provision in the Law for trying."

The Council Members traded looks.

Above their heads Nicholas heard what sounded like scraping. Someone was on the roof. But it was a minor distraction compared to the increasing strain within the room.

He leaned toward the group. "It was my impression that the Law was the Law."

The men nodded guardedly.

"Yes," Learis agreed. "The Law is the Law."

Others murmured, "The Law is the Law, the Law is the Law."

"So, if you break one portion of the Law, even the smallest detail, despite your earnest efforts, does that not instantly turn you into Breakers?" The room grew still except for the scraping, which had moved to the far corner.

Nicholas continued, "And doesn't your Law say any Breaker must make payment?"

No one replied. No one had to. What had been tension before was turning to hostility. He wasn't surprised. Earlier, back at the camp, Nyrah and Kallab had sufficiently warned him ...

"Be careful," Nyrah had said. "They wouldn't agree to meet with you unless they thought they could catch you at something."

"And you won't come with me?" he asked.

Patting her ample belly, she replied, "I wouldn't want to soil my brother's pious hands."

Despite the sarcasm, Nicholas felt her guilt, her shame and her love for her brother—all tangled together into an impossible knot. Why did they do this to each other? But, of course, he had his answer. The Law. How could something created to do such good cause so much harm?

Nicholas looked about the room, watching the men calculate their next move. If he could just make them see what their legalism was doing. If he could just open their eyes to how their efforts to hold the community together were tearing it apart.

He reached for the teapot on the table before him when Orib's wife suddenly appeared and helped. She picked up the pot and poured, the porcelain lid clattering in her nervous hands. Nicholas gave her a smile, but she did not look. The pressure she was under was no less than her husband's. So much appearance to maintain. So much perfection to pretend. Nicholas scowled, wondering how—

There was a ripple of light and he sucked in his breath. Travis had just entered her biography. In some ways Nicholas wished he hadn't. Such fear and anxiety. How many times had she tried taking her life? Two? Three? Nothing obvious, not even to herself. Just a carelessness in her day-to-day living—the way she handled kitchen tools, where she chose to walk at night. And more.

He thanked her for her help and she forced a nervous smile before fading back into the room.

"So tell me, sir," Learis said, subtly changing the subject, "when you speak of Law, which one do you consider the most important?"

Nicholas nodded, grateful to clarify what he'd spoken to Alpha so long ago at the funeral pyre. It had been only a few days, though it felt like lifetimes. He cleared his throat and answered, "Be stewards, obey Programmer, and treat his people as sacred."

The Council nodded, seeming to approve.

In the corner, Nicholas noticed dust sifting down from the ceiling. He took a drink of his tea, saw how flat it looked without the reflection of light. Others had also noticed the change in lighting, many attributing it to the weather. He directed his attention back to the group.

"But again," he said, "my question to you is, who exactly are his people?"

More glances were exchanged.

Suddenly the ceiling gave way. Tile and wood crashed to the floor, billowed up in a cloud of dust. Members leaped to their feet, shouting, coughing... as a gaping hole of daylight appeared through the haze.

Orib raced to the opening and shouted, "What is the meaning of this?"

A cot appeared. It scraped against the edges of the hole, then slowly dropped inside, swinging by ropes attached to each of its four corners.

"What are you doing?"

A Breaker lay on the cot, his lavender robe caked in dust, his body twisted and paralyzed. Nicholas joined Orib as a young man stuck his head through the opening.

"Look what you've done to my roof!" Orib shouted.

The young man said nothing, but silently worked the ropes.

Another head appeared, dirty blond hair, matted. "Sorry 'bout the mess."

"Do you know who I am?" demanded Orib.

The second man ignored him and spoke directly to Nicholas. "He's been tryin' to get to you for days. But the crowds, they been impossible, so we figured—"

"Look what you've done!" Orib cried.

The cot came to rest on the floor. Nicholas approached the Breaker and immediately Travis downloaded his bio— the man's fall during a drunken stupor, his broken neck, the gradual twisting and atrophying of his limbs, the deserting of his wife and children.

"Remove him!" Learis shouted. "This is an important meeting!"

The Breaker's eyes locked onto Nicholas's. Such desperation. He tried to speak, but was too weak to be heard. Nicholas knelt down to him. When the words finally came, they were hoarse and raspy.

"Help ... me." He licked his lips, trying to swallow. "Please..."

Moved with compassion, Nicholas rose to his feet and turned to the group. "Tell me, is this man not also one of Programmer's people?"

"He is a Breaker!" Learis argued.

Nicholas focused on the old man and repeated his question. "Is he not one of Programmer's?"

The Council Member raised his chin, refusing to look away.

"Please." Orib gestured toward the ceiling. "We're talking about the destruction of private property here."

"No." Nicholas turned to him. "We're talking about your heart." Then, to the group, "All of your hearts."

"We are followers of Law!" someone shouted.

The youngest Member stepped forward. "If you knew this man, you'd know why he is sick."

"He is a Breaker," Learis repeated. "Look at him. Look at him!"

Nicholas turned to the man on the cot.

Learis shuffled closer, practically hissing. "He is full of sickness. And death."

"A direct result of disobedience," Orib explained.

Others nodded.

"Tell me," Nicholas asked, "if he was made well, if the sickness was removed, would you consider his payment made, his breaking forgiven?"

"Payment can only be made upon the Grid," Orib answered.

Learis's voice quavered as he added, "Only Programmer can forgive!"

The group agreed.

Nicholas looked at them, their faces hard, drained of compassion. Without a word, he knelt back to the Breaker and placed his hands on his chest. The man looked up to him with fear and anticipation.

Nicholas smiled and softly spoke. "Friend, your payment is made. Your breaking of Law is forgiven."

The group erupted in anger, but Nicholas paid little attention. He closed his eyes and willed the transfer to begin.

He was grateful Travis had not bothered to remove the ability. And he knew he'd have much explaining to do. But for now he felt the heat, the pain rippling into his back, and the cramping of muscles.

A hand was on his shoulder, trying to pull him away.

"This is blasphemy!" Learis shouted.

"Heretic!" another yelled.

The room was filled with shouting.

And, clenching his jaw against the pain, Nicholas realized the sad and obvious truth. Though the outward results of breaking Law were far more visible, the inward results of keeping it were just as destructive. Perhaps more. Because, unlike the Breakers, who knew they were infected by the virus, the Keepers acted as if they weren't.

* * *

TRAVIS SWORE and slapped the console.

"Why did you let him do it again?" Nicholas asked.

"He gave us his word. Why bother reprogramming if I got his word?"

Nicholas continued staring at the screen. "Do you have enough energy to restore him?"

Travis was already typing. "Small potatoes—but their world is definitely gonna get drabber." He shook his head. "This is insane, man. We gotta make him see reason!"

Nicholas nodded, but he had another, much larger concern. Like his digital self, he'd clearly seen the truth unfold in Orib's living room. These were the experts of the Law. If they couldn't be made to understand the thinking behind it, who could? His computer double could talk until he was blue in the face. But the pride and division created by following the Law was just as toxic as the effects of breaking it.

Travis had seen it too. "So we're back to square one. Got the same problems we had at the beginning. Same hatred, same division, same killings ..."

Nicholas nodded. "Which will ultimately lead to the same result."

"Glorious self-annihilation." Travis muttered another curse. "Only this time it'll be in our name." He shook his head. "Hatred, bigotry, murder—and now it's all for us." He sighed and looked back at the screen. "No wonder you hate religion."

CHAPTER 19

A LPHA LAY IN BED, unable to sleep.

He'd been mulling over his son's report about the afternoon meeting with the stranger. It hadn't gone well. Instead of clarifying misunderstanding and building bridges, the stranger had actually created more of a division. Of course, there had been other teachers in past seasons who attempted to twist the Law to their own advantage (though most recanted when faced with making payment on the Grid). But Alpha sensed no twisting in this man's teaching. A deepening of its meaning, yes. But no twisting.

Except when it came to his claims regarding Programmer.

Then there was an entirely different matter. The weather. It was a phenomenon that no one seemed to understand. The most learned individuals suggested an invisible haze had settled over the land, diffusing light in every direction so reflections were no longer visible. Others suggested it was a change in the sun. Then, of course, there were the superstitious who insisted it was a sign of Programmer's displeasure with who knew what, perhaps even the stranger.

The pounding on the front door startled Alpha from his thoughts and brought him upright in bed. Saida, who found more and more reasons to avoid retiring when he did, was still awake in the living room. The pounding continued. He heard her unlatch the door and open it.

A thick, husky voice spoke. "Your daughter."

"Nyrah?" Saida exclaimed.

"She's asking for you. The baby is—"

Alpha threw his feet over the side of the bed. "Saida?" He slipped on his tunic, crossed to the bedroom door, and opened it. "Saida, who is—" He came to a stop.

A redheaded Breaker with scraggly goatee stood shivering in the doorway. He was breathing hard, plumes of breath encircled his head. He had the good sense not to enter the house, though his presence on the porch alone would have called for payment.

Saida turned to her husband. "It's Nyrah! She's given birth. But the baby, he's—"

"Baby?" Alpha asked.

"A boy," the Breaker said. "But somethin's wrong. And the doctor won't come to the camp this time of night."

"Hold on." Saida brushed past Alpha and grabbed her wool cloak from the bedroom.

"Saida."

She ignored him and returned, buttoning it. "When was he born?"

"Couple hours ago. He ain't good. Nyrah, she keeps callin' for you. She keeps—"

Alpha repeated his warning: "Saida."

She turned on him. "She needs me! Our girl needs her mother!"

If he had a response, the fury in her eyes stopped him.

"No one's asking you to dirty your holy hands, but that's my daughter!"

"No," Alpha said.

"Yes! And my grandson. Our grandson. And I won't sit back and do nothing. Not for the love of you, or Programmer, or anybody else!" She turned to the Breaker. "Let's go."

The man hesitated, looked to Alpha.

"It's not his decision!" Saida exclaimed. "She asked for me. Not him. Me! Let's go!"

The Breaker nodded and turned. Saida pulled up her hood and followed him into the night.

Alpha stood a long moment, feeling the cold rushing into the room... until resolve set in. He turned and headed back to the bedroom, grabbing his cloak. By the time he arrived on the porch, Saida had long disappeared. But he knew where the camp was. He'd never been there, no Council Member had ever been there, but he knew, they all knew. He moved down the steps and into the night.

It was too cold for any citizen to be outdoors. He held his hands to his mouth, breathing into them, using the heat to warm his face. Soon he was outside the village and on the rural road. The frozen mud crackled under his sandals. Eventually he crested the ridge and the camp came into view. By then he was shivering hard.

He entered the grounds, saw men and women standing outside their shelters, trying in vain to warm themselves around small, pitiful fires. Hollow-eyed and gaunt, their bright and gay colors belied their worn and weary bodies. Some stepped back as he approached. The drunk, and there were many, barely noticed or didn't care.

Within moments he heard muffled, choking cries. They came from a lean-to whose opening was covered by a thin blanket. A fire smoldered in front of it, with a Breaker kneeling before the flames, adding twigs and coaxing it along.

"No!" the voice screamed from inside. "Please ..."

Other Breakers glanced to the shelter, traded looks, but they did not move.

"Nooo..."

Alpha approached the shelter's opening. The Breaker at the fire spotted him and quickly rose to block his path. Alpha looked up at the big man. The Breaker did not speak, only shook his head.

The screaming continued.

Again Alpha tried to pass and again the man stopped him, making it clear there would be no admittance.

But that was his daughter. He would not desert his daughter. He turned and crossed to the fire. He knelt down and pretended to warm himself. He would wait. And if there was an opening he would find it.

The screaming rose to a shriek, then abruptly stopped. A moment later it was replaced by quiet, heartbreaking sobs.

Alpha closed his eyes and began to pray.

* * *

"Look out," Kallab shouted. "Look out, coming through!"

Men and women stepped aside as he escorted Nicholas past the shelters. Some gave nods of recognition. Others couldn't care less. Some fell in behind and followed.

Meanwhile, the protests from the lab rang loudly inside Nicholas's head:

You must not interfere.

Come on, bro, we talked about this!

"The baby's dead," Nicholas whispered under his breath. "I can help."

"Step back!" Kallab yelled. "Coming through!"

No more transference! We agreed!

"It's Nyrah's baby," he argued. "Alpha's grandchild."

She'll have others.

The debate had begun the moment he received word of the child's death. Its intensity grew as he ignored their protests and made his way through the camp. The one voice, his own, remained calm and rational. The other, his brother's, was outraged.

Where will I get the power?

"You'll find it."

"Coming through!"

The balance, the program's integrity. We've discussed the logic.

But there was the deeper logic. Nicholas was certain now. Just as there were deeper truths within the Law, there were deeper truths within the logic.

They arrived at the lean-to. Nicholas spotted Alpha standing near the fire. They connected only for a moment, but the hope and shame in Alpha's eyes spoke volumes.

Kallab pulled the blanket aside and Nicholas stooped to enter.

Nyrah lay on a mat in the center of the room, covered in quilts. She was shivering and lit only by a flickering oil lamp. Her skin glistened with sweat and her black hair was plastered to her face. Saida sat cradling her daughter's head on her lap, wiping her face with a cloth. Dortha stood with another woman in the shadows. And at the foot of the mat, placed in a small wooden crate, lay the baby.

This is insane, Travis's voice shouted. *I'll stop you. I'll put an end to this whole thing right now.*

Nyrah opened her eyes. Recognizing Nicholas, she gave an involuntary sob.

"Shh." Saida stroked her face. "Shh ..."

This serves no purpose.

Kallab, who had knelt and looked inside the crate, turned to Nicholas and slowly shook his head.

Nicholas turned to the others. "Clear the—" His voice caught with emotion and he tried again. "Clear the room."

Kallab rose. "What?"

"I want everyone to leave but Nyrah and her mother."

Kallab traded looks with Saida, then with Dortha and the other woman.

Come on, man!

"Now. I want everyone out. Now."

Reluctantly, the two women turned and ducked out of the lean-to. Kallab was the last to leave. He hovered a moment at the opening. "I'll be right outside, if you need me."

Nicholas gave no answer and Kallab stepped out to join the others.

Now it was just the three of them. And the baby.

I understand your feelings, his lab voice reasoned, *but this is not a solution.*

He crossed to the crate and lowered to his knees. Even as he did, he felt his fingers and hands suddenly grow numb. It had to be Travis. He was trying to stop him, to paralyze him and shut him down. If Nicholas could not touch the child, he could not transfer his energy. It was a smart decision and he would have done the same.

Quickly, Nicholas changed plans. Without speaking, he pulled his robe up over his head. Saida gasped, averting her eyes from his nakedness.

"Remove the child's blanket," he told her. As he spoke, he lay on his back, stretching out beside Nyrah on the straw mat. "Place him facedown upon my chest."

Saida hesitated, confused.

"Spread him on top of me. Quickly."

What you are doing? his brother shouted.

He knew exactly what he was doing. It was one thing to paralyze his hands, but they could not paralyze his torso—his chest, lungs, heart. Not without killing him.

"Hurry!"

Saida raised the limp child from the crate.

"Stretch out his arms. Stretch—" Suddenly Nicholas's mouth lost feeling. His lips and tongue could no longer speak. But that was okay, they were too late.

This is absurd!

Nicholas watched as Saida laid the baby on top of him, spreading out its tiny arms and legs, pressing its cold chest and belly against his own.

We will not allow—

He concentrated, focusing his energy, directing it up into his chest. Heat began radiating from his ribs, his sternum. He could feel Travis shutting down other areas of his body—his legs, his arms, his face. It was even growing difficult to think.

But it made no difference.

The voices continued to protest, but they were too late.

His chest was on fire. It became difficult to breathe. Colors around him faded. The light from the lamp dimmed. His lids became impossibly heavy. He closed them, only for a second. But when he tried reopening them, he couldn't. Now there were only the voices.

You have not weighed the consequences!

Stop it, bro. Stop it now!

But even they faded. His thoughts became thick, sludgy. He was losing consciousness. And then, just before he was gone, he heard off in the distance, far, far away, the faint sound of a crying baby.

* * *

"Idiot!" Travis shouted as he continued working the controls.

"Will he survive?" Nicholas asked. He caught himself

leaning over the console for support and with effort rose back up.

"I've shut everything down 'cept his vitals."

Nicholas looked up to the monitor as Saida lifted the crying baby from his counterpart's chest. Tears of joy streamed down her face.

"Anyone ever accuse you of being a stubborn cuss?" Travis said.

"Is he going to be okay?" Nicholas repeated.

"Good thing it was a baby. Anything bigger would have killed him." For the first time, Travis glanced over to his brother. "You look like crap."

"I look better than I feel."

"Just emotions, don't sweat it. Nothing beats good ol'-fashioned empathy."

Nicholas ignored him. "What do you propose now?"

"I guess we restore him ... again"

"You have the power for that?"

Travis motioned to the screen. "They do. But things are gonna get weird, I'll tell you that."

"What will they lose?"

"Background info. Mountains, hills, any depth of vision that's not essential." Travis pulled out a roll of mints and bit one off.

"And this time you'll lock him out. For good."

"All extra powers will be gone. Bye-bye, baby, bye-bye."

The statement gave Nicholas some comfort, but not enough. There was still the truth they'd seen displayed in Orib's living room. The toxicity of Law. To continue down the current path would prove an exercise in futility—with or without his double's constant meddling. It was time to regroup, to reevaluate their approach. "We need a serious, sit-down discussion."

"What good will it do? Your boy's got major issues."

Nicholas shook his head. "He's just distracted. Is there some way to isolate him from all this emotional input? Can we bring him back into our world so he can think more clearly?"

Travis looked at him and cocked his head.

"What?"

"We're real, bro." He motioned to the screen. "He's just pixels and teraflops."

Nicholas glanced away, embarrassed at the oversight. Another idea surfaced. "If you can't bring him here to meet us, can we meet him?"

"Like in a dream?"

"It might take more than a dream. Like you said, I'm a stubborn cuss. Can you make it more real, more substantive?"

"Such as ..."

"He hears our voices; can you tweak the program so he sees us?"

"Audio and visual," Travis said. "Like a vision or something?"

"Can you do that?"

"I can do anything, you know that."

Nicholas nodded. "Then do it."

Travis turned back to the console and began working as Nicholas limped toward the back counter for some water. On second thought, he opted for juice. Whatever had happened on that screen had taken more out of him than he'd thought. But he'd no sooner opened the refrigerator and pulled out a bottle of apple juice than he heard banging on the door at the top of the stairs.

"Nicholas?" a voice shouted. "Travis?"

"Annie," Nicholas said.

The banging continued. "Anybody down there?"

Travis frowned, then reached into a drawer and pulled out a small handgun.

"What are you doing with that?" Travis set the gun on the console beside him and continued entering data. "Just in case she's not alone."

CHAPTER 20

WITHIN FIFTY MINUTES Annie had arrived at the remains of the compound. The car had barely slid to a stop before she was out the door calling, "Rusty! Rusty!"

The smell of smoke and burnt wood made it difficult to breathe. Or maybe it was her memories of the carnage. Probably both.

"Rusty!"

The sun was low and would be setting soon. She picked her way over the debris, stumbling more than once and nearly falling. She headed to the back hillside where the laboratory had been and called his name again.

Once she arrived at the hill, she worked her way along its side. The door had to be there somewhere. She saw a man's shoe sticking from a pile of rubble. She kicked aside the burnt wood and spotted a charred leg, its pants bubbled and melted into the flesh. Her stomach lurched, and she turned to the side and vomited. She wiped her mouth, but doubled over and vomited again. She dropped to her knees and retched a third time. That's when she saw the glint of reflection. Rising to her feet, she started toward it. It was the door. She arrived and banged on the blackened steel.

"Nicholas? Travis? Anybody down there?"

A moment later she heard an electronic click and a bolt unlocking. She stepped back as the steel door scraped open.

"Nicholas!" Before she could stop herself, she threw her arms around him. He patiently endured the outburst, may have even returned a slight embrace of his own. Only after they had separated did she see how worn and tired he looked. Then, of course, there was his shaved head.

"Your hair. What happened to your hair?"

"Long story."

He opened the door wider and she stepped inside.

"Is Rusty here?"

"Here?" Nicholas asked. "Of course not."

The door thudded shut behind them.

"Is she alone?" Travis called from below.

"Yes."

They started down the girder steps. Because of Nicholas's bad leg, she offered to help, but he would have none of it. "Why would the boy be here?" he asked.

"He left a message with my mother. Said he was heading up here to try and find ..."

She slowed to a stop as her eyes fell upon the main monitor. There, on a large boulder, at the top of a muddy hill, sat an exact replica of the man she had just met at the door. Absolutely identical, except for the hair.

She stepped from the stairs. "That's ..." She turned to Nicholas, then back to the screen. "Incredible."

"What can I say?" Travis shrugged. "Everything's exact to the smallest detail. Least it was."

Nicholas turned back to Annie. "You're certain Rusty is coming here?"

"He traced my cell phone. The one the guards took, before they were ... before they..." she let the phrase drop.

"Bright kid." Travis rose and moved to a small video camera attached to a tripod.

"Actually, it's his babysitter, she's an electronics wiz."

"If she's pretty, tell her to call me," Travis said as he looked through the viewfinder. "I have an immediate opening."

Nicholas ignored him. "If the phone's in the rubble upstairs and if the boy is tracking it, don't worry, he'll show."

Annie gave an appreciative nod, then threw a look back up the steps.

"Actually, it's a good thing you dropped by," Travis said, focusing the camera on them.

Still sensing her concern, Nicholas added, "As soon as we finish our conference, I'll help you look."

"Smile," Travis said.

Annie glanced over and saw a tiny red light above the camera lens. She turned to the big-screen monitor and to her surprise saw both Nicholas and herself standing on the hill next to the onscreen Nicholas, who seemed oblivious to their presence.

She stepped closer. "Travis, what are you—" But as she moved, she stepped out of the picture.

"Back," Travis ordered. "You need to stay in frame so he can see you."

She obeyed and her image returned to the screen. It felt awkward looking at a duplicate of herself. She was used to seeing her reverse image from a mirror.

"Hope he's still got a strong heart," Travis quipped as he crossed to the console. He hit a single key and instantly the onscreen Nicholas saw them both and gave a start.

"Easy, bro," Travis said as he stepped forward and also entered the frame.

The on-screen Nicholas rose and stepped closer. He reached out his hand and waved. It passed through their projected images. "A hologram?" he asked.

"Sort of," Travis said. He turned to Annie and the in-lab Nicholas. "Say something, guys."

The in-lab Nicholas gave a simple nod.

Annie cleared her throat. "Hi, uh, Nicholas."

"A little louder," Travis said, "so the mic can pick you up."

"Hi, Nicholas," she repeated. "How are things?"

The on-screen image looked at her and smiled. "Better, now that you're here." The comment caught her off guard. Before she could respond, he motioned to his double. "Nice haircut."

"Thanks," the in-lab Nicholas replied. "I did it just for you."

The on-screen Nicholas turned to Annie. "Where's Rusty? Did you find him?"

"He and Fran traced my cell phone. I'm guessing they're heading up here."

"Here?"

"Listen, bro," Travis said, "we got that covered. Right now we need to have ourselves a little talk."

"Yes," the on-screen image agreed. "Absolutely." He paused to look out over the camp. "What happened to the mountains? Weren't there mountains over there?"

"Not anymore," Travis answered. "You been a bad little boy."

The image nodded. "I know. And I apologize. But as I told you—"

"I know, I know," Travis interrupted. "'We gotta be there, we gotta feel it.'"

The in-lab Nicholas spoke up. "We've removed your ability to make any more transfers."

His image nodded and sadly returned his gaze to the

camp. "Not that it matters."

Annie glanced to the group. Everyone seemed to understand but her. "What do you mean?" she asked.

The image turned to her. "Our attempts have not succeeded at any level."

"Why not?"

The in-lab Nicholas answered, "We thought by explaining the thinking behind the Law, we'd better equip them to fight the virus."

"And?"

He shook his head. "Those who follow the Law and resist the virus are just as sick as those who have given in to it."

Travis pulled out a piece of gum and popped it into his mouth. "Religion at its finest."

The on-screen Nicholas agreed. "Our results will be no different from any of the other models we've tried ... eventual self-annihilation."

The in-lab Nicholas added, "The Law may slow the deterioration and extend their existence a bit longer... but self-destruction is still self-destruction."

"Bottom line," Travis said, "their world is screwed."

Nicholas added more slowly, "As are we."

Annie paused a moment, then made the connection. "Because their model is a duplicate of our own."

Travis threw the on-screen image a look. "Except for the occasional magic trick or two ... yeah."

The on-screen Nicholas began shaking his head. "I'm not so certain."

The group looked to him, waiting for more.

"What if those magic tricks are part of the solution?"

"What's going through that little digital head of yours now?" Travis asked.

"I've been giving this some serious thought." He hesitated, unsure how to continue.

"Go ahead," in-lab Nicholas said. "Let's hear it."

The image cleared his throat and began. "Instead of just telling them to overcome the virus ... what if we transfer the negative effects of following it?"

"You've been doing that," Travis said.

"Exactly, but on a singular basis. What if we did it over an entire lifetime? For anybody who was interested?"

"You'd have total chaos," Travis argued. "There'd be no penalty, no order. Nothing to restrain them from giving in to the virus again and again. They'd see it as carte blanche."

"I don't think so. From what we've seen, there may be enough appreciation, enough gratitude, that they start resisting the virus—not because they have to, but because they want to."

"Because they know we're picking up the tab?" Travis asked.

"Yes."

"Talk about wishful thinking."

"No, listen. Wasn't that what happened with Alpha? Wasn't it our personal contact and help that motivated him to build the Temple? Wasn't that why he dedicated his life to honoring us and treating his fellow citizens as sacred?"

The group grew quiet, silently digesting the thought.

"So, what are you saying?" the in-lab Nicholas asked. "Instead of resisting the virus to avoid punishment, they'd be resisting it out of... appreciation, gratitude?"

"That's right," his on-screen image said. "It would no longer become a matter of the Law. It would become a matter of the heart."

More silence followed.

"Relationship instead of Law," Annie quietly concluded.

"Precisely."

"Well," Travis said, "no matter what you call it, it's still impossible."

"Why?" the on-screen Nicholas asked. "It's the same transference of energy we've used before. But instead of removing the results of one breakage, you remove it over an entire lifetime."

"And replace it with what?" in-lab Nicholas asked. "We still need to balance the equation."

"It's identical to the healings," his on-screen image replied. "We replace their payment with energy from my life."

"Come on, man, get real," Travis argued. "We've got nearly a thousand citizens here. You have any idea how much power that would take?"

"We'd only do it for those who ask."

"Because we're still dealing with free will," in-lab Nicholas said.

"Correct."

"But the power," Travis repeated. "You have any idea how much it would take?"

"A lot?"

"Nearly everything."

"Nearly, but not all?"

Travis shook his head. "You've felt the pain of absorbing a few of the virus's effects. You got any clue what it would be like to experience it for multiple people?"

"I lost consciousness with the baby," on-screen Nicholas said. "I imagine the same would happen with the people."

"Yeah, until you die," Travis said.

"Unless . . ." In-lab Nicholas turned to Travis. "We've always transferred energy into him after the fact."

"Yeah, so?"

"So ... would it be possible to transfer it into him before? Or during?"

Travis sighed in exasperation. "This is insane. The whole idea was to create a world like ours. This would eliminate any similarity."

"Not necessarily . . ." All eyes turned to Annie as she spoke. "A Creator paying for His creation's sins? Am I the only one who sees a parallel here? I don't know about you guys, but from my perspective, that makes all the sense in the world."

"No, Annie." In-lab Nicholas shook his head. "That makes no sense in anybody's world. There is absolutely no logic to it."

"Unless ..." the on-screen image said.

The group turned back to him.

"Unless there's a deeper logic—what I've been experiencing here, what I've been trying to explain." He turned to the in-lab Nicholas. "And what you are either unwilling or incapable of understanding."

Nicholas stared at the image a long moment. Not in defiance or anger, but in quiet evaluation. He pushed up his glasses. Then, glancing away, he looked at the ground, deep in thought.

Annie turned back to the on-screen Nicholas. "And this is something you'd want to do? This transference?"

"Want to?" The image forced a laugh. "Hardly." He paused to look out over the camp. "But unless there is some alternative ..."

"They're just a program," Travis argued. "Bits and bytes."

The on-screen Nicholas turned to his brother and quietly answered, "Not for me. For me they're real. Thanks to your handiwork ... they're family."

Once again there was a long moment of silence. Travis took a deep breath and blew it out.

"So what do you think?" the on-screen Nicholas asked.

"I think it's still absurd," Travis said.

"But is it possible?"

"That's a boatload of power, bro. And to be running it all through you ... I don't know."

The in-lab Nicholas turned to him. "But it is possible?"

Travis hesitated. "Let me noodle on it. Answer a few pesky questions like where and when and how."

"Do you have the resources?" the on-screen Nicholas persisted.

"It's off-the-chart crazy. And I'm only gonna consider it till you brainiacs find a real—"

"Do you have the resources?"

Travis gave another long, weary sigh. "Yeah. If push comes to shove, I'll get it wherever I can. But it's gonna be—"

Suddenly they heard the opening bars to "Light My Fire." Travis checked his front pockets, then his back. Annie saved him the trouble. She pulled the stolen cell phone from her jacket and handed it to him.

He took it and answered, "Yeah?" His face clouded. "Hang on." He passed the phone back to her. "It's for you."

She took it. "Hello?"

"Mom?"

Her heart leaped. "Rusty?" The connection was bad, but she clearly recognized his voice over the static. "Where are you?"

"Where are you?" Rusty asked. "We're outside some burned- down place. It really stinks."

"You're here? At the compound?"

"We're in the mountains, it's all burnt up. Mom, Fran's—"

"She's there with you?"

There was no answer.

"Rusty?"

Nothing.

"Rusty, are you there?"

The static stopped. She hesitated, then shoved the phone back to Travis and spun toward the stairs.

"Where you going?" he called.

"My son—he's here!"

PART IV

CHAPTER 21

"RUSTY?" ANNIE FOLLOWED the base of the charred hill, once again picking her way over burnt wood and crumbled plaster. "Fran?" Through the blackened timbers, she spotted two cars. Her rental and, directly behind that, a Lincoln Town Car. She moved faster, stumbling over the rubble, until she rounded a broken retaining wall and came face-to-face with Matthew Hostetler.

"Hello, Annie."

She caught her breath and stepped back. Only then did she see the gun in his hand. More angry than frightened, she demanded, "Where's my son?"

"Great kid. Smart as a whip."

She started at the man until he raised the gun and brought her to a stop. Struggling to contain her rage, she said, "If you've hurt him, I swear to God I'll—"

"Oh, he's fine. Your son is fine."

"Where is he? What have you done with him?"

"First things first. Where exactly is this laboratory?"

"What?"

"I know it's here."

Pieces started fitting together. "You're with the group that attacked us?"

"No."

She frowned. "Then what? I don't understand."

"Those were the big boys. I'm a much smaller fish ... but just as determined. And not so stupid as to think your friends actually moved their operation." Any trace of the thoughtful, sensitive Matthew Hostetler was gone.

"What do you want?" Her voice was higher, thinner than she intended.

"Your boyfriend and his brother are a couple of popular guys. People want to meet them, assist them. And you're going to help me make the introductions."

She hesitated, unsure how to respond.

"I know it's here." He kicked aside a chunk of debris. "But folks have made such a mess of things. Still, I'm sure it's down below somewhere, all nice and tidy." He looked back up to her. "And you're going to help me find it."

"Or what? You'll shoot me?" She bit her lip, regretting the words before she'd finished them.

"Shoot you?" He chuckled. "That would defeat the whole purpose, don't you think?"

She stood her ground, her anger returning, fueling her courage, or foolishness.

"No," he continued. "There are better ways to solicit your help. According to the medical records at your son's preschool, he's allergic to bees."

Coldness gripped her gut. "Where is he? What have you done with him?"

"He's fine. He's right over there in the car with my colleague."

Annie turned toward the Town Car.

"I believe you two have met."

"Fran? Is he with Fran?"

"I'm afraid Fran was not all that helpful."

Annie's mind raced.

"In any case, we found a local beekeeper—not real diffi-cult, considering all the orange groves in the area—and we managed to collect a few." He pulled back his sleeve, revealing a welt on his forearm. "Not without a casualty or two, I might add."

"Rusty? Did he—"

"He's fine. They're sealed up in a jar, all nice and safe. Not happy, but safe. Unless, of course, for some reason you choose not to help."

* * *

THE CONVERSATION WITH TRAVIS, Annie, and Nicholas's in-lab counterpart continued to fill Nicholas's mind. So many questions. Even if Travis could work the program, what if nobody in the community took him up on the offer? Worse yet, what if those who did turned into self-righteous hypocrites like the Council Members? And what of those who might use the offer as a free ride so they could keep on breaking the Law? Granted, the act of compassion should have the same effect as it did upon Alpha. But still...

Then there were the other issues—his pain and possible death. Ironically, death didn't frighten him as much as pain. After all, his counterpart would still continue to live, and that would be the same as if he did... wouldn't it? But the pain. It had been unbearable in the past. He had no reason to doubt it would be any different—at least until he lost conscious-ness. But with that amount of transference, losing conscious-ness should be immediate. At least he hoped. All this, of course depending upon Travis's ability to transfer energy ahead of the event, or during it. If he could accomplish that, then Nicholas would merely be a conduit and the exchange should be smooth and effortless.

At least he hoped. The thoughts continually churned in his head. His only relief, his only peace, came when he stopped to consider the impact of his actions. Not only upon Alpha, Nyrah, and the baby... but on all the others in the community. He had not exaggerated when he told Travis they were family. By his brother's own admission, Mikey had been the model for every one of them. And in every one of them he could see a small portion of himself.

Although these thoughts never ceased, another concern now occupied him. He was lumbering across the manicured grounds of the Temple. Up ahead, a crowd of citizens had already gathered, pressing around the Grid for a better look. On the stage beside it, several Council Members stood, solemnly presiding.

Earlier, at camp, Kallab and Big Red had raced in and told him that Enforcers had arrested young Dortha. They were heading out to rescue her and invited him to come along. Nicholas had joined them and did his best to keep up, but after one hundred yards of thick, gummy clay clinging to his sandals he was definitely feeling his age. After two hundred yards he had to stop and catch his breath, letting them continue without him.

By the time he arrived, the men were already at the Grid, their long knives drawn, holding back a couple of hulking Enforcers. Directly behind them, wrists strapped to the iron mesh, hung Dortha.

As Nicholas approached, he heard a familiar voice shouting at the Breakers from the stage. "If you interfere, your penalty will be equal to hers." It was Orib. Beside him stood several other Members. Among them was Learis, the old man with the white beard, and Alpha.

He continued working his way through the crowd until Learis spotted him and called, "You!"

Heads turned. There was a murmur of recognition. People stepped aside, allowing him to pass.

"Have you come to see justice served as well?" Learis shouted.

Alpha raised his eyes to meet Nicholas's. There was no missing his recognition.

Still breathing hard, Nicholas arrived at the front of the crowd. Carefully, he stepped past the two burly Enforcers to join Kallab and Big Red. Dortha twisted on the Grid behind them, disheveled and frightened. "Get me out of here," she cried. "Cut me loose!" Nicholas turned to the stage and shouted, "What are her charges?"

A younger Council Member answered, "What concern is that of yours?"

"I'm her friend."

Orib stepped forward, trying to take charge. "Friend? Does that mean you have committed adultery with her as well?"

Nicholas's face flushed in anger. His eyes shot a look to Alpha, who stared sadly after his son.

Kallab leaned to Nicholas. "Be careful, they're tricksters of words."

Nicholas called back to the stage, "Why do you insist upon only seeing evil?"

"Easy, friend," Big Red warned. "This is our battle, not yours."

But Nicholas had witnessed enough. He'd tried diplomacy. He'd tried reasoning. He'd witnessed more than enough. He continued, "Do you only see evil because that's what fills your own heart?"

Learis bristled. "How dare you? She is an adulterer. The Law clearly states adulterers must pay for their breaking."

"And what about you?" Nicholas shouted back. "Do you never think of committing adultery? Does it never cross your mind ... or are you too old?"

The crowd chuckled. The man's face reddened.

Nicholas motioned to Dortha. "Look at that beautiful body. So young. So lovely. So enticing."

Learis's face darkened as Council Members exchanged looks.

Orib came to the old man's defense. "Thinking and doing are not the same."

Nicholas shook his head. "No. Your mind controls both. You cannot be one person on the inside and another on the outside." The crowd began to mumble.

Nicholas turned to them. "These men before you are actors. They strut on their stage and pretend to be what they cannot be. On the outside they look clean and perfect, but on the inside their sickness is no less than this girl's."

The crowd listened intently. Some began to nod. Taking advantage of the distraction, Kallab turned and cut the leather restraints holding Dortha's wrists.

If the Members were angry before, they were downright livid now.

"How dare you defile the Law?" Learis shouted. "How dare you defile this holy Temple?"

Big Red called to Nicholas, "It's time to go."

But the Members weren't the only ones angry. Nicholas could barely contain his rage. "Do you honestly think Programmer cares one whit about a building? Do you think that's what Programmer values?"

"Uh"—Kallab stepped closer—"fun as it's been, we've gotta go."

Nicholas gestured to the Temple. "This building is just a building! You are the ones I care about!" He swept his arm across the crowd. "All of you!"

Blood pounded in his ears. It had been years since he felt such passion and he wasn't about to back down now.

He spotted the life units on a table before the stage and crossed to them. Reluctantly, Kallab and Big Red followed, Dortha in tow between them. Their knives were drawn, holding back the two Enforcers who remained just out of reach, looking for an opening.

"But you!" Nicholas shouted up at the stage. "You are more concerned with your holiness than their welfare!" He reached down and picked up a unit. "You exploit the very ones I instructed you to honor!"

In disgust he threw the unit into the crowd. Those nearest scrambled for it.

One of the Enforcers made his move, but Kallab sliced the air with his knife, holding him back. Big Red crouched into a fighting position, keeping the other Enforcer in check.

"Stop it!" Learis cried. "I order you to stop this blasphemy!"

But Nicholas was in no mood to listen. He reached for another unit. "You ignore the very thought behind the Law." He leaned back and threw the unit into the crowd. More people dove for it. "You're so focused on its letter that you've become its slave."

Kallab spoke into Nicholas's ear. "Time to fly."

"The Law is the Law," Learis yelled over the commotion.

Other Members agreed. "The Law is the Law."

"No." Nicholas reached for two more units and threw them into the crowd. The people lunged and fought for them. Dortha joined Nicholas's side. She picked up one and then another, throwing them both. The crowd became even more agitated.

"The Law kills," Nicholas shouted. "By itself, it is a murderer. Don't you understand? It is the spirit behind it that enables you to survive! Survival! That's all I've ever wanted for you!"

In his anger, he grabbed the table and tried to overturn it, but it was too heavy. Dortha reached to help and, with her effort, the two finally toppled it. Dozens of life units tumbled to the ground. The crowd scrambled after them, shouting, yelling, crawling over one another.

"Now!" Kallab grabbed Nicholas's arm. Big Red took the other. "We're flying now!"

They moved into the crowd. The Enforcers tried to follow but several citizens stepped in to block them. Only when they reached the back did Nicholas take a final look over his shoulder. And there, amid the noise and chaos, he spotted Alpha standing on the stage. Sorrow filled the Law Giver's eyes as he watched in silence.

* * *

"You can't leave now," Travis called over his shoulder. "Things are finally heating up."

Nicholas stopped at the foot of the girder stairs and turned to his brother. "Annie should have been back by now. If Rusty was outside, they should be back."

"But you're gonna miss all the fireworks."

Nicholas frowned, not understanding.

Travis motioned to the screen. "I think your alter ego has stumbled on the answer—the how, when, and where of transferring all that power."

"And that is ..."

Travis motioned to the screen. "Right here. The Grid."

Nicholas looked back to the monitor.

Travis continued, "If you're going to make the exchange, this is the logical place, if logic still has anything to do with it."

Nicholas continued staring at the screen. Of course. The Grid. Why hadn't he thought of it? Maybe his alternate had. Without a word, he gripped the rail and pulled himself up the steps. It wasn't easy, leaving the events that were unfolding on the monitor. And he wouldn't have left for anyone except Annie and her son.

The past hours had been exhausting, to say the least— watching and living two separate lives at the same time. Seeing a version of himself stripped of its defenses as layer after layer was peeled back. Watching the raw vulnerability he had worked so long and hard to protect being exposed.

He grimaced at the pain in his leg and paused halfway up the steps, waiting for it to subside.

But, of course, the on-screen version of himself was no longer himself. Not anymore. Oddly enough, it reminded him of his student drinking days. Part of him, the sober, rational Nicholas, standing off to the side, watching and shaking his head over the impulsive, out-of-control one. Standing outside and, in this case, if he was honest... envying.

Because as much as he understood what his alter ego was doing in Alpha's world, he knew he could never achieve it in his own. Those days had long passed. It saddened him, knowing he would never be able to experience that depth of emotion, that intensity of love. It saddened him, but it didn't surprise him. And with that fact, he reached for the railing and continued pulling himself up the stairs, one painful step after another.

* * *

"HERE IT COMES," Nyrah said with a sigh as she held the baby with one hand and poured a cup of wine with the other. "Now you're gonna tell us all that we have to do."

263

"No, that's my point," Nicholas said. "You won't have to do anything."

Kallab took a stick and poked at the flat, monocolored light that was supposed to be fire. Sparks, now simple pinpoints of brightness, rose and disappeared into a blackness where the stars and moon had once been. Apparently, mountains and hills weren't the only elements Travis had removed from the program.

"So what's the catch?" Kallab asked. His words were growing thick and slurred. It had only been a few hours since they'd returned from the Temple. The celebration had been loud and raucous, the wine abundant. But things were already dying down. Dull fatigue and numbness were once again settling in.

"There is no catch," Nicholas said. "You must simply allow me to do it."

"Allow you?" Dortha asked.

"Yes. You must give me permission, otherwise my hands are tied."

"Permission to pay for our breaking?" Big Red belched skeptically.

"Yes."

The group exchanged looks. Nyrah's baby started to fuss and she gently began to bounce it.

"And what do you get out of the deal?" Dortha asked as she poured herself another cup of wine.

Nicholas replied, "Your survival, your welfare."

Kallab laughed. "Sounds like you get the short end of the stick."

The others chuckled, but Nyrah pursued. "What difference does it make to you whether or not we survive?"

Nicholas hesitated, then turned to her. "In ways you cannot understand, you're all a very real part of me."

She stared back at him, unblinking.

Big Red scratched his beard. "We've tried following Programmer's Laws."

"I'm not—" Nicholas cleared his throat and tried again. "I'm not talking about Laws."

"What's left?" Kallab asked.

"If you let me make payment in your place, we become . . ." Nicholas searched for the word. "Partners. You and I, you and Programmer, form a relationship. And it's that relationship which will help you overcome the virus."

"A relationship with Programmer?" Nyrah asked. "Sounds scary."

"And boring," Dortha added.

"No," Nicholas said, "it's just the opposite. Programmer was the original source of your life. You'd simply be reconnecting with that source so you can live it more fully."

The declaration drew puzzled expressions. He looked about the group, searching for an illustration. Spotting the jar of wine at Nyrah's feet, he motioned to it. "It's like ... replacing that wine with him."

They looked to the jar, some to their own cups. He continued, "That wine is the best your current life has to offer. One of the few joys it can provide. And for a few hours it succeeds. But it is a cheap counterfeit of the real thing. It has a bite and a price you must eventually pay."

"So we have to be like the Council Members now," Kallab said. "Never to drink again."

"No. The Members have their own wine."

The group looked to him with surprise.

"Their wine is the Law."

The surprise turned to looks of confusion.

He pressed on. "But if you let me pay for your breakage, and you enter into a relationship with Programmer, you'll have something much better than wine."

"Better than wine." Big Red lifted his cup in a toast. "I'll drink to that."

Kallab and Dortha chuckled, joining in.

Nicholas continued, "As you come to know Programmer, you won't be living by the Law, but by his thinking behind the Law."

"And when we break it," Nyrah asked, "the Law?"

"We are experts at breaking," Big Red said.

Nicholas leaned forward. "My payment will cover all you have broken and all you will ever break."

"But"—Kallab frowned—"you just said we won't be living by the Law."

"That's right," Nicholas said, excited that Kallab seemed close to understanding. "You won't overcome the virus by trying to live the Law. You'll overcome it by living in relationship."

Kallab sat a moment thinking before his frown slowly faded and dullness again settled over his eyes. Nicholas turned to the others. They appeared equally confused. Or worse, uncaring. He felt a heaviness, a sad sinking feeling.

Bro?

He ignored Travis's voice and continued pursuing his point with the group. "So ... what do you think?" he asked.

Big Red grunted, Dortha fidgeted, obviously hoping for a change in topic. And Nyrah's baby started to cry. Nyrah shifted the child to her other hip as Kallab motioned for a refill. "All this talk about wine is making me thirsty."

"Me too," Dortha said, holding out her cup.

We got it, bro.

Nicholas continued watching the group, hoping against hope for some response. Except for the baby, there was only silence.

We know how to pull it off.

Finally, sadly, Nicholas closed his eyes. He nodded ever so slightly, making it clear he was listening.

It's all figured out. But you better buckle in, cause it's gonna be one crazy ride.

Imperceptibly, he moved his lips. "When?"

Now. The wheels are already in motion. Course, I can stop 'em, if you want.

"Why would I want?"

'Cause it ain't gonna be pretty, bro. Not pretty at all. Now, listen up...

CHAPTER 22

NICHOLAS EXCUSED HIMSELF from the group, and walked about a stone's throw from Nyrah's shelter, where he sat on a boulder carefully considering Travis's plan. As far as he could tell, it made perfect sense. What better place for transference than the Grid? It was the logical choice. Even his in-lab double agreed.

"And the pain?" he asked.

If I got this puppy timed right, I'll be pumping energy into you at the same rate the Grid is sucking it out. Best-case scenario, you'll just be a conduit. No pain, no death.

"And the worst-case?"

Travis did not answer.

"And the worst?"

If you don't pass out you'll experience more pain than you can possibly imagine.

The information hit Nicholas hard. He nodded, rising from the boulder, and began to pace.

It's still your decision, just say the word and it's over.

Nicholas felt perspiration break out on his face. The muscles at the base of his skull began to tighten. It was as if all the doubts and fears he'd been wrestling with were suddenly coming together. No longer was he debating some philosophical model in some classroom. This was real life and, despite Travis's assurances, the possibility of real death. Or worse.

They're on their way, bro. I need to know.

"Right." He nodded. "Right." He continued to pace, his head beginning to throb. There were no guarantees, he knew that. The slightest miscalculation on Travis's part, and the pain would be unbearable. And if they succeeded? Even as a conduit, he wondered if Travis had considered whether his system could really handle all that energy. And to what purpose? Really, what was the reason? So Travis could continue his little experiment? So giant corporations could better exploit people and make more money?

No. It wasn't worth it. He would quit now. No one of importance would care. Granted, it would be a setback for Travis and the others, but it would not be the end of the world.

At least not theirs ...

He heard laughter and looked over to Nyrah's shelter. Once again Dortha was bragging about her exploits at the Grid. Young Breakers had stopped by, hanging on to every word, as she increased her heroics with every telling. He watched Nyrah rocking her child, cooing and speaking to him. He saw Kallab dozing by the fire. Big Red, with his head back, mouth open, snoring loudly.

As he watched, his throat tightened. Could he really give up on them? Could he leave them stranded in a world that only grew darker and more hopeless by the day? And not just the Breakers. What of Orib and his struggles? His young wife's?

What of Alpha?

They'll be here any second, bro.

Nicholas nodded and resumed his pacing, fighting to think through the pounding in his head. Surely there had to be another solution. There had to be another way.

"Travis." He swallowed. "Listen, I—I'm—"

Scared?

"Yes."

You should be.

He closed his eyes, trying to squeeze the pain from his head.

We're talking blue-sky, baby. Uncharted territory. Not some simple raising a kid from the dead.

Nicholas nodded, tripping over a rut in the mud.

But if you're calling it quits, it better be now.

It was growing difficult to breathe. And getting cold. So cold, he had started to shiver.

In or out, bro?

They'd discussed it. This was the only solution. If these people were to survive, this was the only—No! This was not his concern. This was not his responsibility. He wasn't the one who chose the virus. They must pay for their own actions. Cause and effect. They must pay, not him.

In the distance, he heard the snorting of horses. Men's voices.

And even if the plan did succeed, who would tell the rest of the community? He turned back to the camp. Drunks? Murderers? Whores? Even if they understood the plan, let alone accepted it, how could they be trusted? The survival of an entire civilization depending upon them?

"Trav—" His voice caught and he tried again. "Travis?"

Right here.

"I think ..."—he took a breath—"we need to abort."

You sure?

"It's their responsibility. They chose the virus. It's their worry."

So we're talkin' game over?

The baby began to cry and Nicholas looked back to the group. "What will happen to Nyrah? To the others?"

I could fast-forward, but we both know the answer.

The hammering in Nicholas's head grew worse. "And Alpha?"

There was a pause.

"Travis?"

He's failed every model.

"What do you mean? Travis, what are you saying?"

If we start again ... it would have to be from scratch.

Nicholas closed his eyes. The pounding in his head was relentless. A salty brine filled his mouth. He looked back to Nyrah, saw her tenderly cajole her baby. He heard Dortha laugh, watched as the half woman, half girl took another drink, so frightened, so lost.

More brine came and he spat onto the ground.

The baby continued crying and Nyrah began singing to him— softly, gently. So much love here, so much suffering—

He doubled over and retched. He wiped his mouth and rose just in time to see four horses cresting the ridge in front of him.

Another thought surfaced—more unnerving than the others. Even if he survived the ordeal... he would lose. Even if the plan succeeded and the Breakers understood, even if they spread the word and people actually accepted his payment for their breaking ... it would prove his own life back in the other world had been a complete waste. That the God he hated and railed against ever since he killed his son in the plane crash might actually exist. Worst yet, He might actually have cared.

The horses came to a stop and the Enforcers dismounted.

I need a clear yes or no, bro.

And yet. . . He turned back to the camp. If Annie was

right, if there really was a personal God whose model he was inadvertently following, then it might actually be possible to save Alpha and the others. If the compassion her God felt for His creation compelled Him to save it, then maybe, just maybe, Nicholas's own love could do the same for his. Because he did love them. There was little doubt. He had entered that deeper logic and experienced a compassion more intense than he'd ever thought possible.

"You there!" The Enforcers approached, their leathers creaking as they walked.

Their voices were loud enough to startle even Kallab and Big Red from their stupors. The two men staggered to their feet and drew their long knives as the women instinctively huddled closer together.

So are we blowin' this popsicle stand? Travis asked.

The Enforcers strode toward Nicholas. Their leader, a tall muscular man, shouted, "By order of Temple authority, you are under arrest."

Kallab and Big Red broke toward Nicholas.

Spotting them, the Enforcers drew their swords.

"What are you doing?" Kallab yelled. "What are your charges?"

The Enforcers arrived the same time as Kallab and Big Red. Now, both groups stood facing each other, less than three yards apart.

"The charges are heresy and blasphemy."

Yo, bro?

Nicholas's head was exploding, his mind reeling. He no longer trusted his thinking. But, from somewhere, a word rose into his throat. Before he could stop it, he shouted, "No!"

No, we don't continue?

The leader stepped forward and reached for Nicholas's arm. Kallab lunged and, in one swift action, sliced the man's hand. Light spilled from the wound as the leader cried out in surprise. His companions crouched, ready to fight.

"No!" Nicholas shouted. "We will continue!"

Kallab turned to him. "What?"

Nicholas stepped between them. "We will continue fighting ... but not this fight."

Kallab and Big Red traded looks.

"If you fight like this, you will die like this!" Nicholas pointed to the leader. "This man is not your enemy." He turned to the leader and motioned toward Kallab and Big Red. "Nor are they yours. You have another enemy, common to both of you. But we can overcome it. If you let me, we can defeat it."

The men shifted, unsure how to respond.

Nicholas's eyes dropped to the Enforcer's injured hand. He was holding it with his good one, light seeping between his fingers.

"May I see that?" Nicholas asked.

The man scowled.

"I can help."

The Enforcer searched Nicholas's face. He turned to his own men, then to Kallab and Big Red, then back to Nicholas.

"Let me," Nicholas said softly.

The man hesitated. Nicholas nodded in encouragement. Slowly, cautiously, the Enforcer withdrew his good hand and let Nicholas take the injured one.

Oh, brother. He heard Travis sigh. *Hang on.*

There was a flicker of light and then the spread of heat into Nicholas's hands. The Enforcer flinched, started to pull away, but Nicholas held on. The pain was what he expected, sharp and searing. He gritted his teeth so he wouldn't cry out. But even now he feared it might only be a foretaste of what was about to come.

* * *

NICHOLAS LEANED OVER HIS CANE, catching his breath. The afternoon sun had dropped behind a wall of fog pushing in from the Pacific. There were no shadows now, just dull light that would turn to darkness within the hour. He scanned the charred remains of the compound for Annie and the boy, but saw no one. He straightened himself and was about to continue when he heard voices— Annie's and a man's.

He hobbled toward them, picking his way through the rubble. Two cars came into view—a cheap compact, most likely Annie's rental, and a black Town Car that was disquietingly familiar. He slowed.

The voices drifted to him from beyond a retaining wall thirty feet away. Instead of directly approaching it, he changed course and made a wider arc until he could see around it from a distance. Annie came into view first. She was followed by the Homeland Security Agent who had assaulted him just a few nights earlier. He was holding a gun.

Nicholas drew back out of sight. He slowly eased forward again, this time searching for Rusty. But there was no sign of him. So, if he wasn't with his mother and if he wasn't out in the open...

Nicholas looked back to the cars, the likeliest possibility.

As silently as he could, he backed up, then circled around, doing his best to keep the wall between himself and the couple. It was a much longer route and he could feel it in his leg, but if he wanted to remain unseen it was his only choice. By the time he reached Annie's rental, the pain in his thigh was unbearable.

He looked into the vehicle. Nobody was there.

With a cautious eye on Annie and the man, he moved to the Town Car. Only then did he notice it was idling. The windows were heavily tinted and he saw no movement... just a strip of blond hair through a two-inch opening of the front passenger window.

"Who's there?" a woman's voice demanded from inside.

The window rolled down and Nicholas limped closer. It was Rebecca. She wore a pair of large octagon sunglasses over bandaged eyes. Her right cheek was dark purple, her nose taped and swollen. Another bandage covered part of her neck.

"You're ... alive," Nicholas said.

She turned to his voice. "Hello, Doctor. For the most part, yes, I suppose I am."

He heard banging on the tinted glass partition between the front and back seats. A child's muffled shouts. "Nicholas ..."

He looked but saw only shadowy movement. "Is that Rusty?"

"Nicholas..."

He stepped to the back door and saw the boy's face pressed against the window, pounding his little fist. "Help me!"

Nicholas tried the handle, but it was locked. He moved back to Rebecca. "Where's his babysitter?"

"She wasn't as cooperative as we'd hoped."

Keeping himself calm, he concluded, "You and your boyfriend are looking for the lab."

She adjusted her glasses. "As you may have noticed, my visual resources are somewhat limited."

He paused, evaluating the situation. "And you are doing this because..."

"For the money, of course. What we'll sell the program for on the open market will be astronomical."

"That's all? Simply the money?"

"That's all there is. Survival of the fittest. Anything else is fantasy and wishful thinking."

Nicholas didn't miss the barb. The boy resumed banging on the partition, shouting.

"You introduced the virus," Nicholas said.

"A stopgap until we got the program." She almost smiled. "I hear it's been keeping you busy."

"Nicholas ..." Rusty cried.

"Let me have the boy."

"Not until we have the program."

"And if Travis refuses?"

Rebecca raised a canning jar she'd been holding in her lap. It was sealed. Inside, crawling on the glass, were nearly two dozen bees.

"I don't understand."

"Of course you do." She gave the jar a shake and then another, until the bees buzzed so angrily he could hear them through the glass. "It's called incentive."

Without warning, Nicholas lunged at her through the open window. But his leg betrayed him, giving her time to pull away. He reached farther inside, catching the arm of her coat. She slipped out of the sleeve and dove for the steering wheel, where she began honking the horn.

Annie and the agent spun toward them. The agent hesitated, then started for the car ... until Annie leaped at him and tackled him to the ground.

* * *

"I DON'T THINK this is such a good idea," the jailer, barely out of adolescence, said. He remained at Alpha's side, guiding him down the dimly lit stone corridor.

"I'll be fine."

"But—did you check with the captain of the guard?"

Alpha smiled. "I'll be fine, son."

"Then ... well, all right, then."

They arrived at a heavy door made of thick wooden planks. The youth slipped a key into the lock. Tumblers clicked into place and he pushed it open, its hinges groaning. Alpha stepped past the young man and entered the cool room. The only light filtered in from a tiny window high above their heads. The stranger sat by himself on a crude bench in front of a wooden table.

Alpha turned to the youth. "Thank you."

"I'll be outside. You need anything, just holler." For the stranger's benefit he added, "Enforcers are just down the hall, they can be here in a second. And they won't be nearly as kind as—"

"Thank you," Alpha repeated. "We'll only be a few minutes. Call us when the Council is ready."

"Well, all right, then." Reluctantly, the youth stepped outside. He pulled the door behind him and it closed with a dull, echoing thud.

Alpha turned back to the stranger. The man seemed oddly serene for a person about to appear before the Council.

"May I get you anything?" Alpha asked. "Water? Tea? Do you need any medical attention? Sometimes Enforcers can be a bit... overzealous."

The man looked up, a soft steady gaze. "I'm fine. Thank you."

As before, the sound of his voice stirred something deep inside Alpha. He crossed to the table, unsure where to begin. There were so many questions he'd planned to ask. But now, standing before the stranger, seeing those eyes, hearing that voice, they seemed less important.

Finally, clearing his throat, he began, "I've waited a long time for this."

The stranger smiled. "So have I."

"But sometimes my office..." Alpha glanced down at his

hands. "Sometimes because of my position, people feel a need to protect me."

"I understand."

Silence filled the room.

"You're certain I can't get you anything?"

The man shook his head.

Somewhat awkwardly, Alpha fumbled with his chair and pulled it out to sit across from the man. "First of all, I want to thank you—for what you did for my daughter, I mean. And for my grandson. I hear they're both doing well."

The stranger nodded. "Yes, they are."

Alpha set his hands on the table, then folded them. "Our reports indicate you're a good man—a follower of Programmer." Smiling, he added, "No surprise there. How could a person do what you do unless they were a follower? Of Programmer, I mean."

The stranger returned the smile.

"But this business of... 'coming from Him—'" Alpha dropped off then shook his head.

"Why is that a problem?"

"By itself, it isn't. In a sense, we all come from Programmer, don't we? But it can be confusing. And, quite frankly, that's why you're sitting here. Some Council Members say you hear Programmer's voice. While others insist you claim to be His equal." Alpha smiled at the absurdity of his last statement, hoping the stranger would join him.

Instead, not unkindly, the man asked, "Would you know his voice if you heard it?"

Alpha hesitated. "It's been—it's been a very long time."

"I know," the man gently replied.

Alpha shifted in his chair. "There have been frauds, tricksters, from the beginning. Men and women who claimed to come from Programmer."

"And I'm sure there will be more."

"So you can appreciate our problem. How do we . . ." He paused, searching for a diplomatic approach.

"How do you know I'm from Programmer?"

"Yes." Alpha leaned forward. "I mean, if we had some type of proof. If Programmer had provided some indication, some word in advance. But, as it is, all we have are your words . . . and, of course, the miracles."

The stranger nodded, seeming to lose himself in thought. Then, staring at the table, he whispered, "I agree. Insert information."

There was a flicker, so brief Alpha thought it was his imagination. "I'm sorry? What did you say?"

The stranger looked up to him. "You asked for proof?'

"That's right."

"What about the prophecies?"

Alpha blinked, stunned that he'd not thought of them until that moment. All those prophecies that spoke of Programmer sending a deliverer to save His people. How odd that until then he'd completely forgotten.

"You are correct." Alpha nodded. "I'm not sure why I hadn't thought of them before." He hesitated. "And yet, the Easterners continue to plague us."

It was the stranger's turn to appear puzzled.

Alpha explained, "The prophecies speak of a great deliverer coming to destroy our enemy. But the Easterners grow stronger every day and you've not lifted a finger to stop them."

The man smiled sadly.

"What?" Alpha asked.

"The Easterners are not your enemy. Your enemy is the virus. Its power over you. That's what I will destroy."

Alpha stared.

The man continued, "But I can only do so if you let me."

"I... don't understand."

"Programmer's commitment to you is so great he will do whatever is necessary to free you."

"Are you saying..." Alpha frowned. "Are you saying Programmer will destroy the virus?"

"No, the virus will remain. But he will pay for the penalties of following it."

"I'm sorry... He would pay for all Law Breakers?"

"No. Only for those who ask."

Alpha tried not to show his incredulity. "And you believe this is true because you feel Programmer has told you?"

The stranger held his gaze. "I know this is true because Programmer and I are the same."

Alpha's heart sank. This was the dilemma. Every time the stranger spoke, the problem arose.

"You find that hard to believe, don't you?"

"If the Council hears this claim, you will pay for it on the Grid with your life."

"Alpha..."

The sound of his name spoken by that voice ... it brought back so many memories, feelings from so long ago. But how was that possible?

"To make payment on the Grid is why I'm here."

Alpha swallowed, blinking back his emotions. No, it simply was not possible. He glanced down to his hands, then back up. The man's eyes were still staring at him.

"And what do I do?" Alpha was surprised at the hoarseness of his voice. "Am I to just stand by and watch a good man suffer?"

"No."

"Then what?"

"Allow me."

Alphas frustration continued rising. Unsure what to do, he leaned back from the table. "Allow you to what?"

The man gave no answer.

Alpha rose to his feet. He turned, then began to pace. "The Council makes these decisions. Not me. I'm merely a figurehead. I have no power to—"

"No, my friend."

Alpha turned to him.

"You must allow me."

"To what?"

"To make payment for your following the virus."

"You? To make my payment?"

"If I'm not allowed to make your payment, then there is nothing more I can do." Again, the man held his gaze, this time with such intensity Alpha could not look away. "But it must be your choice. It is a decision each member in the community must make on their own."

Alphas chest tightened. "How can one man pay for so much evil?"

"One man can't. But Programmer can... if you let him. If you let me."

Alpha closed his eyes. There was no helping him now. He was a good man, doing good things. And that voice, such stirrings. But this was blasphemy. Alpha sighed wearily. He gathered his robes and sadly sank back into his chair. This was heresy and there was nothing he could do.

For a long moment the two sat in silence. Finally, there was the scrape of a key, the sound of the lock opening.

"Sir?" The young jailer pushed open the door. "The Council is ready."

Alpha could only stare at his hands.

"Sir? The Council?"

Alpha nodded, his throat aching. The young man entered and Alpha looked to the stone walls, to the table, anywhere but to the stranger.

Taking his cue, the stranger quietly rose to meet the jailer. He offered no resistance as the young man directed him around the table toward the door. Only as they passed Alpha's chair did the man slow and bring them to a stop. Alpha remained staring hard at the table as the stranger bent down and, ever so gently, kissed him on top of his head. It was a simple act. And it broke Alpha's heart. As the man raised back up, moisture splattered onto Alphas hands. He looked down at it, unsure if it was his tear or the stranger's.

CHAPTER 23

NICHOLAS WAS STILL clutching Rebecca's empty coat sleeve when the popping of a gun drew his attention through the window.

Rusty screamed from behind the partition, "Mom!"

Neither Annie nor the agent appeared injured. Both were wrestling on the ground. But Nicholas's distraction had given Rebecca time to scramble for the set of buttons on the driver's door. She madly groped for the right one, momentarily unlocking Nicholas's door, then relocking it, until she found the control for the glass partition separating them from Rusty. It began sliding down.

Rusty was at the opening, screaming, "He killed Fran! He's got a gun!"

Nicholas squirmed farther inside the passenger window. The edge of the glass jabbed into his gut, making it difficult to breathe. Rebecca reached for the jar of bees, her hand on its top, ready to twist off the lid. Adrenaline surged through Nicholas. With near-superhuman effort he lunged forward, grabbing her arm just enough to knock away the jar. It fell to the floorboard.

She bent down, fishing for it as Nicholas continued to wiggle, suspended in midair by the window, his feet no longer touching the ground.

"Nicholas!" The boy's arms reached through the partition.

"Back!" Nicholas shouted. "Get back!"

"Help me!" he screamed.

"Rusty, get back!"

The woman found the jar and twisted off the lid.

Nicholas froze in fear. It was only a moment, but it gave her time to throw the jar at the partition's opening. It hit the edge and bounced back falling onto the seat beside her. Bees began escaping.

Rusty cried out and drew back into his seat.

With reflexes faster than Nicholas's, Rebecca scooped up the jar and threw it again. This time she succeeded. It sailed through the opening and landed in the back seat.

Rusty screamed.

Nicholas spun to the partition. It was too small to crawl through and too narrow to drag out the boy. The only way to save him was through the back door. But like his own door, it was power-locked from the driver's side. He either had to reach those buttons and unlock it or . . . His eyes shot to the keys still in the ignition.

"Help!" Rusty screamed. "Help me!"

Nicholas stretched for the keys, but they were just out of reach.

Hearing his struggle, realizing his plan, the girl fumbled for the ignition and yanked out the keys.

Roaring in rage, Nicholas gave one last lunge. The pain in his thigh was unbearable as it dragged across the window and he tumbled down into the car seat.

Rebecca reached for the door and barely had it open before he grabbed her shoulder. He had to get the keys. He pulled her closer. She fought, yelling and swearing, then drew herself into a fetal position, clutching the keys to her gut.

Rusty continued screaming.

Nicholas pressed in as the woman kicked and threw punches, more than one finding his face. She pushed the door farther open, exposing the keys for the briefest second. Nicholas reached out, nearly had them, before she freed her arm and threw the keys out into the brush.

The boy kept screaming.

* * *

"Did you or did you not say the Law is no longer valid?"

Nicholas stood in the center of the marble auditorium. Circling him were four rows of men seated on risers. Among them were Orib, Learis, and a dozen others who had listened to him when he spoke to the crowds. Near the back, as unobtrusive as possible, sat Alpha.

"Well?" one of the youngest Members demanded. "Answer the question."

For the last several minutes the discussion had grown more and more heated. Despite their goading and obvious traps, Nicholas had been able to respond with calm assurance. The answer to this question was no exception.

"The essence of the Law is valid," he said. "It is good and just."

"That's right," another agreed, "The Law is the Law." Others nodded, repeating, "The Law is the Law, the Law is the Law."

Nicholas continued, raising his voice to be heard. "It is profound in its simplicity. But..." He waited until he had their attention. "None of you here understands it."

The Council's anger grew.

Nicholas shouted louder. "You keep looking at it from the

outside. To fully understand the Law, you must step inside it. It is useless if you ignore its spirit."

"He's a spinner," someone yelled. "A trickster!"

"No!" An older Member rose to his feet. "A mere trickster cannot do what he does. A trickster cannot bring the dead back to life." The intensity of the debate increased. Several began turning to Alpha.

But the Law Giver continued looking down, busying himself with his hands, his robe. Nicholas didn't blame him. He understood and was saddened, but there was no blame.

"The Law is the Law," Learis repeated.

Once again the chant filled the chamber. "The Law is the Law, the Law is the Law."

"Yes!" Nicholas yelled over them. "The Law is your tutor. It is like the training wheels on the bicycles your citizens are starting to ride."

Those who heard him grew quiet, puzzled at the analogy.

"As training wheels, it has taught you Programmer's principles. It has taught you how to ride and not fall."

Others began listening.

"But once you master the art of balance, once you understand it in here." He tapped his chest. "Then the training wheels are no longer necessary. In fact, they can actually hinder you."

Again the room erupted. "The Law is sacred! It is just!"

"I agree!" Nicholas shouted. "The Law is sacred and just. The problem is none of you can live it!"

The discord grew louder. Only a few remained listening.

"What of the prophecies?" someone yelled. "Look at the prophecies this man has fulfilled!"

"Trickster!" Learis shouted. "He has purposely set out to make them happen."

"Impossible!" another cried. "There are too many!"

"Proof!" the youngest shouted. "We must have proof!"

"Yes," others agreed. "Show us proof."

"Proof?" Nicholas called out. "You wish for proof?"

"Yes, proof! Show us the proof!"

Nicholas gathered his robe and walked around the room, waiting as the Council settled. When he approached Learis, he slowed to a stop and spoke directly to the man. "You are not interested in proof."

The old Member glared at him in contempt.

Nicholas turned to the rest in the chamber. "Each of you ... every person here has erected two walls."

The Council grew even more quiet.

"I know this because . . ." He hesitated. "Because I also have built them."

A handful of Members leaned forward to listen.

"First, there is the outer wall, your primary defense. This is the wall that demands what you call proof. The wall of arguments and debates—cleverly disguised as logic and rational thinking. But it is a false wall. Its real function is to defend the inner wall. The real wall."

"And what wall is that?" Orib called from across the chamber.

Nicholas turned to him. "The one surrounding your heart." He slowly surveyed the room. By now everyone was listening. "Your outer wall, your false wall, is nothing but smoke, a facade to protect you from the real question."

"And what is this 'real question?'" Learis demanded.

Nicholas turned back to him and answered, "The real question is, who is your ruler?" He turned to the rest of the room. "Is it you? Or is it Programmer?"

The murmuring resumed.

"And who is yours?" a Member called out. "Who is your ruler?"

"That's right," another demanded. "Who rules your life? You or Programmer?"

Nicholas turned to the Member. Instead of answering, he asked, "Who exactly is Programmer?"

"Who is Programmer?" another asked incredulously. "The one who created us," Learis shouted.

"The one who spoke to Alpha," another yelled, "who instructed our beloved Law Giver."

Once again heads turned toward Alpha.

"Yes." Nicholas nodded. "You are correct. And I tell you this. Alpha heard my voice and he was glad for it."

Alpha's head shot up in alarm.

"That's not possible," Orib sputtered. "My father was just a youth when he heard Programmer. And he's older than you by several seasons. What do you mean, he heard your voice?"

Nicholas turned back to Alpha, whose eyes pleaded with him to say no more. Smiling quietly, Nicholas answered, "I tell you this. Are you listening?"

The room grew absolutely silent.

"Before Alpha existed, I existed."

The group exploded in anger.

"What?" Learis cried over the noise. "What are you claiming?" Nicholas calmly turned to him.

"Say it!" the old man shouted. "I demand that you say it with your own lips. Tell us. Are you or are you not Programmer?" Nicholas quietly looked about the room—their angry faces, their confusion, their pride, their fear.

"It's a simple question!" Learis cried. "Are you or are you not Programmer?"

Once again Nicholas waited for the noise to settle.

When he had the room's attention, he answered quietly and clearly,

"I am."

The Council was on their feet. Men yelling, pointing, hurtling insults.

"We've heard enough!" Learis shouted. "Take him away!"

Orib motioned to the two Enforcers who stood at the door. They approached and grabbed Nicholas. He put up no resistance as they spun him around and pushed him toward the exit. He staggered out into a long stone corridor. The clamor continued behind him as the Enforcers shoved him forward. He stumbled, nearly falling, until they dragged him to his feet and continued pushing him along.

Finally, they reached a pair of giant bronze doors. Opening them, they escorted him onto the Temple grounds.

* * *

"Get them away!" Rusty screamed. "Get them away!"

Nicholas turned to the partition, saw the boy in the seat swatting at the bees. "No!" he shouted. "Don't move!"

"They're all over."

"Get down on the floor."

"But-"

"Now! Get down on the floor. Bury your face in your knees. Now, Rusty. Do it now!"

The child dropped out of sight.

Nicholas spun around and grabbed the steering wheel. Using it for leverage, he scooted Rebecca out the open door until she tumbled to the ground. He reached for the control panel in the door, hitting one button after another, trying to unlock the back. But with the ignition off, it was impossible.

He crawled out the driver's side, stumbling over the girl. He grabbed the handle to the rear door, but as he suspected, it would not open. Turning, he dropped to all fours and began searching for the keys. The dried grass and under-growth were impossibly thick. He winced as his knee struck a large rock. But it gave him an idea. He scooped it up and rose to his feet. Staggering back to the car, he raised the rock and slammed it hard against the rear passenger window.

A second gunshot fired from behind him.

"Mom!" The boy was up and looking.

"Get down!" Nicholas shouted.

"He shot Mom!" Nicholas threw a look over his shoulder and saw Annie on the ground, holding her arm. The agent scrambled to his feet. He hesitated over her a moment, then raced toward the car. Nicholas turned back to the window and hit it a second time. The third time it spiderwebbed.

"Mom!"

"Stay down!"

On the fourth blow the window exploded, throwing pebbles of safety glass into the car. Nicholas dropped the rock and reached through the hole, hoping to manually release the lock.

"That's enough!" the agent shouted as he continued toward him. "Stop right there."

But Nicholas had other plans. And worries. With his bare arm and hand exposed to the bees, memories of his own childhood rushed in—his throat swelling shut, the panic of not being able to breathe, the horror on his mother's face.

At last his fingers found the door's latch. He pulled and pushed, but the autolock remained fast. Withdrawing his hand, he stooped back down for the rock.

"I said stop." The agent was much closer.

Nicholas broke the remaining glass away. Another shot fired. But to his surprise, he felt nothing. And then another shot. And another.

He looked back and saw the agent sprawled on the ground ten feet away. The man's eyes remained open, staring, a pool of blood spreading across his white shirt. Beyond him, Nicholas spotted Travis scrambling over the charred rubble. In his hand was the gun from the lab.

The boy screamed and Nicholas spun back to the

window. Rusty, who was huddled on the floor against the opposite door, swatted at his arm.

"No!" Nicholas yelled. But he was too late. Rusty killed the offending bee and started brushing it away. "Rusty, don't —" As he did, he ripped out its stinger, releasing an alarm pheromone, cueing the rest of the bees to attack. They wasted little time.

They landed on the boy's hands, his bare arms, his neck. Once again, Nicholas felt himself slowing, freezing. But, refusing to give in to the memories or weigh the consequences, he ducked through the window and reached into the car.

CHAPTER 24

"**I**S THAT TOO TIGHT?"

Nicholas turned with surprise to the Enforcer who had just cinched his left wrist to the Grid. The big man appeared all business, at least for the gathering crowd. But his words relayed something different. He crossed to the other wrist, speaking so quietly only Nicholas could hear.

"My nephew, the kid you healed? He's like this new person. So's my brother. We can't thank you enough."

Nicholas nodded, then tried to shake away the sweat dripping into his eye. He was sweating, but ice-cold—far more frightened than he'd anticipated.

"It'll only hurt a moment," the Enforcer said. "Then you lose consciousness. They don't feel nothing 'til they wake up."

"If they wake up," grunted the second Enforcer. He was at Nicholas's feet, tying his ankles.

Nicholas nodded, and tried to swallow, but his mouth was leather. He closed his eyes and took a deep breath, and then another, trying to reclaim the confidence he'd felt just minutes before in front of the Council. Of course this was the right decision. He'd thought it all through. This was the logical choice. The knowledge gave him some comfort. And each time he focused on that logic, his fear subsided.

Still, doubts continued washing over him. Like waves from an incoming tide, the fears kept recycling, each swell a little stronger than the last, each claiming a little more beach, a little more confidence. Would the transfer really work? Would anybody be willing to accept it if it did? He scanned the faces of those closest in the crowd. Not one of the Breakers was there. Not Kallab, not Big Red, not Nyrah. He saw nobody from the camp.

Though there were plenty of others ...

"Where are your tricks now?" someone shouted.

"If he's from Programmer, let Programmer save him," another yelled.

The Council Members began filing onto the stage. Quiet, sober, exhibiting none of the rage they'd displayed earlier in the chamber. He craned his neck until he spotted Alpha on the far side. The man's face was drawn and troubled—creating even more doubt in Nicholas's mind. If he couldn't reach Alpha, who could he reach? Was this action so foreign that even the most committed to Programmer could not understand?

What if the transfer was too much for his body? What if Travis had miscalculated? What if his life drained away too soon, before Travis could replenish it? What if the energy came too early? Would he explode, blow up?

So much depended on his brother.

"Travis?" he whispered.

There was no answer.

"Travis?"

Still nothing. Maybe he was pushing, fast-forwarding again. If so, would he accidentally skip over this moment and entirely abandon Nicholas?

"Travis!"

The panic continued rising, drowning him in its fear. He closed his eyes, trying to return to that place of logic. But it had slipped away, out of his grasp. His heart began to pound. The shivering grew worse.

"My nephew, the kid you healed? He's like this new person."

The memory startled him, so clear that he nearly opened his eyes to see if the Enforcer had repeated himself. Other memories followed, equally as vivid. The woman whose amputated leg he had restored ... the joy of the man lowered through the roof... Nyrah's tears over her baby coming back to life.

It was the deeper logic. The other had fled, but this was still present, this he could still cling to.

"Open your mouth," the Enforcer ordered.

Nicholas obeyed. The man shoved in a leather pouch filled with sand.

"Keep it between your teeth."

Nicholas nodded, wide-eyed.

"Good luck," was all the Enforcer said as he stepped back.

Nicholas turned back to the stage and the barely concealed hatred on the faces. Why? For speaking the truth? For offering to make payment? He turned to the crowd and saw many with the same expression. What more did they want? He was giving them everything he had. What more could he possibly do?

"Are we ready?" Orib called from the stage.

"Secure!" the Enforcer shouted back.

Nicholas watched, his heart racing, as Orib seemed to hesitate. He looked to his fellow Council Members as if for encouragement. Then to his father. But Alpha would not meet his son's gaze. Finally, Orib turned back to the Grid and gave the order:

"Let payment begin."

Nicholas shut his eyes and clenched his teeth into the pouch.

There was a dull click. Suddenly he was sucked back into the Grid. The leather restraints dug into his wrists and ankles, but they stopped his body from convulsing as indescribable pain ripped into his flesh and tore through his mind.

* * *

Nicholas leaned into the car, stretching toward Rusty. "Here! Take my hands."

The bees crawled over the squirming child, attacking and stinging. Several more circled the air, just as agitated but not yet landing.

"Rusty!"

The boy's face was wet with tears, his eyes filled with terror.

Nicholas reached farther inside, watching as one bee hovered, then dropped and landed on his own bare arm.

"Take my hands! Hurry!"

Rusty hesitated.

The bee, not twelve inches from Nicholas's face, wiggled its abdomen onto his skin, then plunged in its stinger. The pain was sharp and clear, but was nothing compared to what would soon follow.

"Hurry!"

Rusty made his move. He leaped up and threw himself at Nicholas. The man wrapped his arms around the child, feeling a burn in his wrist, another in his forearm, from bees being crushed. A third, that had been in the boy's hair, stung him on the neck as, with effort, he pulled Rusty through the broken window and out of the car.

"Sweetheart!" Annie arrived and took him into her arms.

Nicholas saw where a bullet had grazed the left shoulder of her jacket. There was a trace of blood, but she didn't seem to notice. Instead, she hugged her son tightly, then held him at arm's length, examining him, trying to hide her panic. And for good reason. There were several welts on his arms and two on the back of his hand.

"Mom ..." Tears streamed down his face.

"You're okay, baby," she said as she ripped off her jacket. She batted away the remaining bees and threw the coat around her sobbing child. "You're okay."

Nicholas glanced down at his own arms and hands. He counted, three, no, four welts.

Travis appeared at his side and saw the same. Without hesitating, he grabbed Nicholas's arm and pulled him toward Annie's car. "Let's go. We gotta get you to the hospital."

Annie looked up. "It's an hour drive."

"What's that got to do—"

"They have thirty minutes, tops."

"They?" Travis asked.

"The boy's allergic too," Nicholas said.

Travis swore.

Rusty clung to his mother, crying.

"Shh." She wiped the hair out of his eyes. "It's okay, it's okay." She looked back to Travis. "What about the R.E. Lab?"

"What about it?"

"I saw medical supplies. Wouldn't they have epinephrine?"

Travis turned and started for the lab.

Annie rose. "Hang on, I'll help you look."

But Rusty, more frightened than hurt, would not let go.

"You stay here with Nicholas," she said. "I'll be right back."

He clung more fiercely.

"It's all right, sweetie. I'll be right back, I promise."

"Here." Nicholas stooped down to the boy with outstretched arms. Rusty hesitated until Annie pried herself away, then he turned to bury himself into Nicholas's chest. Annie and Nicholas exchanged a brief, sober look before she turned and hurried off to follow Travis.

"Mom!" Rusty tried to break free, but Nicholas held on.

"She'll be right back. She has to get us some medicine."

A stray bee buzzed by and he waved it off.

"Mom!"

"She'll be right back."

"I want my mom!"

Already Nicholas could feel the thickening in his throat. The swelling had begun. Knowing they only had minutes before anaphylactic shock set in and knowing panic only accelerated it, Nicholas thought of a diversion for the boy. "Hey, you want to see something cool?"

"I want my mom."

"She's coming right back, I promise. But here..." He rose, taking the boy's hand. "You want to see a computer game?"

"I want my mom."

"Come on, Squirt, let me show you. It's really cool." He tugged at his hand.

The boy looked at him through his tears.

"Really. And the best thing is I'm the star of it."

Rusty blinked.

"No kidding." It was growing harder to breathe. The clock was ticking. "Honest, let me show you." He gave another tug. "You'll love it."

Finally, reluctantly, Rusty gave in and they started back toward the lab. Not running, but not exactly walking.

* * *

EVERY NERVE in Nicholas's body was on fire, the pain so

intense he hoped to pass out. But he didn't. He spotted Nyrah and then Kallab doing their best to blend into the crowd. Their heads were covered, but when they looked up he saw their eyes. And when his gaze locked onto Nyrah's, it began.

He is fourteen. He is Nyrah, thrilled at Tomar running his hands over her hips, hungrily kissing the nape of her neck, she marvels at the desire she can ignite in another. So much passion and it's all for her as she feels her own desire rise, the yearning to yield, to be free and lose herself to him, losing herself, freedom in losing . . . until the door flies open, Daddy's voice yelling, her scrambling for clothes, her cheeks flushed with shame, the hurt in his eyes, tears in her own, the promise she'll never do it again. And he believes her. But she does do it again, easier the second time, and the third, each time easier, guilt piling upon guilt, drowned out by losing herself to others, surprised when one offers to pay, guilt upon guilt, embarrassment with old friends, thrill with new ones, a hole growing inside her, dark and gnawing, increasing, deeper and deeper, no bottom in sight.

Nicholas struggled to breathe, but the weight of guilt was suffocating. The joints in his wrists and fingers began to knot, his back twisted, the gums in his mouth throbbed as a tooth fell out, then another. Suddenly he could no longer control his bladder. Brittle bones began snapping in his wrists from his weight until he hung by tissue and ligament, struggling to breathe, to think. No longer able to remember his name, his mind was going, and just as he was ready to expire, grateful the pain would finally end—

His back arched as new energy raced into him, resuscitating every nerve and thought. Only they are not his thoughts, or Nyrah's. His eyes have locked onto Kallab and suddenly he is sixteen, chugging palm wine, friends chanting, cheering, the relief it brings from school pressure, so welcome, so freeing, as he loses himself until he is vomiting, head pounding, vowing never again, but pressure builds, the need to escape overwhelms, and he yields, the heat sliding down his throat, burning his stomach, such relief, such freedom. Once a week, twice a week, during the days, grades falling, goals fading, lost in the freedom, drinking to drown the guilt, the self-loathing, as his emptiness grows, the abyss opening, dark and unending.

Nicholas's gut exploded in pain, his bowels discharged, excrement ran down his thighs, he shivered with fever, his vision grew cloudy, then dim, then gone, his thinking faded, muddled, until he could barely think at all, only grateful that it was over, when—

Nicholas's body arched as new power surged into him, and once again he was fully alive and fully conscious this time as someone he doesn't know, a nine-year-old, jealous of his sister's attention, finding his glory in grades, copying papers, cheating, Mother's praise unending, the cheating continuing into business, lying so easy, so freeing. Cheating his partners, cheating on taxes, cheating on wives ...

And so it continued. Milliseconds becoming lifetimes in Nicholas's mind and body, as he experienced the freedom of breaking, then its cost and death and bottomless darkness . .. until he became alive again with new energy and experienced another life and death. And another. And another. Hoping each time would be his last. But each time being wrong.

CHAPTER 25

DARKNESS HAD SETTLED over the compound, making it difficult for Annie to work her way across the rubble. She was panicking, she knew that. She also knew her baby was in serious danger and every second counted. Directly behind her, she heard Travis snapping his cell phone shut with an oath.

"What's the word?" she called.

"Medivac chopper won't be here for twenty minutes."

"Twenty minutes!"

"It's the best they can do."

She slipped, nearly falling over a mound of drywall, but it barely broke her stride. Having ransacked the R.E. Lab, they'd found a cupboard with the epinephrine—two autoinjectors, the size of large test tubes, gray with yellow wrapping, the type all schools and most workplaces have in their first-aid kits. The search had taken seven, maybe eight minutes. Another half minute was spent patching her arm to stop the bleeding. As they headed back to Travis's lab, she estimated they had, at best, fifteen minutes left.

"Who's there?" a voice shouted.

She squinted through the dark and saw Rebecca, the lab assistant, stumbling blindly across the debris.

"Somebody help me!"

Travis shouted to Annie, "Go on, I got her."

Annie needed no second invitation. She continued along the hill until she arrived at Travis's open lab door. Ducking inside, she called, "Rusty! Nicholas!"

"Down here." Nicholas coughed. His voice was thick and raspy. A bad sign.

She raced down the steps, nearly slipping, catching herself on the handrails. The room was bathed in the usual blue-green light of the monitors. Rusty and Nicholas lay on the concrete floor, Nicholas against the back wall of cupboards, holding her son's head on his lap. The boy's eyes were closed, his face red and swollen.

"Rusty?"

His eyes fluttered open. "Mom ..."

"It's okay, baby, I'm here, I'm here."

"My stomach hurts."

She dropped to her knees in front of them. Nicholas tilted back the boy's head, trying to keep his air passage open. The massive quantity of histamines released inside both of them was causing fluid to leak from their blood vessels into their tissue, swelling their bodies, filling their lungs. If not treated, they'd be dead within minutes.

With shaking hands, Annie ripped off the gray top of the auto injector. Now it was armed. She grabbed Rusty's right thigh with one hand and slammed the injector into his leg with her other. There was a soft click as the needle shot out, passing through his pants and into the leg muscle. The boy yelped and tried to pull away, but she held him, pressing the applicator against his leg as she counted the required seconds:

"One ... two ... three ... four—" He tried to squirm. "Hold still, baby, hold still. "Five... Six ... seven ..."

She heard Travis and Rebecca enter the stairway above them. Looking over her shoulder, she caught sight of the monitors and the other, on-screen Nicholas, fastened to the Grid, his body jerking and writhing. She turned back to Nicholas watching himself up on the screen through swollen eyes.

"Eight... nine ... ten."

She pulled the applicator away and dropped it to the floor. She scooted closer to Nicholas and ripped off the safety cap of the second, preparing to inject him.

"No," he wheezed.

"What?"

"How much?"

She didn't understand.

He nodded to the applicator. "Dosage?" He was struggling to breathe.

She looked at the yellow label on the cartridge and read, "Three-tenths of a milligram."

"He'll need—" Nicholas broke into a choking cough. "He'll need more."

"I gave him the adult dose."

"Multiple stings ..." He took a gulp of air. "He'll need more."

Annie's mind reeled. He was right. Despite the dangers of an overdose, one injection might not be enough, even at adult strength. But what about Nicholas? She turned to Rusty, searching for any sign of improvement. It was too early. She looked at the autoinjector in her hand, then to her son, then to Nicholas.

"I—you'll . . ." She couldn't say the word. "I just can't let you—"

"Five minutes." He closed his eyes, laboring to breathe.

She searched his face.

"Give him ... five."

She understood. Within five minutes they'd know if the dosage had been enough. If not... She looked down at the applicator, torn with indecision.

Travis suddenly appeared above them, his face showing the strain. He began to nod, making it clear he had heard his brother and that he agreed.

Rusty groaned. She moved to his side, squeezing between the two of them. She held her son, praying, searching for the slightest improvement. She looked back to Nicholas. His eyes were closed and he had started to shiver. He was going into shock. Her heart rose into her throat. Five minutes could be too late.

As if reading her mind, he tried to smile, then mouthed the word,

"Five ..."

Rusty convulsed once, twice, then vomited, spewing liquid onto the floor beside them.

"It's okay, baby," she said, wiping his mouth and holding him tight. "It'll be all right."

"Travis!" a voice cried through the speakers.

She looked up to the monitor. The on-screen Nicholas was screaming from the Grid.

Travis hit a switch and spoke into the mic. "Right here, bro. I'm right here."

"Travis, can you hear me?"

"I'm right here!" He adjusted some switches, then spoke as he quickly typed. "Can't you hear me? I'm right here."

The picture froze, then continued, then froze, pixilating into bursts of tiny squares like a bad DVD. The audio broke into static.

"What's happening?" Annie shouted.

Travis said nothing, frantically working the keyboard.

"You're overloading!" Rebecca cried from across the room.

"What?" Annie yelled.

Incredulous, Rebecca shouted at Travis, "You're transferring energy through him into the Grid?"

"Travis…" The voice cut through the static. "Travis?"

"The system can't handle that," Rebecca yelled. "No way can you transfer that much power through a single source!"

Travis read the panel and continued to work feverishly.

"You can't do it!"

He kept working.

"It's not possible. You can't do it and you know it!"

He hesitated, double-checked the readouts, then finally began to slow. Almost imperceptibly he started to nod. "Right... you're right." He reversed course, hitting a different set of switches. "It's a no-go. We have to abort."

"No ..." Nicholas wheezed from the floor. "Travis, no!"

Travis turned to him.

"Keep ... going."

"It'll destroy him!" Travis argued. "He can't handle it."

"Keep—" Nicholas broke into a gasping cough, then nodded, insisting.

Travis stared at him. He turned back to the screen and hesitated.

"The only... way," Nicholas wheezed.

Travis continued to think.

"Only…chance…"

"Travis?"

Another moment passed, longer than the last, until finally, slowly, he lowered his hands from the controls.

"Are you crazy?" Rebecca shouted.

Travis answered quietly, "No, he's right. It's their only hope."

* * *

ALPHA WATCHED with guilt and pity. In all his seasons he had never seen anyone experience such agony when making payment. The convulsions continued, one after another—each accompanied by a look of horror on the stranger's face.

"How can one man pay for so much evil?" Alpha had asked.

"One man can't. Programmer can."

The light flickered—not on the platform, but everywhere. As if the entire sky, the sun itself, had blinked. At first Alpha thought it was his imagination. But the concerned look of other Council Members said otherwise.

So did the murmuring crowd gathered around the stage.

It happened again, this time longer. When the light returned, something had changed. It was subtle, but everything surrounding Alpha appeared just a little rougher and jagged. Not the straight lines; they were still sharp. But the smoothness to anything curved was gone. Even the faces. Instead of roundness, everything looked as if it was made of overlapping angles. Thousands of them, almost appearing as curves, but not quite.

"What's happening?" Learis shouted.

Others on the platform exchanged frightened looks as the crowd grew more agitated.

Alpha stole a look at the Grid. The stranger had turned to the platform and spotted him, his gaze so compassionate Alpha could not look away.

Suddenly he remembered the Killing Wall—as clear as if he were there.

He is standing atop the ledge, looking down on his newborn daughter, hearing her whimper, hearing his wife's begging, "No, Alpha, please..."

Now he is climbing down the cold, slick stones to the

street, struggling to contain his guilt, and turning to see the stranger standing, his arms outstretched as they are on the Grid, his face filled with pain and empathy. It's as if he too were there, participating in the awful deed.

Now Alpha is before his shelter, thrusting his battle-ax deep into the attacking father, watching light gush from his wound, then spinning around and slicing open the neck of the man's son. He stretches and opens his hands, absorbing the breathglow until he sees the stranger standing nearby, eyes filled with moisture, stretching out his own hands.

Now he is at the crib of his dying son, a rat scurrying across the railing, feeling the emotion clutch his throat, so powerful he cannot breathe. The death of his child, the death of his wife, everything is destroyed because of him, his ignorance, his stupidity. He swallows back a sob, and then another, lowering his head, until he feels a hand on his shoulder, the stranger's ...

"Daddy..."

He raises his head to see Nyrah in their kitchen, frail and pregnant.

"I'm the one at fault, Daddy, not you."

Tears run down his face. How can he be so heartless? And beside her, he sees the stranger with the same tears of guilt and shame.

The stage moved under his feet. Pulled from his memories, Alpha turned and saw that the trees covering the Temple grounds had vanished. So had the grass. Now the people stood on a flat, green plain. He turned to the Temple behind him. No, it wasn't possible! Giant slabs of stone were blinking in and out. One minute they were there, the next gone, then back again, until they disappeared for good ... and the blocks of stones they supported began to fall.

"Earthquake!" someone shouted.

The stones crashed onto the platform, shattering wood,

throwing debris, pounding the air with a thunderous roar. Council Members screamed. Pieces of the stage started to vanish—replaced by gaping holes. Alpha was thrown from his feet as the platform lurched and lunged.

"Father!"

Through the dust he saw Orib crawling toward him. "Are you all right?"

The remaining stage listed, then collapsed to the ground. The fall knocked the wind out of Alpha. Rolling onto his back, he saw the entire north tower flicker, then disappear. A flash of light exploded around him. Like an electrical storm, but there was no storm. The sky was black as ink. Not from clouds or lack of light, but from lack of color. Another flash. Blinding. And another, brighter still. The earth had turned liquid, rolling in giant waves. Blocks of the Temple continued falling, crushing Council Members, their mouths opened in screams that Alpha could no longer hear.

He peered through the rubble and dust toward the Grid, hoping for a glimpse of the stranger. But the Grid was empty. The iron mesh glowed an eerie blue-red. The leather restraints remained fastened, tendrils of smoke rising from them. But no one was present.

The stranger had vanished.

* * *

"SCORE!" Travis swiveled in his chair to face Nicholas. "We did it, bro! We nailed it!"

Nicholas struggled to open a single, swollen eye. Annie couldn't tell for certain, but he might have smiled.

"What are you talking about?" Rebecca demanded. "You've lost contact. There's no way of knowing—"

Travis cut her off. "We did it!"

"Everything went according to plan. It's beautiful, bro. Everything went exactly like we hoped."

Only then did Annie realize the sad truth. Travis had failed. Their eyes connected the briefest moment before he turned back to the keyboard and continued frantically working away.

"Mom..."

She turned to her son. "How are you feeling, sweetheart, any better?"

He shifted his weight and broke into a gagging cough. "A ... little."

Annie's heart sank. She looked at her watch. They were at seven minutes. Nearly two beyond Nicholas's deadline.

Rusty continued coughing.

"Lie back, sweetheart, try to relax."

Nicholas rolled his head to her, his whisper so full of air, she barely heard. "Better?"

She tried to lie, but couldn't.

"Time?" he wheezed.

She gave no answer.

"Annie.."

She swallowed. "Seven minutes. Look," she argued, "the chopper's in the air. They'll be here any—"

"Now."

"Nicholas, there's no—"

"Mom..."

"Relax, baby. Re—"

"I'm freezing." Rusty was going into shock. She held him closer, adjusted her coat around him.

"Now..." Nicholas gasped.

She looked away, swiping at the tears spilling onto her cheeks.

"Ann . . ." But it was too much effort for him to finish her name.

She turned to him, his face a blur through her tears.

He tried to nod, his voice more gurgle than words. "It's . . . okay..."

The ache in her throat was unbearable.

"Mom..."

"O ... kay..." He struggled to smile.

Tears streamed down her face.

"...kay..."

She started to nod. She tried swallowing, but couldn't. She gulped in a breath and then another.

"Mom..."

She fumbled with the injector, then raised it into the air. She wiped her face with her free hand, then angrily ripped off the top of the applicator to arm it. Hesitating, hands trembling, she glanced back to Nicholas.

With closed eyes, he gave the slightest nod.

She looked back to her son, summoning resolve. Then she grabbed the boy's leg and, before changing her mind, plunged the injector into it.

Rusty barely flinched.

She started counting, "One . . . two . . ." Tears dripped from her nose, her chin. "Three ... four ..." She swiped at them with her arm. "Five ... six..." She could barely breathe, barely speak. "Seven... eight..." Her voice caught as she whispered, "Nine... ten."

She pulled out the applicator and threw it across the room. She took Rusty's head into her arms, while turning to Nicholas. "I'm sorry," she whispered. "I'm so—"

He did not answer.

"Nicholas?"

"Mik...ey...?" he asked in a breathless whisper.

She frowned. "Who?"

"Mike..."

Her mind raced. Mikey? There was no Mikey. The only Mikey she knew of was—

He struggled to open his eye, to look past her. "Where's ..."

Suddenly she understood. "Here, Nicholas... he's right here." She flattened herself against the wall so he could see past her to Rusty. "He's right here."

Through the tiniest of slits his eye spotted the child. He gave a faint smile before closing it.

Annie wiped her nose, could not stop the tears. "The chopper will be here any second," she choked. "Hang on. Just hang on." She moved closer, raising her hand to stroke his cheek. In all their years, it was the first time she had ever touched his face.

There was a gurgling wheeze. Still holding her son, she gently laid her head on Nicholas's shoulder. He took another faint, ragged breath. And then another. Each more shallow than the last.

And there she stayed, through the final, wheezing rattles. Eventually, the sound ceased. So did the movement. Everything grew still except for her quiet weeping and silent prayers.

EPILOGUE

"**B**ODIES JUST DON'T vanish," a younger Member of the Council argued.

"Nor do pieces disappear from the Temple," Orib countered, "or the grounds, or our surrounding community."

"The leather restraints were still locked and fastened."

"It's a trick," another insisted. "Some sort of illusion."

"Or..." All eyes turned to the aged Learis. "His followers used the diversion to steal the body."

"From under our noses?" Orib asked. "With Enforcers standing right there?"

And so the argument continued. With the Temple destroyed and pieces of land literally missing, the remaining Council Members were meeting in Alpha's home. But Alpha had found it difficult to focus on the proceedings and excused himself. He had drifted over to the front window, where he parted the curtains to gaze outside.

Two days had passed since the disaster. Already work parties had formed and were beginning to rebuild the community. Starting first, of course, with the Temple. Good, dedicated men who were sacrificing their time and resources.

"We'll have it completed by the end of the season," they boldly proclaimed.

Maybe they would. But even if the Temple was rebuilt, Alpha doubted things would ever return to what they had been. There was just too much missing. Not only of the Temple ... but of reality. Trees, random chunks of buildings, even pieces of ground, had disappeared. Gone.

Not destroyed. Gone.

In the background, he heard the Council continue.

"We'll order the Enforcers to testify," a Member suggested. "They'll say the body was stolen."

Orib disagreed. "The payment for such dereliction of duty is death."

Once again Learis spoke; slowly, ensuring the subtext was not missed. "I'm certain, in this matter, the Council would be lenient."

Alpha quietly shook his head. Even with all that had happened, they were still concerned about the stranger's disappearance. Then again, maybe they were right. Maybe there was a connection. Continuing to gaze through the window, he looked to the porch. Nearly half of the left side was missing. The rest of the steps were perfectly intact, but those to the left simply weren't there. The same could be said for the fireplace behind him. The entire right side—hearth, stones, mantel—were gone. But, equally as strange, pieces of it were slowly beginning to reappear—not always as they had been, but often duplicating what remained. Just this morning another picture frame showed up on the right side of the mantel. An exact replica of the one that had been untouched on the left.

There was something else, as well. The ancient breathglow, once so vivid in the beginning, was supposedly return-ing. But not to everyone. Only to a handful of the stranger's followers. Rumors, of course. More imagination than fact, but still...

Through the window, he spotted a woman coming down the lane. It was a foolhardy venture. Other than work parties, few stepped outside. There were just too many dangers. A person could walk down the street and suddenly come upon a giant hole, another missing piece of reality. Even the sky had gaps. As the sun slowly arced across, it would disappear behind patches of emptiness—not clouds, not any type of obstruction. Just... emptiness.

The woman was closer now. A Breaker, by the bright, garish colors of her clothing. She held something in her arms. At first he thought it was a package, perhaps a gift. As the Law Giver, his home was filled with such presents. But as she approached, he saw it was wrapped in a quilt. And the way she carefully held it and spoke to it clearly indicated it was no gift, but a child, a baby. And the mother s determined and purposeful stride just as clearly spoke of her identity.

Both fear and excitement rose inside Alpha. What was she thinking? It was too dangerous for her to be out walking. And with the baby? To the very home where the Council was meeting?

He pulled from the window and started toward the door.

"Father?" Orib called. "Where are you going?"

He cleared his throat. "Outside. For some air."

"Be careful."

He nodded. But as he approached the door, his feet grew heavy. It would be better that his wife handle this. He turned toward their room and called, "Saida?"

She did not answer.

"Saida?"

Apparently she was resting, something she did more and more these days.

He turned back to the door and hesitated. He had not communicated with Nyrah since before she gave birth. As Law Giver, it would set an unthinkable precedent. It had been bad enough he entered the Breakers' camp the evening the child was born. But to actually speak and communicate with her? No. All contact had been through Saida's visits. Visits everyone pretended not to notice.

"Father, are you all right?" Orib asked.

"Yes, fine."

He opened the door. The afternoon air smelled fresh and green. The cherry tree beyond the porch was purple with buds. He looked up to see her approaching the white picket gate.

He shut the door behind him and headed down the steps, holding on to the rail, staying as far from the missing portions as possible. Once he reached the bottom he started toward the gate. As before, his feet grew heavy, like lead.

She did not speak. She reached for the latch, then pulled back her hand and looked to Alpha. She would not enter without his permission.

Through sheer will, he forced himself to continue, stiff and self-conscious under her gaze, but determined.

Nyrah waited. The baby stirred, but did not fuss.

At last he arrived. His heart pounded in his ears as he looked to her.

Her eyes glistened, but she did not look away.

Orib called from the front door, "Father, what are you doing?"

Alpha said nothing. Nor did Nyrah.

"Father!"

The baby yawned. Nyrah adjusted the quilt and Alpha

dropped his gaze to the child. The infants cheeks were cherub and flushed, his eyes pale blue like Saida's. He cooed and stretched his hands, tiny fingers clutching the air.

Alpha's heart swelled until he thought it would burst. He reached down to the gate.

"Father, she cannot come here!"

Without speaking, he unlatched it.

Nyrah looked to him, making sure this was what he wanted. Only then did he notice the glow coming from her mouth.

"Father!"

Without hesitation, he pulled open the gate and stepped aside, allowing his daughter and his grandson to enter.

* * *

"He's been playing computer games all morning," Annie's mother complained.

Annie glanced over to Rusty as she loaded dishes into the dishwasher. "I think he'll be okay," she said. "Everybody deals with grief differently."

Her mother's silence voiced disapproval. So what else was new? Still, it was good things were finally getting back to normal.

Yesterday's funeral had pretty much ended the adventure. At least she hoped. It had been a simple affair, with only Travis, Annie, Rusty, and a handful of faculty members attending. The turnout saddened Annie, but didn't surprise her. The man was as unpopular in death as he was in life.

Two Homeland Security agents (real ones this time) hung back by the cars to observe and note any strangers who might happen to drop by and pay their respects.

None did.

She'd been interviewed by the agents on two separate occasions. Once at the hospital as she stayed with Rusty, the other time here at the house. They assured her there would be other visits and on more than one occasion she caught glimpses of what she thought was a car following her. But overprotection was better than no protection. At least that's what she told herself.

Originally, she'd been surprised at the lack of news coverage. It would seem the destruction of a high-tech lab in the Santa Barbara mountains, not to mention a half dozen killings, would be hard to miss. But so far everything remained eerily quiet.

The silence left her both appreciative and suspicious.

Travis had reported that the program was pretty well ruined. The fact that federal authorities had moved in and shut down what was left of it hadn't helped. Still, there were those bits of information scattered around the world from the tens of millions of SETI home computers and the other networks. And someday, given permission and, of course, the money, he hoped to salvage what was left and rework the program. Even at that, he suspected some pieces were reconnecting and repairing on their own, since repair and reproduction were a natural part of the program. Or, as he enjoyed quoting, "Nature abhors a vacuum." Until then, there was nothing more he could do, or was allowed to do—except keep his head low and pray he wouldn't be charged with whatever dozen Internet laws he'd broken.

Rusty's recovery had been fairly quick. He bounced back just as Annie had hoped, though she still kept a close eye on him and a healthy supply of antihistamine available in the medicine cabinet. Of course, she was equally concerned about the psychological effects of Nicholas's death. The two had been so close. On the surface Rusty seemed unfazed. But she knew that wasn't the case. She'd tried getting him to talk about his feelings, but so far he wasn't interested. And for now, she wasn't worried. When the time was right, she knew he would open up.

Until then, he'd found his own way to cope ...

"Shoot!" he cried from the computer.

Annie closed the door to the dishwasher and wiped her hands. "So how's it going?" she asked.

"Lost again." He sighed. He set his elbows on the desk and rested his chin in his hands as he'd seen Nicholas do a hundred times. "I should have seen it coming."

He'd been playing Go for almost two hours—the same game he and Nicholas were so fond of. Earlier, she'd checked out the website. It was an association of players who competed with each other over the Internet in real time. Of course, she'd looked over his shoulder now and then to make sure everything was safe. And it was. Unless she counted the opponent who kept bruising her son's ego with multiple defeats unsafe. Earlier, she'd been half tempted to go online and ask him what it felt like to beat a five- year-old.

"You sure you don't want to give it a rest?" she asked.

Rusty shook his head, marveling. "He's real good."

She smiled and turned on the dishwasher. "As good as Nicholas?"

He didn't answer and readjusted himself for yet another game.

She strolled over to him and set her hands on his tiny shoulders. "So is he as good as Nicholas?" she repeated.

He shrugged. "'Bout the same."

She watched as the pieces from the old game disappeared, leaving a blank board on the screen. Rusty reached to the keyboard and typed:

Okay, I get to go first this time.

He hit Enter and waited. The reply appeared underneath the board:

As if it matters.

Rusty stared hard at the screen, considering his first move. More words appeared:

Anytime you're ready, Squirt.

Annie blinked. "Squirt? Did you tell him to call you that?"

Rusty shook his head. "He just knew."

A faint chill crept across her shoulders as her son typed:

I'm thinking.

The reply was immediate:

I thought I smelled smoke.

Her chill turned colder. "Rusty, did you tell him to say that?"

"Mom, I'm trying to—"

"Did you tell him?"

"No."

Keeping her voice even, figuring it was leftover paranoia, she asked, "Who is it?"

"Mom..."

"Rusty, what's the name of—"

More words appeared:

Any century you feel like starting, let me know.

The chill tightened her stomach. Some creep was playing with her kid's head. She sat down on the edge of Rusty's chair. "Scoot over."

"Mom..."

"Scoot over."

Reluctantly, he obeyed, as she reached for the keyboard and quickly typed:

Who is this? What do you want from my son?

"Mom, what are you doing?"

She hit Enter and waited.

There was no answer.

Fear turning to anger, she typed:

I want to know who you are and I want to know now!

There was a long pause. And then, just before she fired off another salvo, just before she threatened to call the cops or the FBI or her new friends at Homeland Security, another set of words appeared on the screen:

I miss you, Annie.

SOLI DEO GLORIA

The Bug Parables

For a further list of Bill's work as well as sample chapters see

www.BillMyers.com

CPSIA information can be obtained
at www.ICGtesting.com
Printed in the USA
LVHW041158141019
634125LV00006B/2626/P